BETA: THE SCORPION AND THE BULL

Phillip Wallace

Tyler Anderson

Black Rose Writing
www.blackrosewriting.com

© 2011 by Phillip Wallace and Tyler Anderson

All rights reserved. No part of this book may be reproduced, stored in a retrieval system or transmitted in any form or by any means without the prior written permission of the publishers, except by a reviewer who may quote brief passages in a review to be printed in a newspaper, magazine or journal.

The final approval for this literary material is granted by the author.

First printing

All characters appearing in this work are fictitious. Any resemblance to real persons, living or dead, is purely coincidental.

ISBN: 978-1-61296-063-0

PUBLISHED BY BLACK ROSE WRITING

www.blackrosewriting.com

Printed in the United States of America

Beta is printed in Calibri

Thank you to all of our Beta testers.

Special Thanks to Jon, Brady, and Jordan.

BETA: THE SCORPION AND THE BULL

Johnny's hand hovered above his chip-stack while he sucked in air through his gritted teeth – a tell-tale sign that something was up. "Raise to five thousand," Johnny said as he looked across the table at his competition. Dash, his best friend and business partner, looked down at his cards and folded with a smirk.

"Well when I'm beat... I'm beat," Dash replied as he thought back to his pocket nines. Shaking his head at the way Johnny was playing his hand. Johnny's eyes moved to his other competition, his Uncle Dylan and good old Fat Montey.

"Too rich for my blood kid," Uncle Dylan responded and mucked his cards. Uncle Dylan gave a little smile to Johnny as he tossed in his cards. Johnny had been having his ass handed to him all night and was down to his last ten thousand yen out of a hundred thousand yen buy in. But this time was different; Johnny had been dealt a pair of aces. On the other hand Johnny wasn't the greatest at poker and everyone at the table could tell.

"Ya know what kid. Even though everyone here knows you have a monster hand I'm gonna call you. This just ain't your night." Fat Montey laughed as he puffed on an over-sized cigar. Fat Montey swirled his glass of whiskey in his hand while watching the dealer turn over the flop. The game was Texas Hold'em and when another ace was revealed Johnny had to hold back his excitement by biting his tongue.

"A grand," Johnny said as he cleared his throat, trying to hide the fact that he had hit the best possible hand with the combination of cards.

"A grand," Fat Montey scoffed. "Seems like you're hiding somethin', but I got somethin' as well. I'll raise you whatcha got left," Fat Montey said with a thick Irish accent and a sinister chuckle.

"You're in over your head Johnny; you just don't know it yet."

"That's what you think Montey; I call," Johnny said with gusto and pushed his remaining money into the pot. Johnny smiled as he flipped over his cards. "Beat that!" He yelled.

"That's pretty good Johnny, but let's see how the cards land." Fat Montey again chuckled as he turned over his pocket pair of deuces. Fat Montey had also made three of a kind on the flop with the spare card being a six of diamonds. Johnny was stoked as the turn card came out it was the eight of diamonds.

"Well, it looks like I'll be hangin' around a little longer," Johnny said with cocky confidence.

"Ya shouldn't count your chickens, Squirt. Look at the cards again," Fat Montey said as he leaned back and took a huge drag off his cigar. Johnny examined the cards closely. Johnny had the ace of spades and clubs in his hand with the ace of diamonds, the two of clubs, the six of diamonds, and the eight of diamonds on the board. Johnny then noticed Fat Montey's pocket pair which claimed the two of diamonds. As the river card came out Johnny could almost sense what was coming. His confidence slumped as the jack of diamonds fell on the river. Fat Montey had made a flush and beat him.

Johnny dead panned, "I fucking hate this game. I don't even know why I play."

"Just wasn't your night," Fat Montey said as he scooped up the pot. "But I got a way you can make a hundred times more than what you just lost, if you're interested." Dash's ears perked up as dollar signs danced in his head.

"Really?!" Dash interjected wanting to hear about the opportunity. "What kind of work do you have for us?"

"We still got a few more hands left. We'll talk after the game," Fat Montey said as he began to shuffle the cards.

The game continued while Johnny grabbed a smoke outside. He took a long drag and thought about how the cards played out. One hundred thousand yen was a bucket of money to Johnny and he really shouldn't have been playing. Many of the folks on the south side owed Fat Montey. His gambling dens and bookies helped him keep control of Southern Neo-Hiroshima. If Takahara Security shut one down another was opened within a matter of hours.

Fat Montey balanced lining his pockets and keeping the 'Ochikobore's' happy, making himself rich. 'Ochikobore' - leftovers, was the name given people who lived south of Old Interstate 90 in Neo-Japan. The people who lived there clung to the old regime of the United States. There were very few Ochikobore's on the south side that didn't have anything to do with Fat Montey and the Irish mob. The Irish mob kept peace and order with an iron grip. Most lived in poverty, but they were kept alive and working because Fat Montey made jobs for his side of town.

Johnny flicked his cigarette butt into the street and quickly lit up another, it wasn't long before his Uncle joined him outside. Johnny was still kicking himself for the bad beat he just received.

"Hey, Uncle D. Come to rub it in," Johnny said as Dylan joined him outside of Dylan's pawn shop.

"I think you're beatin' yourself up enough. Though it was a little funny to watch the deuces tear your bullets apart," Dylan said with a smirk.

"Ha ha. I'd like to see your face when that happens to you," Johnny retorted, not amused at his Uncle's comment. "So what do ya know about the job Fat Montey's offering? Is it legit?"

"The money seems like an extreme over payment, but I did some research on my own. It looks good. A pretty easy job, something I could have done back in the day," Dylan answered. "This job will keep you goin' for a while..."

"But...?" Johnny asked and waited for his Uncle to respond.

"I don't know. It seems a little fishy. I can't put my finger on it." Dylan replied with a little worry in his voice.

"Sometimes I think you worry too much Uncle, but thanks for lookin' out for us," Johnny said with a smile.

"You're the only family I got left kid, and I want to keep you breathing," Dylan replied with concern.

"I know Uncle. Dash and I have been around the block a few times now. You've even said that yourself. If the job is too fishy then we'll bail. I assume you set this up?" Johnny asked while trying to alleviate his Uncle's concern.

"Montey asked if I knew a couple of guys with skills and balls. Naturally I thought of you two. I haven't been given too many details, but I'm sure it's something you can handle. I'll also be expecting my normal percentage," Dylan responded.

"Never could give me a break could ya?" Johnny joked.

"What's family for, if not to give ya a hard time? Besides just think of all the money I spent getting ya to where you're now. I deserve a little compensation," Dylan replied with a small laugh.

Dash stepped outside carrying three beers. "I just made the deal of the decade," Dash said proudly as he handed out the drinks.

"Should we toast?" Johnny joked.

"Yes. To Fat Montey... a sucker and his money are soon parted," Dash said as he raised his bottle.

"So you ended up winning my money back?" Johnny asked hoping that Dash would throw a few Yen his way.

"No, but after this job a hundred thousand Yen will be a drop in a bucket," Dash answered.

"Well then, to Fat Montey." Johnny raised his bottle.

"To Fat Montey... and my ten percent." Dylan clanked all their bottles together with a smile.

It was the biggest job they had ever taken and everything was going as planned -- the smoothest sailing they had in a long time. Johnny had big plans for the money he had yet to earn, and the Yen for this job was as good as spent. Some booze, new improvements for his motorcycle, replacement gear, maybe pay for the warehouse garage door to get fixed. The money had already burned a hole in his pocket.

Life for Johnny and Dash was about to hit easy street. They had been runners, thieves, acquisition men, and muscle on occasion. While they may not be the best, they always got the job done but they should have known better when they took this job. The money just seemed too good.

Johnny hit the button on the door to exit the building. Thinking no was around to hear him he sighed with relief and shared his excitement with his partner in crime.

"Dash, this was the easiest boost in the last three years," Johnny said, as helped carry the case to the van. Johnny wasn't a big guy standing only at 5'8" but hidden under his clothes was strong runner's physique. His hair was a dark brown and kept shaggy. His eyes are a dark blue and his face showed his five o'clock shadow.

"God damn it, you fucking loud mouth! These cameras can pick up your voice from a mile away," Dash whispered through gritted teeth, then promptly slugging Johnny in the shoulder, which he knew would cause a bruise later. There always was when Johnny screwed up. They continued through the cold paved parking garage as a chill breeze swept through the structure. They scored a nice parking spot on the first floor which would make it a little easier to get out if they needed to make a quick escape. The place was packed with cars that lined the parking lot of the Mika Labs making it easy to hide their van. All part of their careful planning that Johnny had just ruined. They began to load the case before Johnny felt it was safe to reply.

"You're worried? That's a laugh. The merchandise is already in the damn safety harness and we'll be out of here in two seconds flat. There's no way that they can respond in time to stop us. That money is as good as ours," Johnny replied back, smirking as he propped himself up and leaned on the side of the van. The bark of three gun shots rang out and bullets slammed into the side of the panel van next to Johnny's hand. Johnny jumped at the unexpected gun fire and took cover.

"You had to fucking say something didn't you!" Dash growled angrily as he slammed the driver side rear door shut and went for the driver's door, keys in hand. Dash was taller than Johnny, standing at 5'10". He was muscular with broad shoulders. His hair a light brown which was kept short. His eyes were smokey gray which, when combined with his chiseled, clean shaven jaw line, made him look like one serious mutha-fucka.

"Oh! So it's my fault. You're the one yelling at me like I had done somethin' wrong," Johnny responded, hopping in the back of the van shutting the door. He crouched next to the removable panel and popped it off grabbing his Scorpion machine pistol from the compartment. It was loaded, cocked, and ready to rock. Dash turned the key bring the van roaring to life as Johnny flipped the safety of his weapon. Dash quickly shifted the van in reverse and slammed on the gas. With a crank of the wheel Dash made it so the rear of the van was facing the oncoming security guards. Bullets began to chew up the doors damaging the latch on the driver's side rear door. Dash threw the van into drive and slammed on the gas. The tires squealed as the van peeled out and began to speed away, causing the driver side rear doors fly open. The jolt from the acceleration made Johnny stumble, but with a quick adjustment he prevented himself from falling out of the van. More bullets hit the rear door shattering the back window. The thumping sound the bullets made as they impacted the back of the van sounded like a drum solo during a rock concert. The security guards were shooting something a little heavier than their normal pistols.

"Holy Shit!" Johnny yelled, pointing his pistol out the broken window, and letting loose a full clip in a matter of seconds. The rounds chewed through concrete and made an expensive bill for the executive cars that were parked close to the doors, making the guards take cover. Johnny reached out, shut the rear door, and began to reload.

"You know Johnny, if it weren't for me you'd be shit splattered all over the side of that building!" Dash yelled over his shoulder with a laugh.

"Really fuckin' funny, Dash!" He shouted back, trying to be heard over the van's squealing tires. "Driving like that you'd be the reason why I could've been splattered in the first place and you were the one bitching about the sensors. Use my fucking code name." Dash slipped the van into drive and began to speed up. He busted through the candy cane striped parking garage meter maid arm.

"You and your super spy code names. Why don't you throw on some spandex and a cape?" Dash joked, catching a glimpse of how serious Johnny looked in the cracked review mirror. "It will be a cold day in hell before I call you Berith. Just get your fucking head down!" Dash yelled as a few sporadic bullets connected with the van before they were out of the line of fire. Johnny made his way up to the front seat and sat down with a sigh. He flipped down the visor and grabbed the pen that was strapped to it, and then opened up the mirror that was attached to the visor and a piece of paper fell out. The paper was covered with tally marks. Johnny added another one.

"That makes fifty in less than three years. Most people like us are dead or in Nagasaki Prison by now," Johnny said with a smile.

"That almost wasn't your fiftieth job," Dash said with a sigh, his words a mixture of both frustration and relief.

As Dash began doing his best impression of a street racer in a full size van, they began blaming each-other as to who screwed up the tail end of the job. Dash put the blame on Johnny for being heard by the security sensors and Johnny tried to fight it by saying that Dash almost got them killed with the stunt he pulled with the van. In the end Dash was right -- as usual it was Johnny's fault. He had messed up big time and could have gotten them killed. The ass reaming that Dash was giving him was one he had heard before. Sometimes he thought Dash would eventually stop, but it had been 3 years and still, every time Johnny messed up, the speech came out. Johnny could almost recite it word for word.

"Life lessons as told by Dash McBragg," Johnny thought, chuckling while Dash continued to rip him a new one. Johnny stared out the window while Dash bitched him out. The buildings of the Northside reflected the sun's bright rays. The streets were free of any debris. Street sweepers passed by like clockwork. Everything and everyone had its place on the Northside and all of it was Takahara owned or licensed. It was easy to spot the people who didn't belong and if they hung around in one spot for too long, the Takahara Corp. Security would be there to give them a bad day. The TCS kept the street clear of the riff-raff. Hookers, dealers, hustlers, bums, and Alphas never made their way to the Northside unless they were looking to straighten up. Being caught on the Northside doing anything illegal could earn you short stay in prison – it was only a short stay because most prisoners only lived a few months. Dylan had told Johnny of many friends he lost inside the walls of Nagasaki Prison.

    Dash crossed over old Interstate 90 and into the Southside. The change of scenery was dramatic. Rundown buildings, dirty streets, dealers, and hookers of every color were just some of the sights that littered the area. The criminal element of the Southside made it hard to see the law abiding folk. Most residents were people that had lived there since they were born. Others moved to try to avoid the Takahara Corporation. Working for Takahara Corp. meant that they owned you and that didn't sit right with these people. The people on the Southside may have had to struggle to get by, but they argued that it was better than the alternative. Johnny drifted back to the conversation as they neared their exit.

    "Almost dying may be part of the job but it's not something I want to make into a habit," Dash interjected after Johnny's chuckle. "And wipe that stupid smirk off your face."

    Dash would forgive him later he always did, and of course Johnny had to pay for the repairs for Frankie -- their van. Johnny didn't really know why the vans name was Frankie, but that's what Dash always called it. Frankie was a nice van. Dash and Johnny broke the vehicles cherry on its first time out, barely made it back in one piece, but it always remained a smooth ride. Johnny suspected that there was a girl in Dash's past of the same name that completed the analogy.

After about an hour of hairpin turns, a near collision, and running red lights they finally made it back to the industrial district were, if you found a Takahara Security Agent, he was taking a nap and security cameras were mostly for show. They owned a warehouse in the area and used it for a base of operation. Calling it a warehouse was a little bit of an exaggeration. The warehouse was basically an oversized two car garage. The paint was peeling off the outside walls and the door stuck every once and a while, but it fit the van and their motorcycles, a desk with a small computer, and room for about ten good size boxes in which were loaded with large weapons, additional small arms, bullet proof vests, and a few extra essentials. Also in the back room was the "Trophy Wall". Dash has always been one to show off a bit. He kept something from each of the jobs. Most of the time people didn't notice. This time would be no different.

"That makes sixty three for me. Not bad if I say so myself," Dash bragged a little while he showed the shipping form to Johnny. Dash had done a few side jobs that Johnny wasn't a fit for. Johnny lacked a certain charm that Dash had naturally. Johnny normally referred to those jobs as shower jobs because afterward you needed a shower because of all the bull shit you have to wade through. For this boost the trophy was a packing slip. For shower jobs most of the time the trophies were a set of panties.

Johnny and Dash had trained together for over a year before they began taking jobs. They built a reputation on finishing any job no matter what it was. Some jobs were less than glorious but they had to pay the bills. Dash even played escort a few times for the rich and famous. Normally on those nights Johnny drove the car. Dash had been part of the crowd before the incident. He was able to fit right back in with the Northside yuppies. Johnny never held it against him sometimes Dash would come out with another job afterwards. Dash made connections left and right at those parties, but always kept a wary eye out for Takahara goons.

"Dude we're gonna get raided some day and end up in prison for a long, long time," Johnny replied.

"You got your tally sheet I got mine," He replied.

"Whatever. Can you say consecutive life terms?" Johnny responded.

As they pulled up to the side of the warehouse with the garage door Dash signaled the door to open with his headlink. A headlink is just some of the upgrades they could get these days. The human body is, for lack of a better word, an apparatus. Companies come out with better devices to plug into you every year. Cybernetics is the cash crop of the 2050's. These days you'd be considered to be in the technologically stone age if you used an external device for communication, that, or socially inept. Technology was fast becoming society's new god – and it had many worshipers. Most cybernetic implants are outrageously expensive. One of the few things everyone could afford is a headlink. Breaking it down to the simplest function it is like having a fancy phone in your head. The signal for a headlink, unfortunately, was not a fix for a faulty door.

Johnny jumped out of the back of the van on instinct and began to try to open the garage door per the usual methods and with a kick and some coaxing. The door finally opening after about the fifth kick and Dash pulled the van into the garage just as the sun was setting. Johnny flipped on the light and closed the garage door after the van rolled by him. That is when he noticed the damage on the back of the van. The van looked like Swiss cheese. The handles were shot off, tail lights were nowhere to be found, both rear windows were gone and there were about forty holes that needed patching. Not to mention the bullets that made it inside the van. Johnny realized two things in that moment: that there was more to the job than a simple snatch and grab and that those bullets had Johnny's name written all over them. Johnny became enraged at the sight. Johnny was used to putting his life on the line for a job, but Dash put his life on the line to make a point.

"Man! I could kill you for that stunt you pulled. What if they were armor piercing rounds?" Johnny grabbed Dash by the front of his shirt and pushed him against the van. "I could have been killed!" Johnny paused pointing at all the bullet holes. "Hell, I'm surprised I wasn't!"

"Will you fucking relax man? You weren't even fucking grazed." Dash smirked as he forcefully removed Johnny's hand from his shirt and quickly put him in a painful arm lock.

"Ow! That fucking hurts man. Let go!" Johnny yelped as Dash let go with a little shove. "You know I hate it when you do that," Johnny said as he began to swing his arm around in a circle to relieve the pain. It may not really help, but Johnny thought it did.

"And you know I hate it when you mess up my shirt. Now come on," Dash said in a joyful tone as he straightened collar. "I'm alive, your alive, the van... still runs, and the job is done. Let's go out and fucking celebrate." Dash always had the right words to ease the tension.

"Amen to that, bro." Johnny smiled.

"We'll turn the case into Dylan tomorrow like we're supposed to. So relax and let's have a little fun. First round is on me," Dash said as he extended his hand.

"I wouldn't have it any other way." Johnny smirked, shook his hand, and then began to pull his bike out of the warehouse. Johnny started locking up while Dash finished securing the merchandise in the warehouse. Johnny helped the garage door shut as Dash pulled his bike out. Dash's Harley roared to life. It was a beast of a bike and looked like it could crush Johnny's bike under its wheels like the cars at a monster truck show. Dash was lucky to have it since the American Vehicle Act of 2034 mandated that you couldn't get anything American made. It was a 1999 Harley-Davidson Fatboy - black with red accents, with skull and crossbones across the gas tank that completed the look. Lucky for Dash, Johnny and he weren't exactly law abiding citizens. Johnny kicked his 2010 Honda CBR1000 into gear; the high pitched engine was music to his ears. His bike was black, accented with a pair of orange flaming wings painted on the sides. Johnny's helmet design was of a phoenix. Dash thought helmets were for dumbasses that didn't know how to stay on their bikes. Also, Dash always thought the sound of Johnny's bike was like nails on a chalk board. These two facts made it even more fun for Johnny to rev the engine.

"With the money we make are you finally going to spend it on a real bike, Berith?" Dash joked knowing it was never going to happen. "Or is it ok to call you Johnny now?" Johnny glared at him for the comment about his code name, but shrugged it off.

"This baby is top of the line…" He started to reply.

"For a rice burner!" Dash chuckled.

"Why don't you take your hog and go make some bacon," Johnny replied as he put his helmet on and gave him the finger. "Race you there." Their tires squealed and sent the smell of burnt rubber into the air as they sped off into the night.

"You can send in the security from Maki Laboratories," Mr. Takahara said with coldness in his voice. Five men entered the room, each man wearing a Takahara Corp. security guard's uniform. All the men were nervous and as they entered the room they immediately dropped to their knees supplicating themselves to their boss.

Mr. Takahara sat behind his desk - an older Japanese man, hair that had begun to pepper and the wrinkles on his face showing that he had lived a hard life. He was dressed in a black suit and tie with a red shirt. A picture of his son was the only item that sat on his dark polished-mahogany desk. The picture was decorated with a black ribbon on the corner of the frame.

"We must humbly apologize sir," One of them pleaded. "Please forgive us."

"Stand up. This is not a police state, this is my corporation," Mr. Takahara said, showing no emotion. "Who spoke?"

"I did sir," Said one guard with his eyes fixated on the floor.

"What is your name?" Mr. Takahara asked as his cold glare moved to the man who dared to speak.

"Kenji, sir," He replied. Mr. Takahara raised an eyebrow at the guards name as it was the same as his brother's.

Mr. Takahara walked to Kenji's side, put his arm around his shoulders, and guided him as they walked toward the large section of wall behind Mr. Takahara's desk.

"Kenji. This is a business... We are here to make money. Money equals control and power. It is what every human being strives for. Without money you lose that power. Look at what happened to the United States." Mr. Takahara paused, pointing to a large map of the continent bedecking the wall. "Our company is foremost leader in cybernetics and soon gene manipulation. We are so powerful that we were able to purchase a piece of the crumbling United States. We are so powerful that our yearly profit is more than almost every country in the world. The strong rule the weak. One of nature's many lessons that we would be foolish to forget."

Mr. Takahara turned Kenji towards a bank of top of the line video monitors that filled the wall behind his desk. "And yet, somehow, we can't seem to keep two ochikobores from walking into one of our most secure facilities and leaving with our latest break-through," Mr. Takahara explained as he flipped on the monitors showing the robbery. Pictures of Dash and Johnny filled the screen. "Now, can you tell me what happened?"

"I was at the door sir. I don't know how they got by me," Kenji said as he trembled with fear.

"That part is coming up. Watch closely," Mr. Takahara said as his arm tightened around Kenji's shoulders and pointed to the monitor. The monitors showed an employee walk up, slide his badge, and open the doors. Dash threw a rock which banged loudly against the guard shack wall. Kenji turned away from the door for a second giving Dash and Johnny just enough time to slip in before the doors shut. Kenji inspected the noise and went back to work. "It was very simple."

"Please forgive me sir," Kenji pleaded.

"There is but one honorable path to forgiveness Kenji," Mr. Takahara said, pointing to a rack of fine, antique blades on the far wall. Kenji walked shakily to the wall, hand hovering nervously over one of the short swords. "Do it." Mr. Takahara commanded with an air of menacing authority.

Kenji fumbled with the clasp holding the sword in its sheath - hands shaking like a man suffering with palsy. The four other guards began to fidget, casting nervous glances at each other. Kenji let out a slight gasp as the clasp slid free, releasing the blade. Kenji allowed the sheath to clatter to the floor and grasped the handle with both hands, eyes staring off in the distance, teeth clenched in a grimace. He paused, sweat beading off his forehead.

"Now!" barked Mr. Takahara. Broken as if from a trance Kenji plunged the blade deep into his guts, twisted it, and then tore it horizontally out his side. Shrieking, Kenji collapsed, bleeding out over the lacquered floor.

"You... are... forgiven." smiled Mr. Takahara as he walked to Kenji and retrieved the sword. He wiped the blade on Kenji's writhing body, then slid it back into its sheath and set it back into its place within the rack. "Ichiro," He said, and a medium size man with a Mohawk, black suit, and sunglasses with red lenses walked in with a katana strapped to his back.

Mr. Takahara walked out and, with a glance over his shoulder, spoke two words to Ichiro. "Finish this." As the door shut behind Mr. Takahara the drawing of a sword was heard and the screams of the men carried into the board room which was always unnerving to some of the executives. Mr. Takahara removed a white handkerchief from his pocket and wiped the blood off his wing-tip shoes; once completed he held up the handkerchief the blood was soaked in and was going to stain.

"Ruined another one," He muttered as he threw the blood soaked rag away. "Sorry for the delay. Sometimes I like to let go of employees personally. Now, can anyone tell me how a couple of ochikobores were able to break into one of our most high-tech facilities?" Mr. Takahara asked politely in a chilling tone.

"Actually, Mr. Takahara, we need to discuss who perpetrated the break-in at Maki Labs not how they were able to do it," A woman said as she walked into the room. She commanded the respect of every man in the room as she walked over to Mr. Takahara. Her beautiful black hair was cut at the shoulders. She wore a white lab coat. Her fair Japanese skin had signs of wrinkles. She wore glasses, which are a prehistoric tool with the advances that have been made in cybernetics. "Subject one is of no concern of ours, however subject two is possibly a Beta."

"Dr. Maki, that is preposterous. I was in charge of the Beta project cover up," One of the executives spouted. "The Beta project was destroyed leaving no evidence in a tragic fire almost 20 years ago..." Dr. Maki shot him a glare that caused him to stumble over his words and then became silent.

"Oh really, then do you care to explain this?" She asked as she clicked the button that exposed the wall monitor. The monitor then began to display a picture of a baby that was slowly beginning to age, one year than two years and so on until the age of twenty-one.

"It *is* him, but that is impossible. I made sure they were all accounted for," The executive said with shock as he glanced over to Mr. Takahara to assess his fate. Mr. Takahara showed no sign of emotion as he continued to listen to Dr. Maki.

"Yes it is," Dr. Maki said as she walked over to the man. "Mr. Takahara. I'll be in my lab. Remember I will need him alive." Dr. Maki exited as quickly as she entered.

"Thank you very much," Mr. Takahara politely said as he pressed some buttons on the table consol. The face of a Takahara security agent popped up on a vid screen in the conference room. "Hayao, make sure that the border agents are looking for these men. Make no mistakes or it will be your head." The security agent gulped and bowed. Mr. Takahara turned the vid screen off and folded his hands together.

"With the borders sealed it is only a matter of time. The rest of you will have until tomorrow to find him. You are dismissed except for you." Mr. Takahara ordered as he pointed to the executive that spoke up. The other executives scrambled to get out of the room. Mr. Takahara brought up the vid screen again. "Ichiro, would you come in here for a moment." A grin of devilish pleasure grew on his face.

Johnny didn't remember much of the night, which meant that Dash and he shot whiskey. A black out was almost assured when whiskey was involved. Johnny had a hard time saying no when Dash and he were out partying. After nights like that Johnny always wondered how he got home. He laid in bed looking at the ceiling, praying that the normal hangover wouldn't kick in, a few questions popped into his head as dollar signs appeared in his mind.

"What upgrades should I get for my bike?" Johnny thought. "Should I make Dash pay for half of the repairs on the van since he was the one who backed into the oncoming bullets? Where did my underwear go and who the fuck is caressing his chest?"

"Morning handsome," purred a very sexual female voice.

Then Johnny felt a kiss on his cheek. "Please God don't let this be like the last one," Johnny thought. "Um..... Mornin'," Johnny said as he finally turned to look at her squinting just in case. He opened his eyes fully once he noticed that, lying next to him was the hottest girl he had seen in a long time. Her skin looked soft and was a dark tan. Her long brown hair hung down in front of her bare breasts, and she had beautiful doe brown eyes. Johnny smiled as he caressed her arm. Her skin felt like silk.

"So how are you this morning?" She asked with a little giggle and a wink.

"Could be worse, I supposed I should thank you for the ride home last night?" Johnny said, still holding a shit eating grin. The grin soon faded as he realized that the last time he checked his walls weren't pink. She looked at him and he saw the realization come over her face.

"What?!" she exclaimed. "You don't remember." Johnny got out of bed and began to slowly back away. He noticed his clothes in a pile next to the bed. She grabbed a night gown that was on her night stand as Johnny scrambled to get dressed. Johnny couldn't help but look. She wasn't the girl of his dreams yesterday, but she sure was now. She was hot and just the right height too, a little over 5'. "Johnny!! I don't believe this shit. You finally think you meet a nice guy…" She pouted, unable to finish the sentence.

"Now, listen a minute. I'm really sorry…" Johnny said and she cut him off instantly.

"*You're* sorry?" She huffed in a mocking tone.

"Whiskey makes me back out," Johnny replied sheepishly knowing he was dead in the water and no argument was going to save him. So he finished putting his clothes on.

"I bet you can't even remember my name," She said, waiting for a response.

"Um… Kiyomi." Johnny replied thinking of one of one of the most common names for a woman her age in Neo-Japan.

"Get the hell out of here!" She screamed.

"Come on now. We had fun last night. Don't let a little black-out ruin it," Johnny pleaded while doing his best Dash impression. Johnny could see a little smile creep across her face as she remembered last night. That only lasted for a moment.

"Get out," She stated again.

"Don't be mad. Give me a chance to make it up to you," Johnny begged.

"Fine, get… out… and don't come back until you remember my

name," she replied.

"Okay, I'll leave, but I'll be back," Johnny said as he opened the door and stepped into her living room. "You can count on it. Oh one more thing before I go." Her eyes grew more intense.

"You're soooo hot when you're angry." Johnny kissed her on the cheek and backed away. She scowled at him and then promptly slammed the door in his face, but just before her face left Johnny's sight a cute little smile crept across her face.

Johnny found himself in her apartment's living room. He would have rushed out of there to begin searching for her name, but as the breeze from the door slamming caught her hair he noticed her high dose calcium patch. The hottest girl he had ever seen, let alone slept with, was an Alpha. Specifically, she was an Alpha Echo – or as people on the streets liked to call them, "Echoes". Calcium patches and super model thin bodies were the most telling factors. Echoes had increased reflexes and speed caused by the Alpha Virus, but the price for their neat new tricks wasn't worth the complications. Echoes had to take high doses of calcium because their bones are calcium deficient and very brittle. Their bones would snap due to the massive tension their condensed muscles would put on their skeletal structures without the almost lethal dose of calcium. Echoes were the lucky ones, Alpha Oscars and Tangos couldn't hide their afflictions.

Johnny didn't have much time to contemplate the situation, because just at that moment, he heard a crash come from behind him. He turned around and quickly took cover behind the couch. Peeking out from behind the sofa he saw Dash, buck naked, leaving the second bedroom as a vase went flying passed his head. It crashed hard against the wall behind Johnny.

"Come on, Baby...Honey... You know I care about you," Dash pleaded in his best attempt to convince whoever was in there not to throw anything else. Dash caught a glimpse of Johnny and gave him a wink. Johnny figuring everything was in the clear stood up from behind the couch. "See I knew we could work this out like rational...

Oh shit! Johnny, run!" Dash yelled.

"What?" Johnny asked in confusion, but then quickly made a bee-line for the door just behind Dash who sprinted by him, a blur of nakedness. As Johnny was about to head down the stairs he looked back to see, not one, but two half naked girls wielding new Takahara collapsible longbows. The mechanized bows unfolding from their wrist sleeves caught Johnny's attention for a moment, but with one girl wearing Dash's shirt the other wearing his pants it was a fleeting moment. Dash had really done it this time. One day a cute smile and a sweet ass are going to be the end of him.

Johnny caught up to Dash outside who was hiding his junk behind a trashcan lid.

"Johnny, give me your shirt," Dash stated.

"What the fuck you gonna to do with my shirt?" He asked as he lit up a cigarette.

"What the fuck do you think I'm going to do?" Dash said with a berating tone. "Give it here before the TCS shows up. They'll haul my naked ass off to the clink."

"You know it's kind of funny. Cool, calm, and collected during meetings, jobs, and anything in between. Put the man on the street with nothing more than a trashcan lid to cover his junk with and he needs help all of a sudden." Johnny chuckled as he removed shirt and handed it over to Dash. Dash made quick work of it and fashioned it in to a kilt.

"Nice," Johnny said with a bit of sarcasm in his voice. "You can keep the shirt."

"Thanks," Dash responded.

"Now explain something to me. You somehow convinced two girls to sleep with your dumb ass. You even slept over. Yet in the morning you're chased out by psychos wielding, of all things, bow and arrows? What is this, the Wild West?" Johnny joked.

"Hey, just because 'Pocahontas' and 'Crazy Beaver' in there have a fetish for shit like that doesn't mean they weren't a great roll in the ol' sweat lodge if you know what I mean." Dash laughed devilishly and winked.

"Let me guess. You actually called them that?" Johnny mused.

"Not until this morning." Dash stated innocently.

"One of these days, Sheriff McBragg, you're going to get yourself killed," Johnny admonished, pointing his index finger at Dash and firing it like a gun.

Dash put his hand over his heart and feigned getting shot.

"You never were one to give a shit about being politically correct," Johnny replied. "Reminds me of the time you told that chick that you couldn't hook up with her because you were an alien from Alpha Prime and your superior's only directive was for you not to sleep with ugly whores." Johnny began to chuckle. Dash shortly joined him.

"Good times. You call a cab yet?" Dash asked.

"Yeah, it should be here shortly." Johnny nodded.

The cab that arrived was a piece of shit, smelt like fish and the driver smelled like he had rolled around in the offal of a muskrat den, but it got them home. Johnny was glad to get home and take a nice, long shower. After loaning Dash some clothes, they went back to the bar to pick up their bikes, chatting on the way. More or less Dash bragged about banging two chicks while Johnny listened, though he wasn't really paying attention. Johnny was trying to understand why he couldn't get over the fact that he had slept with an alpha. "Though it could have been worse," Johnny thought. "She could have been a Melt addict, tech fiend, or worse, crazy."

His Uncle always said Alpha-humans were freaks and couldn't be trusted. Johnny guessed he just always believed his Uncle. The pretty girl that he saw wasn't dirty or a freak anymore then he was. She just wanted the respect that any normal woman wanted and he liked her, and from what he remembered last night, she was really nice and pretty funny.

Johnny kept thinking about it as they drove down the dirty streets of South Side Neo-Hiroshima. He had never known a time without Alphas. They first started showing up in the early 2020's, a few years after Takahara Corp. had purchased Washington State from the United States government. Johnny remembered his Uncle Dylan telling him about how. Uncle Dylan never forgave President Burton for what she did to the United States in the name of "getting us out of a financial jam". In the end, it did save the country, or what was left of it. Alaska was sold to Canada and California to Red China - a match made in heaven. Washington was bought by The Takahara Corporation with the support of its home country Japan. When Takahara Corporation took charge of Washington State business had never been better for Uncle Dylan. Otherwise he would have moved out during the Great Panic of 2019 caused by the sale of the states.

Then again Uncle Dylan always seemed a little off. He had told Johnny his conspiracy theory about how the Alphas came to be. During the panic, Takahara Corporation began providing free flu vaccines to the population, many of whom were poor as dirt, homeless, and sick. What Dylan insisted on was that Takahara Corps actual motive was not the distribution of a "vaccine", but getting test subjects for the Alpha drug, or "Virus" as he referred to it. The vaccine was distributed quickly to over 50,000 people and a few short months later there were the first sightings of Alpha Echoes, Alpha Oscars, and Alpha Tangos. The Alpha drug had changed them according to his uncle - their bodies *and* their minds.

Uncle Dylan always talked about the media blitz that came out after the Alpha virus was exposed. The Takahara Corp. media said it was due to a chemical spill from one of the old factories. Some knew better, but most bought it hook, line, and sinker. The media coverage of the Alphas always referred to as a plague carrying filthy dirty ochikobores that had nothing to do with the flu vaccine they had handed out.

The Oscars looked a little more like cave men with large thicken skulls, extended jaws, over sized teeth, but the worse of it was the severe skin diseases they would get. Most Oscars were lucky if they only had acne and warts, but Johnny had heard of others that developed severely dry skin so much so that they couldn't move without it cracking and bleeding unless they covered every inch of their bodies with a special lotion. The only benefit they received from the Alpha Virus was an increase in strength.

Tangos received a major increase in strength beyond that of an Oscar, but their pain was much worse. Tangos bone structure never stops growing developing horn like spike at their joints. There finger nails are all bone, some develop facial spikes and horns growing out of their skin. Their bodies produce a high level of calcium. They have to take a calcium depletion agent or die in a matter of days. Some try to fit in with normal citizen by filing down their spikes and horns, but due to their size there was no place for them to hide. For all the pain they go through to try to fight off their mutations, Johnny started to feel sorry for them.

Something clicked in Johnny's mind at that point; all those years of alpha-hating, all the jokes, pranks, and all around treating them like less than human had lead up to this. What a waste. Sometimes it is surprising what will change the thinking of a man, then again it could just be that she was a the most beautiful woman he had ever laid eyes on.

"Wow, I'm an ass," Johnny stated aloud.

"Yeah you are. You've been zoning out for the past few minutes," replied Dash, "You alright? Hello, Earth to Johnny, come in Johnny."

"Sorry man I was lost in thought," he replied.

"Still thinking about that girl...fuck I would be to if I were you," he said with a chuckle. "I had my eye on her, but I think I made the better choice."

"Why is that?" he asked. "You got chased out of there by chicks toting bows."

"It was worth it." Dash smiled as he turned his back towards Johnny to show him some scratch marks.

"Dude what the fuck?!" Johnny exclaimed as he examined the mauling that Dash took last night. "Some of those are pretty deep. Ya need to disinfect that shit."

"Those kittens weren't playing around," Dash said as he pulled his shirt back down.

"Women are gonna be the end of you," Johnny said smiling.

"Yeah I know, but what a fun way to go," Dash replied with a devil-may-care smile.

"I don't remember you bein' like this in high school, but then again we didn't hang much," Johnny said.

"That is the first decent piece of tail you've had in months. Wait; there *was* that one girl... Bridgette. That was some piece of work," Dash said with a forced chuckle and began to clap.

"Eat shit," Johnny said angrily as he gave him the finger and got out of the cab. It was true Johnny hadn't much luck with the ladies lately and the luck he had managed to gather up had him making trips to the clinic for booster shots a few months prior. Johnny knew that Dash was poking fun, but was pissed that he brought it up.

"Should've left your ass with your crazy squaws," Johnny mumbled back at Dash through his teeth.

"Ha. You wouldn't have left me," Dash proclaimed with a smile. "I know where you live. And it'd be an awful shame to have to wake you up in the middle of the night after I spring a mousetrap on your balls."

They had just pulled up to the bar. "We're lucky we sprung for those biometric ID's on our bikes after our last job, otherwise we'd be walking home," Johnny said, trying to change the subject as the cab came to a stop. Johnny paid the cabbie and got out of the cab. Dash knew he got under Johnny's skin and continued on with his razzing he got on his Fatboy.

"Don't change the subject, you know me, I would have done it. Hell I still might just for the laugh." Dash smirked. Johnny looked a little ill at the thought.

"Um. Right. Look we got shit to do today and although talking about clamping a mouse trap to my nuts sounds fun and all," Johnny said sarcastically. "I just want to make some money today and we're already running a bit behind due to last night's shenanigans." Johnny started his bike and revved the engine.

Dash grimaced at the sound. "You need to go get the van fixed and I'll see you about four." Dash hopped on his bike and took off. Johnny watched him ride out of sight and then powered up his headlink. After a few quick calls and a smoke Johnny ordered the parts for Frankie and had them delivered to the warehouse.

Johnny rode through the crumbling streets of Southern Neo-Hiroshima. Johnny never knew what it looked like before the city became the shit hole it was today, but his Uncle had told him stories about how beautiful the city was back before the riots. He imagined what it was like sometimes as he rode through town. Johnny sped down Interstate 5 heading north until he hit the Bailey Street exit into the old industrial district; it was an easy ride not a lot of traffic since most of the people were at work in the area.

As Johnny made his way through the demolition zones to the warehouse one thing did come to mind. Takahara Corp. did put all these people back to work, but Johnny's praise didn't last for long. Johnny had reached the warehouse and look over the horizon at Takahara's newly completed headquarters, Takahara Tower. Takahara Tower cast a cloak of darkness over the city as dawn passed to dust that could be seen for miles, but there was no time to sit and speculate what the monstrous corporation was doing today. Johnny grabbed his oiled covered work shirt he kept at the warehouse then went straight to work.

It was nice not to have to worry about running into any TCS goons on the Southside. Even though the Southside could use more Takahara Corp. presences to help rebuild, however most preferred they stuck to the Northside of Old Interstate 90. Almost every building in Neo-Hiroshima north of Old Interstate 90 was owned by Takahara Corp. They even purchased the housing, supermarkets, and other building on the Northside for their employees.

Working for Takahara Corp. provided all the comforts that a person needs. The comforts were very lavish as well. Takahara employees didn't live in barracks or dorms. No they have nice full furnished houses, the latest Japanese vehicles, and a nice salary to take care of any need that Takahara hadn't already provided. Takahara Corp. also kept their money in house. They paid their employees in Takahara credits that only worked at Takahara owned businesses. Since Takahara owned 70% of the businesses in Neo-Hiroshima their employees never complain. This also made a very profitable market for currency exchange, which Uncle Dylan had some dealings.

The Northside might have the best in human excess, but the Southside provided more valuable resources. A man could be his own boss on the Southside. Sure you had to deal with the crappy streets, bum filled alleys, the Melt dens on the corner, the abundance of crime, but a man could stand on his own two feet on the Southside.

The Southside was also where what were left of the Alphas hide. Some Alphas can hide in plain sight mostly second generations that had not experienced the full effect of the virus. Those with the more severe mutation try to keep out of sight as much as possible. Most Alphas banded together keeping each other safe and out of the reach of Takahara Corp. Cashing in on an Alpha was very profitable back in the early mid 2020's. Takahara wanted to bring them in for treatment, or so they said. The Alphas refused which lead to a bounty being put on their heads.

Takahara Corp. didn't expect the Southside to take care of its own. The Irish mob pushes back against Takahara Corp. and its loyal businesses by either running the owner off and taking over or making sure that their business never got up and running in the first place. Something Fat Montey's crew has been doing since the 30's.

Johnny tightened the last bolt on the back door and looked up at the Neo-Hiroshima skyline. The immense Takahara Tower reached for the sky standing above all the rest. Johnny raised his hand and pointed his fingers at it like a gun. "Bang," Johnny said then began to put his tools away.

It only took a few hours to do, but being able to fix things himself save him tons of Yen. Johnny finished the repairs about an hour before he had to meet up with Dash. Johnny went back to the bar in search of the girl's name. He knew he would have to keep this from Dash or else he'd catch flack for it. Johnny had a long history of women that had broken his heart. Leaving him kind of jaded to the whole idea of being with someone. Yet he still felt compelled to at least figure out who she was. Johnny knew where he could get some answers and began to retrace his steps back to the bar.

El Diablo Tavern was run by Shamus O'Reily, a friend of his Uncle Dylan. Johnny never quite understood how a Spanish named tavern was run by an Irish guy. There was a story about him winning it in a card game, but Shamus fired a gun better then he played cards and wasn't too bad in a fist fight. Back before he owned the bar he carried around the nick name 'Toothless', but if anyone other than Dylan or Montey call him that, they learned the hard way to never call him that twice. The name of the bar still always made him smile. Johnny headed inside. The bell chimed against the door as he entered. The bar had just opened for the night and he was hoping to get the name of girl before anyone showed up. Shamus was loading cash drawers into the tills.

"What can I get for ya?" Shamus said as he busted open rolls of coins, his back to Johnny.

"Hey, Shamus," Johnny said to get his attention.

"Hello, Johnny. You're in for a beer already? It must be a rough day for ya. I guess after last night's little shindig that ya had I shouldn't be surprised," Shamus said with a smiled.

"Yeah last night was a surprise alright. So anyway, did you see who I left with? My brain is kind of foggy?"

"I told her not to get mixed up with you two, but she and her friends insisted on buying you drinks - *especially* when Dash went on the offensive," Shamus said. "I don't see how he does it. It amazes me some times."

"Shamus," Johnny said to get his attention. "Do you know her name?"

"Of course, she works here," he stated.

"Really? When did start?" Johnny questioned.

"About three days ago," he replied.

"She got a name?" Johnny almost begged.

"Listen. She's a sweet girl and getting mixed up with you would only get her into trouble." Shamus huffed.

"Come on. You know me," Johnny begged.

"You're right. I DO know you. I also know that... Wait a second. You didn't remember her name?" Shamus asked, beginning to sound a little preachy, breaking into an Irish brogue. "Awwwwww fuck it. Never mind. I understand just by looking at your bill from last night. Sixteen shots of whiskey you two knocked back last night. Speaking of which, pay up!"

"What? I paid my tab last night. That I know for sure; I wouldn't just lose 1000 yen in cash," Johnny explained.

"Right. But Dash didn't," Shamus explained. "And since you two are like brothers..." Shamus gave a sly little grin, showing a grill full of missing teeth. The look was completed by his leathery old face that looked like a used up old catcher's mitt. His jaw was rimmed with an orange dyed beard and he perpetually had a pipe dangling between his lips. It was a face that only an Irishman could appreciate.

"Cheap, Son of a Bitch, I'm gonna..." Johnny mumbled. "Here." Johnny handed over the yen reluctantly. The bar tab tapped him for almost all of his funds.

"Good. Now that you two are square with the bar I'll tell you her name." Shamus smirked. "It's Kate and she just pulled into the parking lot". Johnny perked up and looked out the window, grabbed his helmet and exited the bar.

"Hey Kate," He yelled across the parking lot. Kate looked up at the sound of her name. "I think I owe you a date." Johnny smiled as he walked up to her.

"Is this your way of trying to make it up to me?" Kate said with a smirk. Johnny looked dumbfound at her response. His jaw dropped at her comment and he was a little hurt. "Relax Johnny. I think it is kind of cute." Johnny tried to play it cool, but his subterfuge was wasted on her.

"So…" Johnny said. "What time you get off work?"

"Around 11," Kate responded with a sexy smile.

"Got any plans tonight?"

"Well it appears I have a date, but right now I have to get to work."

"See you then." Johnny winked at her and head for his bike.

"Johnny," Kate called after him. Johnny turned to look at the gorgeous woman that called after him. "I'm glad that you didn't give up after this morning." Kate smiled as she approached Johnny and kissed him on the cheek. Johnny smiled and put on his helmet.

"See ya t'night," Johnny said as he started his motorcycle and rode off.

Johnny left the bar in better spirits but still needed to grab a bit of food before he met up with Dash. He barely had cash to grab a burger from a street vendor. He sat on the curb side while he ate. The burger was tasty, but that could have been that fact it was drowned in condiments and toppings. The condiments, mostly mustard, were to cover up the fact the patty tasted like rat, which it most likely was, but with some cheese, pickles and onions it wasn't half bad. Johnny figured out early in life if you didn't like the taste of something cover it with mustard. It always killed the taste right quick.

Johnny watched the people on the street while he ate. The streets were a dirty place especially in southern part of town. Takahara Corp. allowed those who wouldn't join up to live in the dirty and grime of Southern Neo-Hiroshima. Johnny always wondered if it was better when the United States was in control or if it was just the same shit-hole, but under different management. Across the street there were guys slinging quick silver and melt, and tech fiends tripping off their downloads. Those drugs ran rampant in Neo-Japan. Especially in Neo-Hiroshima – the city that once was Seattle.

Quick Silver was an upper like no other. Having a quickie had a whole new meaning. Melt was just the opposite. The drug was called melt because you could barely move when you took it. Most people just sat where they were and melted into their furniture. Tech fiends were the worst. Tech is black market cybernetic software that made people's brains think they were high. He almost went as far as to remove the head link from his skull because of tech fiends and a recent cybernetics bug they infected thousands with. Johnny hated drugs, but could do nothing about it without drawing unwanted attention. Drawing attention would have led to an "early retirement" because of his history with Takahara Corp.

Johnny shook his head and ran his hand through his shaggy hair, his thoughts returning to Kate while he avoided mustard dripping on to his shirt. "I should really try to impress her when I take her out." He said to himself, and then thought about the fact that his bank roll was bone dry. "I'm glad I get paid today. Then I'll have the dough to take her out for a night on the town she'll never forget." He chuckled to himself and thought "Hopefully I won't either."

Johnny finished his burger and hurried back to the warehouse to meet up with Dash.

Dash arrived at Jack's building after a quick drive down I-90 to Mercer Island. Jack lived on the Northside, but didn't work for Takahara Corp. His building was invisible to the eyes of Takahara Corp. Jack had hacked the local camera feeds and digitally removed the building. Dash considered Jack the smartest man he knew, even if he wasn't all there.

Dash looked up at Jack's camera and waved. The buzz at the door let Dash know it was safe to enter. Dash stepped over the booby trapped door mat then went up the stairs. As Dash entered the room he saw the usual sight -- Jack sitting at his computer plugging away, surrounded with empty cans of energy drinks.

"Got another letter and cash for you to deliver," Dash said

interrupting Jack's train of thought.

"Huh, oh hey, forgot I let you in. Whatcha say?" Jack replied prying his eyes from his computer screens.

"Another letter," Dash repeated, waiving the envelope in the air.

"Oh, yeah I'll get that taken care of. You bring back Frankie?" Jack asked.

"Sorry man, I'm going to need her for one more day," Dash said with a shrug.

"Hey she's mine. I just let you borrow her. What are you hiding? You scratched her didn't you? Where is she?" Jack insisted.

"Would you relax. She's back at the warehouse. I'll get her to you tomorrow. There's nothing to worry about." Dash sighed. He had been through this routine several times.

"You better have her back by tomorrow or I'll... I'll..." Jack began to get angry.

"You'll what?"

"I'll do something and you won't like it…. So what was the caper this time?" Jack eyes return back to his computer.

"Retarded fucking Johnny and I nabbed something from Maki Labs… And if there's a scratch on Frankie, it's Johnny's own damn fault."

"Johnny? You know, the amount of times I hear you swear every time you say his name I wouldn't have thought you'd have kept working with him. I don't understand why you would work with the guy who ruined your life."

"That's where the money is. His uncle keeps my pockets full of Yen and soon enough I'll be able to whisk my girl away and head off to Canada."

"Yeah, but…."

"It's nothing Jack. Johnny is a fucking tool. After I get paid today I'm fucking out of here. Fuck him."

"Whatever you say man… So check this out, I've been working on cracking the new retinal scanners the TCS have come up with. All I need to do is get this program in and I'll have access to any and all

Takahara Corp. buildings. The only problem is getting into their system. I've been trying to hack it for months now. All the normal splice commands get destroyed before I even start, but what if I tried to install a program that is already supposed to be there and then slip in a back door." Jack continued to mumble to himself as his fingers flew over his keypad. It was almost five minutes before Jack came back around.

"Jack... Jack... Just make sure to deliver the letter," Dash said with a sigh as he headed for the door. Jack spaced out some times when he was working on trying to take down Takahara Corp. Jack was a conspiracy nut to the core, but some of the elaborate conspiracy that he ran around in his mind sometimes made sense. When Jack started to make sense or was wrapped deep into his work Dash knew it was time to leave. Dash was just about to leave when Jack spoke up.

"If you do it for the money, I wonder what they do it for. I mean the mob normally would have left you to rot to save their hides. I wonder what or who stopped them from dropping you in the bay. Seems with all the heat that was on you three years ago getting rid of you would have been easier. Instead they spent, I don't know, how much money to send you to that training camp, outfitting you, and employing you. Seems like a waste of money to me... Not that I would have thrown you in the bay... I mean it would have just been for profitable to turn you in... not that I would, I mean you and I are friends.... Right?... ah yeah so I'll deliver that letter right away. You can count on me buddy... Dash... Dash..."

"Right Jack," Dash said he turned his back and waved. "See you when I bring Frankie back." Dash went out the way he came. Dash thought briefly on what Jack had said about Johnny and Dylan keeping him around. Dash could only think that he was kept around because he was a good investment.

The training that Dash and Johnny went through was rigorous and like no other training that Dash had seen or heard of. Dash continued to reflect on what Jack said. Dylan probably thought that if the training didn't kill him then maybe Dylan could make use of him.

Dash continued to contemplate his past as he went back to his place.

He ran through the shower to rid himself of the smells of the previous night. Dash was no angel when it came to women, something he again blamed on Johnny. He wasn't like this in high school, but he was trying to fill a void that left a hole in his soul, but no matter how much tail he got nothing healed the pain. Dash dressed in a blue button up shirt and black jeans. He grabbed his keys and went out the door. It was finally time to get his life back on track and leave those sorry sacks behind.

Dash pulled up to the warehouse and parked his bike. Johnny was waiting inside, he had cleaned himself up as well and was now wearing a red t-shirt and blue jeans. It was time to get paid.

"Hey. You owe me for your tab last night." Johnny accused.

"Really? I didn't pay again? Wow!" Dash said, loading each word with sarcasm. "Just put it on my tab. I'll get you back after we get paid," Dash said, hopping into the driver seat of the van.

"You realize that would be your entire cut for this job if ya paid everything you owed me back," Johnny said as he pretended to a little math in the air. "Carry the four, yup all of it."

"Yup." Dash smirked a devious smile.

"Ya ain't going to pay me back are you?" Johnny sighed.

"Nope," Dash stated.

"Why not...." Before Johnny even finished the sentence he knew. Together they said, "Fern."

Johnny sighed again, "You're never going to let that go, are you?"

"Not a chance." Dash smiled.

Johnny never meant for their lives to be this way and had been trying to make it up to his friend ever since, but one small incident changed their lives forever. Their lives before this one were the best that they could be. Johnny and Dash were on the high school football team together. Johnny and Dash had it made. In high school they only knew each other through football. Johnny returned punts and kick offs , but didn't see much more playing time then that, but he didn't really need to since he return about 1 in 4 for touchdowns. Dash was the star quarterback and had lead the football team to the championship game each season since his freshman year. On the field they shared a competitive streak that made them push each other to be the best they could be.

Off the field they stayed out of each other's way. Dash grew up on the Northside of Old interstate 90 and Johnny grew up south of Beacon Hill at the time was considered the worse part of Neo-Hiroshima. It was as simple as that and if it had not been for the incident they probably would have went their separate ways after high school, but life is never that easy. It was just a month before their senior year homecoming game and dance.

Three years ago, in order to earn some easy cash, Johnny ran errands for his Uncle Dylan. He would drop packages off and pick items up. It was how earned enough to pay for his motorcycle. He was doing a delivery for his Uncle in a part of town he had never been in before, but considering what his Uncle's business was it made a lot of sense. Except for school and football, the Northside of town was off limits to him and always would be. According to Uncle Dylan, Takahara Corp. security would have picked Johnny up in an instance if they knew who he was. Being the nephew of a known mob member had its draw backs. Takahara Corp. didn't care much for the Irish mob's influence on the Southside. didn't care much for the Irish mob's influence on the Southside.

It was middle of October 2047; football season was going well so Johnny cut practice to make a few extra yen making a few deliveries for Fat Montey. The deliveries were on the Northside of town, but Johnny figured he would be in and out quick. Johnny made the drop just like he was accustomed to doing when appearing from behind a van, a TCS agent struck with a nightstick knocking Johnny off his bike. Johnny knew that the TCS never travelled alone as he lay on his back he spotted another two agents. Johnny gathered himself and got to his feet, thankful that his leather jacket protected him from getting too banged up. Johnny dusted himself off as he sized up the agents. Being a cocky 17 year old he thought that he could take them.

"You on wrong side of town, Ochikobore," One of them said in poorly spoken English.

"I just got a little turned around. Could you point me in the right direction? Is it that way?" Johnny asked giving the TCS agent 'the finger' as he pointed. "Or perhaps it is that way?" Johnny gave him 'the finger' with his other hand.

"This is last time you show face around here." The man scowled. Johnny tried to move toward his bike but was blocked.

"Kick his ass Joe!" One of the agents shouted to the other.

"This is going to hurt," Johnny said under his breath as he looked at each of the men. Johnny bum-rushed the agent they called Joe. He was smallest of the three and obviously in charge. He tackled him to the ground and stuck him in the face bloodying his nose, but one high school kid against 3 grown men were bad odds for anyone, even Johnny. He fought back as well as he could but it was over in a matter of seconds.

Lying in a heap on the ground, Johnny did his best to protect his three or four broken ribs. His blurry vision and blood stained shirt belied a broken nose and obvious signs of a concussion. Johnny had received and given out enough beat downs to know the agents weren't going to stop. He prepared himself for the end, aware that men as dangerous as these usually didn't leave any loose ends lying around, but as luck would have it Johnny didn't die that day.

Two of the figures that were hovering above his broken body were removed from his vision. Johnny focused as best as he could on the new figure that had joined them. The figure dress in a Mustang football jersey had knocked them flat on their backs. Johnny could barely make out the jersey number. The number "1" clad the chest of his savior and the jersey belonged his team's quarterback, Dash McBragg.

Dash didn't let the two gain their feet without paying dearly for it. Johnny had a hard time trying to make heads or tails of what happened next as his concussion made everyone's movements blurry. Dash moved like a movie in fast forward and placed a front kick into the crotch of the only man remaining on his feet. He emitted a high-pitched gurgling sound and collapsed very close to Johnny.

Dash's retractable metal cleats must have malfunctioned and extended during the kick. The agent was grabbing his groin with both hands, but no amount of pressure was going to stop a man from bleeding out after being ripped open by Dash's cleats. As the other two rose to their feet Dash met them with a solid punches to their faces. His fists connected sending the men staggering back.

Dash had completely surprised the men who attacked Johnny and Johnny took the opportunity to pull his switchblade from his pocket and stabbed the cleated agent in the throat as he went for his gun, putting him out of commission for good. One of the other men stepped too close to Johnny who lashed out, kicking him in the knee cap, bending his leg sideways while ripping every ligament in his knee. The sound the man's leg made Johnny will never forget. If it weren't for the adrenaline surging through his body the grotesque noise would have made him puked. Dash moved in quickly on the crippled man and put him in a choke hold. Johnny tried to help fight off the other security guard, but was too weak to do anything. He just kept hitting Dash, over and over again, but Dash wouldn't let the choke hold go. Dash continued to squeeze tighter and tighter.

That's when the last man stopped punching Dash and pulled out his gun. Johnny reacted as fast as he could. Gripping his knife tightly Johnny made it just in the nick-of-time.

Dash twisted to the side in order to put the man he was choking between him and the gunman. Everyone left alive was greeted with the sound of walking on dried twigs in the forest as the man's neck snapping in three places.

Johnny used the last of his reserve of strength and stabbed the gunman in the head. The thrust was weak but it was enough to take him down. Dash let go of the man he had grappled with who lay limp on the ground like a rag doll. All three bodies lay still and lifeless. Pools of blood had formed around the men. Johnny glanced down at the man he had just stabbed in the back of the skull. The man blinked but was immobile otherwise, amazingly still alive. A lucky nick by Johnny's blade was enough to cause spinal damaged. The man wasn't dead yet but soon would be. They had vanquished the Takahara Security men. Being just high school kids they had no clue what to do, so they fled. Johnny and Dash stumbled back to Johnny's uncles, both being in a state of shock. Neither had ever seen a dead body let alone killed someone.

The death of the three agents was all over the 5 o'clock Takahara news before they got to Dylan's place. No names were released and no suspects were mentioned, but that didn't mean anything coming from a Takahara owned station. Those stations only reported the news that was approved by the company. After getting cleaned up Dylan tried to drive Dash home, but after Dash explained what happened to his parents. They kicked him out. At least that is the way he saw it.

Dash always said it was his choice. If he would have been caught they sure would have imprisoned his parents or worse. Dylan and Dash never spoke again about what happened that day. Dash swore Dylan to secrecy. Dylan knew Dash was troubled by what his parents did, so he did his best to take care of him.

Uncle Dylan cleaned up the mess as best he could, getting them new ID's, new names, new everything. After some training they became package runners. The only job they could take without being found by Takahara Corp. That is when Johnny's alias Berith was born. Dash refused to change his name. He figured that within a few months things would be back to normal so what was the point.

Dylan was quick to enlist Johnny and Dash into his crew. They had a rep now and wouldn't be messed with and with some training from the right guys they could make some real money. Dash really didn't understand exactly what was going on, but he did notice the money and the respect that he got, but that still never made up for ruining his life. Dash saw what had happened as a normal day for Johnny, while he had to give up everything. This never sat well with Dash. When he was not learning his new trade he was looking for some way to clear his name. Dash needed to clear his name so he could get back to her.

Dash was dating a girl named Fern and they were pretty serious; more serious than any eighteen year old should be at that age. Johnny and Dash had to disappear for a while and didn't know when they could return to their old lives Johnny and Dash needed a little cash to help get them out of town for a while, so they took on an easy delivery for Dylan's friend Fat Montey. They were going to make enough to take care of themselves until it was safe to come back. During the delivery Dash went off job, saying he had to be somewhere. Johnny did his best to befriend Dash. Dash had saved his life and Johnny was a little awe struck that someone would do that for him, so Johnny told him he would take care of the delivery and come back to pick him up afterwards.

Dash gave Johnny an address hastily scribbled on a piece of paper and told him to pick him up there when he was finished.

Johnny completed the job -- no big deal, as it wasn't anything that Johnny couldn't handle by himself. Afterwards, Johnny headed to the spot he was supposed to pick up Dash. It wasn't until he saw the "Charging Mustangs" sign when he realized that the address was to the high school and to make matters worse it was on the Northside.

Dash had been waiting for a chance to steal Fern aside and had finally found his moment. This particular night was the homecoming dance - one more event in Dash's life that he had to give up for the sake of staying under the radar. Dash waited patiently for a couple hours in the dark until he finally saw Fern walking outside alone to have a smoke. She wore an emerald green dress, cut high in order to show off her perfect legs and cinched tightly beneath her ample breasts. Her fiery hair was done elegantly. She was a beauty to behold that night and dressed to impress one man in hopes that he would be there that night. She slowly exhaled a drag of smoke and leaned against the wall before burying her face into the crook of her arm and sobbing. Dash's heart broke as he watched her, tears welling up in his own eyes. Dash couldn't take it any longer and stepped out of the darkness, arms sliding around her from behind.

"Ssshhh. It's okay my love," Dash said as she started to scream, but she recognized his voice and quickly became silent, melting into his embrace.

"Where? How...?" She murmured as she pressed herself into Dash, enjoying the emotions that were washing over her.

"It doesn't matter. I'm here now," he stated fighting back his emotions.

"You disappeared. I didn't know what to do. I was all alone," Fern whispered, tears falling down her cheeks.

"You'll never have to worry about being alone again. Come with me. I'll tell you about everything," he told her and began to sway with the music emanating from the open gymnasium door. "Marry me Fern."

Fern gasped. "Of... Of course...Yes!" She said softly. He spun her around to face him and they embraced each other, holding on to each other as though their lives would be incomplete if they let go. Dash knelt down on one knee and placed the ring he bought on her finger.

"I'm so sorry I couldn't come to you sooner, but I had to make sure it was safe," Dash said as he pulled her close and kissed her deeply. "I'll tell you about everything later when the time is right."

Fern pulled away, "Are we leaving tonight?"

"Yes," he stated.

"Let me say goodbye really quick?" Fern asked, her sparkling green eyes breaking down Dash's defenses.

"Sure, be quick. I have a ride waiting," he said and waved into the darkness. Across the parking lot a pair of headlights flashed twice and an engine roared to life. Fern ran inside and Johnny drove up to the sidewalk. Dash walked over to the driver side window. "We got room for one more?"

"Um...sure," Johnny said uncertainly. "You know Dash; we were supposed to leave this shit behind. Uncle Dylan isn't going to like this and, besides, this is no life for her. You know it and I know."

"Fuck you and your damn Uncle!" Dash yelled as he slammed his hands against the van. "And how do *you* know what is best for her?!"

"I don't. But come on man, think about it," Johnny said hoping that Dash would really think about what would happen if she came with.

"I can't!" Dash yelled as a tear ran down his cheek. Johnny had never seen Dash cry and knew that this was one of those moments that would make or break the friendship he was trying to form. Johnny felt that he really had only one friend left in the world. So he did what all friends should do in this kind of situation.

"Okay, but I ain't covering her rent," Johnny said jokingly. "Hurry up and go get her. We were due back five minutes ago. I don't like being out on the Northside too many TCS roaming around."

Dash smiled as he ran back to the high school's door. As Dash was standing at the door waiting for Fern, a burnished-silver Honda Civic pulled into the parking lot and shut off its head lights. The car was custom; the frame and been dropped a few inches and the windows were tinted black as night. The car slowed as it began to creep closer towards the van.

Johnny noticed a vehicle in the side mirror and knew that this wasn't just some stupid high school kids. His side of town saw at least a drive by a week and he knew how to deal with them. He got out from the opposite side of the van and circled through the bushes in order to get behind the car. As he got nearer to the car, light from a street lamp gleamed off of a gun barrel pointed out a side window at Dash.

"Gun!" Johnny yelled and Dash instinctually ducked behind the nearest cover.

Johnny drew his pistol out from his hidden holster and emptied his clip through the rear window. Bullets plunged into the back of the driver's head smashing it open like a fat, ripe melon. He then reloaded and ran up beside the passenger side, staying out of view of the gunman, and pumped five bullets into the man's neck, shoulder, and head.

"Dash we've got to go - now!" Johnny shouted over the screams of high school kids.

They both sprinted to the van. Two more Hondas marked with Takahara Corp. Security emblems came screaming into the parking lot, guns-a-blazing. As they left the parking lot high school kids were running for cover in panic. Dash leaned out the window and fired on Takahara's assassins, catching a glimpse of Fern staring painfully after them as they drove from the parking lot, leaving her behind. Thoughts of Fern raced in his head. Dash knew then that would be almost impossible for him go back to his old life to be with his one true love, but that wasn't going to stop him from trying.

Beta: The Scorpion and The Bull

"**Johnny, snap** out of it!" Dash stated as he punched him in the arm.

"Ow. Fuck!" Johnny shouted. "What was that for?"

"You've been day dreaming for the past 20 minutes. We're here," Dash stated, and pointed at Uncle Dylan's pawn shop. Johnny rubbed his shoulder as he hopped out the van.

"You know you're gonna hit me one too many times and I'm gonna snap," Johnny said.

"*Riiiiiiight*, and Dylan won't try and stick us with paying for our own gas for the job," Dash responded with a chuckle.

"Just help me with the case," Johnny said. They each grabbed a side of the box and lifted it out of the harness. As they walked to the door something seemed amiss to Johnny; the "closed" sign was flipped over. "Uncle Dylan's shop is never closed this early; especially when we have a delivery," he thought.

"Hey Dash, does this look right to you." Johnny pointed at the closed sign and Dash took a quick look around.

"No, it doesn't. Let's put this back in the van for a minute," Dash said. Johnny and Dash re-secured the box back in its harness.

"I know where he keeps the spare key. You want to go in?" Johnny questioned.

"I'd like to get paid. Did you call him this morning?" Dash asked.

"No, didn't you?" Johnny responded

"Why would I call that nasty old fuck?!" Dash said agitated. "And besides, he's *your* uncle."

"Yeah, but you're the one that made the deal," Johnny argued back.

"Sooooo... what's your fucking point?" Dash asked, raising an eyebrow.

"So, that means you make the phone calls," Johnny said equally agitated. This wasn't the first time they have had this conversation.

"But I leave the bitch work for you," Dash said blowing off the argument. Johnny gave him the finger in return. "Are you armed?"

"Do you have to ask? I take a gun to the fucking movies," Johnny joked as he pulled out his Scorpion from the hostler under his jacket and cocked it.

"Well why don't you use it to go knock on the door and see if anyone's home?" Dash said.

They approached the pawnshop and Johnny grabbed the fake rock that his uncle hid the key in.

"Your uncle needs to get better security." Dash dead panned.

"Dude, he's old school Irish mob. No one fucks with his shop," Johnny said scoffing at the comment as he opened the door. "Uncle Dylan, hey, Uncle D, we're here."

"Shhhh," Dash whispered and cuffed Johnny upside his ear. Johnny whirled around and Dash pointed to a shot out security camera. Johnny turned the safety off, and ducked behind a rack of Tech downloads.

"You stay up here and cover my ass. I'll check out the back room," Johnny whispered with a note of worry in his voice. Dash drew his guns: twin Springfield Armory .40 cals - one modified for automatic fire. Johnny also noticed a giant Raging Bull revolver tucked into a chest holster. Johnny understood the Springfield's were excellent guns, but the Raging Bull just seemed a little excessive. Dash always said that if was going to shoot someone important he was going to do it in style. It had been three years since the incident and Dash had made a habit of doing all their jobs with style. Johnny was always kind of impressed how well Dash acclimated to his new life.

Johnny snuck into the back room and found it shot to hell. In the middle of the room was his Uncle bound to a chair with his head slumped against his chest.

"Uncle Dylan. Let's get you the hell out of here," Johnny said with his heart racing. He was glad that he could finally return the favor that his Uncle had given him. Johnny kept an eye on the adjoining office door, which also lead to the back alley. As he untied the cords blood dripped off Uncle Dylan into a pool on the floor.

"Hey Bryan," Dylan said deliriously from blood loss. "Help me out of here."

"Uncle, this isn't Bryan. This is Johnny, your nephew," Johnny said with a hint of worry in his voice. "Just give me a second and we'll have you out of here," Johnny said concerned for his uncle's condition. There was a lot of blood, too much blood.

"I'll get you over to the hospital and everything will be fine," Johnny said, more trying to convince himself than his uncle.

"Get out of here Johnny," Dylan said, becoming lucid once again. Realizing Johnny had walked into a trap. "If the TCS find out you're here you'll be as fucked as a goat with nine assholes." Dylan spat a tooth on the floor. "They can't find you. If they find out your alive you'll have nowhere to run."

"Then we'll just have to hurry up and get out of here together," Johnny said as he finished untying him.

"I'll only slow you down," Dylan muttered through the blood, tears, and unspeakable pain. "They busted my knees. I can't walk. Just leave me."

"Fuck you old man. I'm not leaving you," Johnny said through his own tears as he picked up his uncle and threw him over his shoulder. "You need to lay off the Twinkies, Uncle." Johnny grimaced and began to move back towards Dash's position in the main room.

Just then, the office door opened up.

"They're trying to take him," A voice said, as shots were fired hitting Dylan instead of Johnny. Johnny dropped his slack uncle's body like a sack of Irish potatoes and whipped around bring his weapon in line with his target. He fired a burst of shots that ended the intruder's alarm.

"Uncle!" Johnny screamed as he crouched over to Dylan's body and rolled him over. The shots hit center mass. Dylan's eyes were rolled back into his skull and his tongue lolled out like a basset hound. "No...Uncle... No! No! No!" Johnny sobbed as he grabbed his uncle and held him. Tears started rolling down his cheeks. Uncle Dylan was the only blood family he had left. Uncle Dylan reached up and touched Johnny's face.

"You... you... got to... get..." Uncle Dylan stuttered, spitting out gouts of blood from his mouth, before he passed away.

Johnny sobbed uncontrollably as he hugged his Uncle. A few moments went by as he wept. Johnny's sorrow was interrupted by the cocking of a gun hammer as the barrel of a gun was placed at the crown of his head.

"Well, well, well. The chicken has come home to sleep," A voice in a thick Japanese accent said followed by the cocking of a piston hammer.

"It's roost, dumbass," Dash said and fired his Raging Bull. The TCS agent's brains splattered all over the wall. Dash looked down at Johnny, "Johnny we got to go leave'em."

"They killed him!" Johnny began to sob a little more. "We were almost out of here."

"Dude we're going to end up dead if you don't move your ass. We'll get'em back," Dash stated to try calm Johnny down. "Just remember; Vengeance is best served with a side of cabbage. Or whatever your uncle was so fond of saying". Dash smirked.

Johnny wiped his eyes and let out a broken chuckle.

Dash took a quick peek out the back door. As he did bullets came screaming by his head. Six TCS agents armed with assault rifles were moving towards their position.

"Mother Fuckers are gonna pay," Johnny stated as his chuckle turned to rage. Turning, he grasped the handle of the back door and whipped it open, letting loose the rest of his clip from his Scorpion machine pistol. The rounds connected with an approaching TCS agent ripping through his powder blue uniform. Dash then kicked the door shut as Johnny began to reload.

"What are you fucking crazy? We are outnumbered and out

gunned. We need to make it back to the van and figure this out. Now get your head on straight and come follow me," Dash yelled as he grabbed the chair Uncle Dylan was bound to and braced the door with it. Johnny was still enraged, but Dash knew this was no time to fight. He slapped Johnny across the face.

"Run dumbass!" Dash yelled at Johnny.

Johnny snapped out of it and headed for the van. Dash covered their escape and fired a couple rounds through the back door to the shop. Johnny got in the passenger seat, rolled down the window, and positioned himself to be able to fire over the top of the van. Spotting movement from either side of the building Johnny let loose a spray of bullet at each side causing the TCS agents to back off long enough for Dash to get Frankie going. Johnny wrapped his leg around the seat belt to give him a little support. TCS agents began to emerge around the edge of the building firing at them as they pulled away. Johnny continued to fire at them until Dash turned the corner. A black Honda Civic, clad with the Takahara Corporation Security emblem, peeled around the corner after them. The Civic's driver jumped right on the van's ass. Dash put the pedal to the metal as he weaved in and out of traffic, but his pursuers were not going to give up that easy.

"We have to lose these guys. Where we headed, Dash?!" Johnny yelled from his firing position. Johnny's thought kept creeping into his mind not allowing him to focus on what he needed to do. Uncle Dylan had always been there, gave him jobs, made sure he was took care of, and had saved his life more than once. Johnny couldn't form a thought in his head with the death of Dylan at the forefront of his mind, but there was no time for his thoughts as he continued to firing at the perusing vehicle.

"Get your head in the game. We'll lose these guys and get back to the warehouse in one piece," Dash explained. "Then, we need to get a hold of Jack."

"Who?" Johnny asked, very puzzled.

"My hacker contact, he'll be able to find out why we got this much heat from the TCS, and may be able to tell us what the fuck's in that case." Dash continued.

"I thought I knew all your contacts... just in case?" Johnny questioned, looking a little hurt.

"Not this one," Dash said.

"How do you know him?" Johnny asked.

"He owns Frankie," Dash explained.

"Owns Frankie?" Johnny looked quizzically at him. "I always thought it was yours?"

"Nope. Lost it in a poker game to Jack; I guess you could say it's on "extended lease" to me." Dash finished with a smirk as they entered the Southside Street market off of Rainer Ave. Dash took a hard turn clipping a melon cart sending cantaloupes and honeydews flying all over the place.

"Well since this Jack fellow's your friend, *you* get to explain the bullet holes," Johnny said as his Scorpion roared to life.

Dash checked his review mirror. "Son of a bitch. They're STILL back there!" The loud thuds and shattering glass rang out inside the van. "AND they're fucking firing back!" Dash grumbled as a bullet went through the windshield.

Johnny changed clips and began firing again. Johnny's seatbelt kept holding strong around his leg even though there were a few turns that could have sent him flying into the side of a building. Dash kicked his driving skill into high gear as he began to make left turns, right turns, and avoided traffic as well as possible. The chase had been going on for five minutes which never happened when Dash was driving, even if he was in a crap van with poor handling. Dash was astonished by the fact the Civic was still in his rearview mirror. Dash was known for his get-away driving, three years of hairpin turns, shaking tails, and knowing the streets backwards and forwards will do that.

"I'm out they must have a bullet proof windshield on that thing." Johnny said as he slid back into the car. A set of rounds burst through the back doors of the van and through Frankie's windshield. Johnny ducked narrowly avoiding bullets clipping the back of the head rest on the seat.

"It also might help things if you weren't using a fucking toy for a gun." Dash said as he threw the van into a tight turn. "Fucking Scorpion's are only good up close and personal. Remind me to bring a real assault rifle for you next time."

"I hope this Jack guy has good insurance because no cut rate place is going to cover that many bullet holes. He's probably not going to like being dragged into this."

"You don't know the half of it," Dash responded. "Fuck this shit, Grab the wheel!"

"What? Why?" Johnny asked confused.

"Just do it," Dash said as he undid his seat belt and wrapped it around his arm. Johnny quickly grabbed the wheel as Dash opened his door and leaned out. Dash grabbed two grenades from the side compartment in the door, pulled the pins and skipped them off the asphalt behind them. The first grenade detonated just in front of the car causing the driver to swerve erratically. The second skittered under the rear end of the car making an explosion like a Fourth of July celebration. Inertia carried the car end over end before it landed upside down. The flaming wreck skidded to a stop ending the chase. Dash gave Johnny a "thumbs-up" and pulled himself back into the driver's seat.

"Holy shit! That was fucking sweet!" Johnny exclaimed as he helped Dash back in the vehicle.

"Sweet like your mom," Dash said. There was a moment of silence then they both laughed as Dash headed to the warehouse. "I think we were set up, Johnny. Dylan knew better than to send us after Takahara shit. He was the one that insisted that we never take a job that got us close to that side of town."

"Yeah I know that... which means someone set *him* up," Johnny said. "We better stash the van. This is too hot of a target right now. You think Fat Montey had something to do with it? It was his job?"

"Doubt it, then again... Let's just grab our bikes and head back to Jack's. He should be able to get us some info on what's going on,"

Dash said, but there was some uncertainty in his voice.

"I hope so because Takahara Corp. owns the border police. It would be impossible to get across the border without being turned into meat paste; and short of kidnapping Takahara himself I'm out of ideas." Johnny admitted.

"It might come to that," Dash said with a straight face as he watched the mirrors to make sure they weren't being followed again.

"You're kidding right…. Dash, please tell me that you're kidding?" Johnny asked thinking that Dash had gone off the deep end.

"What else could we give him to save our asses?" Dash mentioned. "This Takahara screwball isn't known for being 'Mr. Nice Guy.' Either we fuck him or… well… you get the picture. We need to lie low and think of a plan."

"Lyin' low and thinking of a plan sounds good. Kidnapping sounds like the worst plan ever," Johnny replied not even believing Dash was actually considering grabbing Takahara himself. He knew that if it really was true about Takahara Corp. being after them, that they were fucked worse than a hooker on two yen Tuesday.

"Listen, how about we kidnap his niece and hold her ransom and then take the job to get her back. Then we return her and we won't have to be on the run anymore. We'll be heroes."

"You know how crazy that sounds. That's almost as stupid as walking into Takahara headquarters and shooting up the place. We'd be dead in half a minute tops," Johnny said. "We could talk to Uncle Dylan's boss, Fat Montey. Maybe he can help us out."

"Fat Montey is a total jerk-off. That grease bag would sell out his own mother if it fetched him a good price. This situation is too hot to trust to anybody outside of us and our closest friends – we better just go straight to Jack. Three heads thinking about this are better than two. Especially since you're still all fucked up and emo over your dead uncle." Dash said without concern for Johnny. He had bigger concerns. This job was supposed to be his last. He needed Johnny's head on straight if he was going to survive long enough to get paid and buy his way out of the Neo-Japan. He knew that after a few drinks he would be square with Johnny. Dash knew that Johnny thought of him as a friend and could use that to his advantage.

"Fine!" Johnny agreed unwillingly, still looking pissed off at Dash's comment. "Let's get our bikes, check with Jack-me-off, and then head down to El Diablo. Shamus will know what to do. We need to get the damn TCS off our backs."

"I can do without those monkeys," Dash said and began to pantomime a primate, jungle calls and all. "But we should probably stay away from Montey's people. At least until we know it wasn't him that set us up."

A few minutes later they pulled up to the garage and, for once, the door didn't stick. Dash stashed the van and they both got on their bikes and rode off to Jack's.

"Who the fuck is Jack and why hasn't Dash told me about him," Johnny thought. "Dash and I have no secrets... What else is he hiding from me?" They headed east on Old Interstate 90 over Lake Hiroshima, old lake Washington, getting off at the Mercer Way exit, and then headed south. The further people lived from the coast in Neo-Hiroshima more people were willing to accept help from Takahara Corp. which made this part of Neo-Hiroshima not a good place to Dash and Johnny to be.

It wasn't long before they arrived at Jack's. They parked in an alley a couple blocks away to keep their bikes out of sight. Johnny was trying to think of a way to ask Dash if there was anything else he should know before they met with Jack, but he kept his thoughts to himself. Johnny trusted his friend even if he Dash didn't seem to trust him back. Dash grabbed Johnny by the shoulder to stop him and pointed across the street from where they were.

"Jack," Dash whispered, and motioned Johnny to follow him. The person ducked into a nearby coffee shop. Through the window of the shop they noticed Jack as he sat at a back table and pulled down the hood of his coat.

Dash and Johnny entered and walked back to where Jack was seated. As Jack flipped open his laptop Dash leaned in. "Hey man we were coming to see you."

Jack was about 6 foot tall and had longer, shaggy hair, but it didn't reach his shoulders - sported square-rimmed glasses and a goatee. He wore a green army jacket over a black hooded sweatshirt. Johnny could only think, "Oh great; a conspiracy nut."

"You bring any *more* friends?!" Jack asked harshly, pointing at Johnny, but as softly as he could as not to draw attention.

"What are you talking about?" Dash asked. Jack then flipped around his laptop. It was security footage of roughly 20 TCS guardsmen and agents tearing Jack's place apart.

"What the hell man? How did the boys in blue find you? I thought you lived off the grid. Those are more than just TCS agents all over your place. There must be a platoon of guardsmen at your place," Dash stated.

"I live off the grid and it's *three* platoons," Jack exclaimed in a whisper thrusting three fingers into Dash's face.

It wasn't too hard to tell the different between TCS agents and guardsmen. Agents were Takahara's privately owned police force. Agents were normally dressed in uniforms similar to what a beat cop from the early part of the century would wear. The uniforms were kept very similar to the United States government except they were a light blue. Johnny suspected that it made people still think they were still part of the States. Johnny never saw many of them growing up on the south side of Neo-Hiroshima because the Irish mob made sure they weren't welcome.

TCS Guard on the other hand was another story. They were the soldiers of Neo-Japan. Brought in whenever they were needed and sometimes when they weren't. Many worker strikes were brought to an end at the rifle fire of the TCS Guard. Guardsmen were better trained, better funding, and better equipped. Most that have confronted them were dead or imprison for life.

Normally Guardsmen dressed in black uniforms and were armed to the hilt. Dylan always told Johnny that they were like a special unit called S.W.A.T. back before the Depression and the panics. Except they were not used to protect and serve the people they were used to removed people that were in the way of Takahara Corp. and the corporation used them on a whim.

Johnny and Dash must have qualified for their whim. They watched with Jack as the agents and guardsmen ransacked Jack's place. Jack grimaced each and every time he saw them break something. Johnny and Dash could only assume that their places were being torn apart as well.

"They must have followed you yesterday when you came to drop off the letter at my place," Jack whispered forcefully. "You know... After your shootout at Maki Labs!"

"Shoot out? We weren't in a shootout," Dash lied. "Besides if we were in a shoot out, I'm sure that you can get most of that fixed buddy." Dash tried to apply a comforting slap to Jack's shoulder, but all he received in return was a sad glare.

"Oh, really. Then explain this," Jack said, taking his laptop back. He then pressed a few buttons, and then flipped it back around. Across the screen, like some amateur vidstream from the internet, flashed a video showing the heist and the shootout immediately following it - fully implicating both Johnny and Dash as their faces scrolled across the screen on numerous occasions.

"You gotta be kiddin' me." Johnny muttered, to which Dash just sighed in resignation.

"Well... long story short, now you know why we're here," Dash said knowing that he had put Jack's life in jeopardy. "But it really couldn't be helped since our fucking lives are on the line!" Dash said with his voice getting louder with every word. "We've been set up and we could use, no, need a little help right now." Dash finished, emphasizing his point by grabbing Jack by the shirt collar.

"Right, look, I just want you to leave me alone. So go away," Jack said timidly, brushing Dash's hand off his collar. "I'll go my way and you go yours and everything will be jusssst fine."

Jack tried to stand up and leave the shop, but Johnny shoved him back into his seat. The ruckus startled the customers. Johnny waved at the people with a forced smile on his face but people continued to stare at them. Johnny then made the hand motion like Jack had been drinking a little too much in order to get them to go back to what they were doing.

"Who's this clown?" Jack asked with distain.

"Clown?" Johnny scoffed at Jack's comment.

"I don't mean that you're a clown as such I mean that you are funny looking...Did I say that you were funny looking I meant that you looked at me funny, but with a face like that I..." Jack continued to ramble trying to backtrack his way out of an ass beating from Johnny, but always seemed to end his ass kissing with a backhanded compliment. Johnny just rolled his eyes at the babbling fool. Dash shook his head trying not to laugh at the gibberish that was coming out of Jack's mouth. Dash always thought that Jack had an interesting way of trying to apologize. Jack's back handed comments had put his ass in the fire a few times.

"This is Johnny. I've told you about him," Dash told Jack.

"Oh. That must have been you firing out the back of Frankie. I've heard a lot about you. By the way, where *is* my van? Where's Frankie? You better take me to Frankie right away. What have you done with my van? There had better not be a scratch on her or else..." Jack said very defensively of his van. Johnny and Dash looked at him and Jack could sense the question they were asking. "...or else I'll have to fix that scratch, so you better take me to her." Jack said who was now extremely concerned about his van.

"It's at the warehouse. They haven't found *that* yet," Dash said. "At least, I *think* they haven't."

"Won't be long until they do and when they do I don't want her to be there. Frankie is very delicate." Jack continued to rant about his van with even more urgency. Jack could easily see that Johnny and Dash were beginning to become a little creeped out. "I want Frankie; take me to her, so that I can see how bad you guys smashed her up." Jack said, trying to sound demanding and less like a pervert.

"Yeah we can do that, but can you find out what is going on

first? We really need to know why what we stole is such a big-fucking-deal," Dash requested.

"Figured you'd ask; NO! Well... Yes! But not until you take me to Frankie, and THEN I'll look into it," Jack stated as he crossed his arms and leaned back in to his chair. Johnny and Dash knew it was the only way to get Jack to help. They looked at each other and nodded.

"We have your word?" Johnny questioned.

"Dash? Have you ever had to ask for my word before?! I've been feeding you information and sending Fern the letters and money for 3 years now. That is important!...right? Yeah it was!" Jack responded. "I don't think it should be questioned now! Especially with Frankie in danger!" Jack said with some finality on the matter.

"*FERN!*" Johnny said loudly, drawing the attention of the crowd again. Dude what in the hell? You knew you couldn't, but you did it anyway! You put her life in danger again! You selfish son of a bitch!"

"Don't tell me what I can, and can't do. I never asked for a life like this. NEVER! This is *your* fault. So fuck off!" Dash yelled and jabbed Johnny in the chest with his finger.

"Excuse me gentlemen, but I'm going to have to ask you to leave." The hostess said as she walked up to the table, trying to remain polite. Johnny looked over at that hostess and was about to try to talk his way out of it when Dash interjected.

"Sure right after this," Dash said as he sucker punched Johnny in the gut, watching him collapse to the ground like the Hindenburg. Johnny got up to his knees and gasped for air.

"You fuck!" Johnny rasped as he swept Dash's legs out from under him. Dash fell to the ground, whacking his head on the table. Johnny jumped on top of him and began punching him. "You think I wanted this. Runnin' for our lives all the time and changin' apartments every couple of months. I hate fuckin' movin' and you always have to live on the third god damn floor."

Dash grabbed Johnny by the jacket, and flipped him into the side of a table. Guests of the coffee shop started to scatter as glass and hot coffee went everywhere. Dash wasted no time and was on him like white on rice, striking him with blows to the face, neck and groin.

"All I wanted was a normal life!" Dash yelled he lifted Johnny up by his shirt collar and head butted him in the face, breaking his nose. Johnny grabbed for the nearest object, a plate, and broke it over Dash's head. Dash slumped a bit and rolled off of Johnny. Dash stumbled to his feet and kicked back at Johnny. Johnny grabbed Dash's foot and shoved Dash back, into the wall. Dash slid down the wall and lay there, stunned, for a moment.

"This is it then! When we're done here we're through," Johnny said as he set his nose, like he had done many times before. The sound of the nose popping back into place made Jack fight feel nauseous. He covered his mouth with his hands like he was about to sing his lunch. "Son of a Bitch!" Johnny said, trying to stem the blood that was gushing out his nose. "Jack could you hand me the napkins." Jack handed over a handful quickly, hoping not to get into the middle of the fight.

Dash slid back up the wall, using it for balance. "That's fine with me dick weed. I was tired of saving your stupid ass over and over again. I was splitting after this job anyway." Dash agreed as he caught his breath.

"*Guys!*" Jack exclaimed, as he scrambled to pack up his laptop. "Agents are here!"

"That was fucking quick," Johnny said with a sigh as he became aware of the TCS Honda outside the shop.

"This shop is probably owned by Takahara Corp, like damn near everything else. They probably have a warrant out for us right now. Back door sounds like a good Idea," Dash said and bolted towards the rear. They ran for a few blocks eventually heading back to their bikes.

"Hang on a second guys, I need to do something before we get out of range," Jack said as he was catching his breath. He pushed a few more buttons on his computer. Jack began to hum to himself as he typed. "There that should do it. Maybe they will get the hint and leave me alone." A few seconds later there was a loud explosion about two blocks away.

"What the fuck did you do?" Dash said a smoke and dust cloud began to rise in the air.

"I blew it up!" Jack said proudly, "Couldn't risk them getting any information from my stuff." Jack shrugged.

"So you blew it up," Johnny said astounded. "You can keep your crazy friend too."

"He's been a better friend than you've ever been," Dash said angrily as he started up his bike. Dash motioned for Jack to get on the back of his bike and he did.

"Do you have a helmet? There is an 85% mortality rate for people not wearing helmets in motorcycle crashes," Jack said hesitating to get on the bike.

"No... just hold on tight," Dash said and grimaced.

"But what if we crash? Head trauma isn't pretty and I don't want to be a vegetable. Maybe we can just go slowly. And avoid sharp turns," rambled Jack. "And make sure to give plenty of space to the vehicles in front of you."

"See you at the warehouse then!" Johnny yelled over the bike. Dash gave him the finger and rode off. Johnny got on his bike, started it up and followed.

"Hayao, report on your progress," Mr. Takahara said as he watched the camera feeds on the gigantic monitors behind his desk. Hayao's profile popped up in the right hand corner monitor. As one of Takahara's best recovery agents his only failure was tracking down the man who killed Mr. Takahara's son.

"We're searching the known associate's premises, and so far no sign of him," Hayao responded, his voice slightly distorted by his communication receiver. "We may need a tech specialist. It seems this one is a bit of a tech head."

"We will have one in route shortly. Don't disappoint me," Mr. Takahara stated as he muted the screen. "Giichi have you tracked their recent purchases?" Giichi's profile replaced Hayao's. Giichi was known for is information gathering skills. The methods of which he retrieved that information never left any witnesses.

"Mr. Takahara, there was a bit of a snag, but we are in route to the El Diablo Tavern," Giichi said as the monitor showed him and his men get into a car and take off.

"Excellent, Giichi, keep me apprised of your progress," Mr. Takahara ordered.

"Yes sir," Giichi responded. Mr. Takahara then muted Giichi monitor. Ichiro entered the room; the tapping of his shoes on the expensive tile work announced his presence. Ichiro bowed as he reached Mr. Takahara's desk. With a slight nod from Mr. Takahara Ichiro began his report.

"Sir, I have two teams ready to deploy as soon as we give them the green light," Ichiro stated.

"Thank you Ichiro, but I'm sure that they will not be needed. From the bios that Hayao provided they should be in our possession by the end of the day," Mr. Takahara said, his voice filled with cold satisfaction.

"I will keep them ready just in case we are able to dig up another lead," Ichiro said with a bow.

"Very well, who do you have leading those teams?" Mr. Takahara asked.

"Tatsuo and Takeshi," Ichiro replied. There profiles popped up on the monitors. They are both leaders of TCS guard forces. Their records were perfect with every man, woman, or child they were sent after acquired or killed. Tatsuo's and Takeshi's teams were a combination of extraction and assassination squads. No one lived when they were sent out unless that was their objective.

"Interesting choice, they are the most violent of the available choices. Is there a reason you choose them?" Mr. Takahara questioned in a maniacal tone.

"They are the best. If you doubt my choice I will gladly take my life now." Ichiro offered with cold look on his face.

"There will be no need for that, but remember we need the one intact. Be sure to keep your dogs on a leash as we do not want things to get out of hand. Those two are like caged bears, you must be careful when you let them out otherwise they will destroy everything," Mr. Takahara coldly suggested.

"It will be done," Ichiro said affirmatively. Mr. Takahara waved his hand at Ichiro dismissing him from the room. Bowing with respect Ichiro returned to his duties. Mr. Takahara continued to watch the monitors. "Please send Dr. Maki in."

Dr. Maki walked into his office carrying a folder. "How is the search going?" She asked as she sat down in one of the two chairs in front of his desk.

"Rather irritating. This city is my maze and they are trapped in it like rats. Though I don't understand how they have eluded us thus far," Mr. Takahara said as he turned around in his chair to face her.

"Well, we did make him. Perhaps we made him too well," Dr. Maki said proudly.

"What have you found out from your research on the Beta Experiments? Anything we can use?" Mr. Takahara asked. Dr. Maki opened the folder she brought in.

"Unfortunately, we do not have much on the Beta Experiments. The lab burnt down during a worker riot about eighteen years ago. What we do know is that at age 3 he showed signs of higher than normal reflexes and that after an initial sickness he had recovered and was progressing as a child should," She replied as she skimmed roughly twenty pages in the file that were mostly filled with test data.

"That is all? There has to be more." Mr. Takahara insisted as he stood up. His face became red and there was fire in his eyes as he approached Dr. Maki. "Find it or I may find myself short a scientist."

"I am your brother's wife. How dare you threaten me like that! Wait until he hears about this," Dr. Maki said as she stood up and turned to leave. Mr. Takahara shot up and snatched her by the wrist swinging her around to meet his dreadful gaze. He clenched her wrist tightly bending her to his will.

"You're hurting me! Stop!" She cried as she dropped her documents and slapped him across the face. The sting of the slap shot through his face, but it did not faze him. He instinctively grabbed her other arm before she was able to remove it from reach. He squeezed harder and pulled her face close to his. She turned her head and attempted to pull away to avoid his icy stare.

"Well, he isn't here now is he? This is my town and if you want to leave here alive then you WILL show me respect. I've been hiding your experimental failures for almost thirty years. Is this how you treat the man who saved you from ruin and the shame that you would have brought to your husband?" Mr. Takahara said as his death cold eyes chilled her to the bone.

"I would have stopped after the Alpha Virus if I would have had a choice and you know that," She said with fury in her voice. Sweat began to bead on her forehead as she tried to twist her wrist out of his hold, but she was at his mercy. Mr. Takahara pulled her closer their noses almost touching.

"Now you and I both know that progress requires sacrifices. Perhaps we should make sacrifices of our own. Perhaps, little Juni would like to volunteer to be part of the next round of testing," Mr. Takahara said wickedly cracking a smile

"You wouldn't," she said with a gasp.

"It would be sad for someone so young to die," Mr. Takahara said as he released Dr. Maki and straightened his tie. Returning to his chair he spun the chair around to face the monitors. "Leave and find me something to work with." Dr. Maki quickly left rubbing her wrists.

"Now where was I? Oh yes, Hayao, report," Mr. Takahara demanded.

"Well it appears that this guy had his computer locked down with some sort of device. The tech team is working on it. We should have it open shortly," Hayao said, briefing Mr. Takahara of his progress. Then, a loud explosion came across the feed followed by a high pitched whine. In a moment of weakness Mr. Takahara covered his ears and muted the monitor again.

"Hayao report… Hayao report!" Mr. Takahara demanded, returning the sound to the monitor.

"Mr. Takahara this is Agent 221 from outside the building. The building's top floors just exploded. We need medical teams. We have wounded and… oh God, there are body parts… everywhere." The sound of vomiting came pouring over the monitor.

"It is so hard to find good help these days," he said with a sigh.

Johnny couldn't believe what Dash had said. It was over; his only friend left in the world just disowned him. He did the only thing he could and decided to take one last ride with his friend. He didn't know if they were going to make it out of this one. Even if Dash had disowned him he was still going to do whatever he could to give Dash that normal life he wanted, perhaps winning his friend back in the process.

"A normal life… what was that?" Johnny pondered. Johnny had been pretty much raised by his Uncle Dylan. His father and mother were killed when he was very young though his uncle never really told him how. All he said was that it was job related. His parents were factory workers. Working in a factory could be as hazardous for your health as doing the jobs Johnny did. Over the last 3 years he has had his Run-ins with street gangs, pimps, and wanna-bee's, but nothing was ever quite as bad as when they ran into to the TCS. Every time they did another dead body would show up. Johnny and Dash were lucky it hadn't been them. Johnny's mind began to wander; they had never been shot, stabbed, or tortured. He had been beaten a few times because he couldn't dodge every punch. He has had bruises, concussions, and a broken bone or two, but nothing ever life threatening. "Guess it was all saved up for now, which means we're totally screwed," Johnny thought.

They arrived at the warehouse without running into any problems, which was good news. That meant TCS hadn't found it yet. Johnny parked his bike outside and got the door open for Dash and Jack. Johnny went to one of the boxes and popped it open. He pulled out a black, white and gray urban camouflage reinforced vest. Little better than your standard police issue vest. Better at taking blades and even arrows, which reminded Johnny of the first run-in they had with strangers wielding bows. They were collecting a gambling debt for his Uncle and the mark was a big-time game hunter that had been to every continent and killed something. The man even had a stuffed penguin. Johnny always chuckled when he remembered that job and as he took off his shirt to put the vest underneath. The fond memory came back to him.

"Watch out, it's the great deadly beast of the frozen south, the evil Emperor Penguin. Watch how they waddle back and forth across the frozen tundra," Dash said doing his best impression of those survival guys on TV.

Johnny remembered the room smelled of wet dog as Dash continued his joke, "They are such vicious beasts..." That was when he got hit in the back with an arrow. The arrow made a 'thunk' as it struck the trauma plate in the vest and got stuck in the mesh.

"I think you got shot with an arrow dude," Johnny said as Dash then turned toward him. The arrow was limp, but was still stuck to him. "Yup."

"You've got to be fucking kidding me." Dash turned to try to see and knocked over a stand filled with trophy bear claws with the arrow. Johnny laughed and he placed his hand on Dash's back and pulled the arrow out.

"We should probably get to him before he gets to elephant guns or something bigger," Johnny said as he snapped the arrow off.

Johnny came back from his thoughts and tightened his clip holster beneath his leather jacket. He tossed Dash his navy blue camouflaged vest and a spare black one to Jack.

"Why do I need this?" Jack asked curiously.

"It is more of a just in case, Jack, just put it on," Dash replied.

"Oh no no no! I'm not going anywhere near bullets," Jack stated as waved his hands in front of him denying the vest.

"Not to be a dick about it, but you're wearing the vest!" Johnny stated and he forcefully assisted Jack with the vest.

"Johnny," Dash said in an authoritative tone. Johnny shoved the vest at Jack and went to back packing up his things, clearly frustrated with the whole situation.

"I'll help him," Dash said as he finished strapping on his vest. "Jack, you've got put it on and come with us. We're pretty sure that this place is next. I'm sorry about your building, but we can't do anything about it right now. We need to get you to a safe place. There's a hotel off the last exit on old Interstate 5 heading south out of town. You know where I'm talking about. Take the back roads to get there. You'll avoid most, if not all, of the cameras that Takahara has in place." Dash told him. It was easy to see the worry in Dash's eyes. Like a ship without a sail he was at a loss at what to do and had no direction in his plan.

"Yeah, but you also told me that I was never ever allowed to go there. I remember you specifically telling me that if I went there you would drop Frankie in the ocean! Which is big...and wet!" Jack replied. "Both Frankie and I like her to be not wet. I don't swim to well, or float...and ... Um... I think I might be allergic...and well... Frankie can't get wet!"

"Yeah, well, it's the safest place I can think of now with computer access. We'll still need you to be our eyes and ears on this one. After this you'll be able to have all that evidence you wanted on our corporate government," Dash said trying to persuade him. Jack perked up a little bit.

"You guys owe me big time for this one," Jack said as he scratched his head through his mop top of hair.

"I'm sure we'll save your life a few more times before this is done," Johnny cruelly joked.

"Ignore him. I know we owe you. Now clam down and get a move on. Take Frankie," Dash said as he tossed Jack the keys. "The hotel has an underground parking lot. Hide Frankie there and whatever you do don't open the box. We don't know what's in there and I don't want to have to scrape whatever's left of you off the inside of the van. I'm serious Jack."

"Yeah yeah I heard you; keep my hands off," Jack said as he looked back at the box longingly wondering what could be inside; was it a new gadget, maybe it was components to upgrade the van, or maybe even his favorite meal. Jack took a few steps closer to the box as sneakily as possible.

"I'm serious Jack!" Dash said once again and pounded the hood of the van with his fist making Jack jump.

"I was just lookin' I promise," Jacks said as he was startled. "All right all right! Hey why didn't you tell me Frankie had been shot up?" Jack said as he moved to the back of the van and started checking out the bullet holes. Dash winced at what was about to happened next.

"How many times have you got Frankie all shot up?!" Jack screamed like a mother whose baby was just dropped as he started to pull back the already shot up paneling.

"Well, Johnny was supposed to have fixed that," Dash said staring at Johnny.

"Excuse me. When the hell was I supposed to have time? Between the car chase and the brawl we had in the coffee shop! I did replace the original doors with new ones," Johnny replied.

"These aren't her original back doors where are the original back doors?" Jack asked.

"I left them over there behind the boxes, figured I could use the doors as scrap if I need to make a quick patch job," Johnny said a little confused as he watched Jack scramble over to the doors. He tried to lift them but was a little too weak. Johnny chuckled to himself as Jack tried to drag the door.

"Dash, we need to put her doors back on, you can't just take the doors off... um... we should hurry," Jack said as if a dark omen had fallen upon him and his beloved van.

"Sure but they're Swiss cheese," Dash said unsure of what Jack was trying to do.

"Frankie is a very special vehicle. Taking the doors off could kill her or leave her damaged permanently," Jack said shooting a death glare in Johnny's direction. Jack became more and more frantic the seconds passed. "We need to hurry!"

"Johnny, give us a hand?" Dash asked. Johnny breathed a sigh of relief when Dash asked for help. It meant that he wasn't mad any more. Johnny was sure that Dash was still hurt and troubled by what had happened over the last few hours, but at least he wasn't going to bite his head off every time he spoke to him. Johnny picked up one of the doors and brought it to the back of the van, then began to retrieve the other one while Dash and Jack removed the new back doors and put the old ones back in.

"I told you to bring Frankie to me if anything went wrong with her," Jack said with as much anger in his voice as he could muster which wasn't a lot.

"I didn't think that included bullet holes," Dash replied with mocking tone.

It didn't take too long to replace the doors with the three of them working on it.

"Ok the doors are switched out now what? Is it going to magically fix itself," Dash mocked Jack jokingly.

"Psh...No. Magic isn't real." Jack popped open the front door and plugged his lap top into the cigarette lighter. "This is just a little somethin' I'm working on that actually works. Problem is I can't get near the nano bots to examine them. They have become aware of themselves and when together, have a hive mind but when separate, become individuals... The nano bots don't really like that because individuals don't get along so well, and have issues like jealousy...and hate... and frustration... and anger... and other emotions...and they beat each other up...and...uh..anyways. Also individuals never really get anything done on their own. So to avoid this, the nano bots go crazy trying to retrieve their missing member before it develops an individual personality and has to be destroyed. Cause if one gets an individual personality then the others would be soon to follow. I had trouble with this when I was first making them. Trust me the outcome was not good. It was pretty much World War Two nano bot style. The battle only lasted like thirty seconds and was sweet to watch, but the lab I was working in was completely destroyed. You see it has to do with both their neural hardware and their programming." Jack continued to ramble about the nano bots while Johnny scratched his head. Dash wasn't so lucky he tried to understand what Jack was talking about, but when he started to talk technical terms Dash's mind blew a fuse and he just stopped listening, but Jack continued on and on.

"They were originally built to do vehicle maintenance and car repair. They adopted this van as their home and pretty much as long as you don't take a rocket to the engine, the van will fix itself if it has the materials. Hello Frankie," Jack finished.

A bionic feminine voice came from the computer which sounded like a million voices talking in unison. "Hello Jack, do you wish for me to begin repairs?" The voice asked.

"Frankie repair mode. It is good to hear you again Frankie," Jack said with utter joy in his voice.

"We will begin repair mode immediately." Right before their eyes silver ooze spilled out of the tail pipe around Dash's feet. The silver ooze moved over to one of the doors. The old doors started to crumble.

"What the..!" Dash screamed and jumped away fearing the ooze would start to eat away his shoes. Both Jack and Johnny looked at Dash, befuddled that such a girlie scream came from a guy like Dash. Dash calmed himself really quickly after receiving the ridiculing looks from them.

"Have they been treating you right Frankie?" Jack asked as he rubbed his hand on the van.

"Not as good as you do Jack," Frankie replied with a seductive feminine voice.

"Ha, ha... um." Jack blushed felling very awkward.

"Is there something I should know about you Jack? Did you get a girl friend?" Dash joked.

"So, yeah after I invented Frankie, Takahara Corp wanted me to make more, but I couldn't hurt Frankie. So they fired me. Little did I know she hitched a ride in my van and they have called it home ever since. Oh and never play games for money with her. She always wants her winning in steel and she never loses," Jack said changing the subject. In short order, the bullet holes, the glass, and everything else wrong with the van was fixed.

"Why didn't she do this earlier when I was fixing the van?" Johnny asked puzzled.

"She will only fix original parts and Frankie is kind of shy," Jack answered as he got in the driver's seat of the van. Johnny and Dash looked at each other dumb founded.

"Shy?" They questioned Jack.

"Didn't sound shy a second ago," Johnny mumbled. Dash couldn't help but chuckle. A good joke was a good joke even if you want to rip the head off the guy telling it.

"Well yeah, and also you need to have a computer linked into the car so she can talk to you. I still haven't figured out how to get her to talk through the radio yet. Well Frankie, we're off to the hotel," Jack said. Jack began to pull out of the garage. Johnny and Dash were still in a little bit of shock from what just happen. Dash thought Jack was just a wicked smart hacker that was a little off his rocker. Johnny was slowly drawing that same conclusion.

"Uncle Dylan always told me there was a thin line between brilliance and insanity. I now know why," Johnny said scratching his head.

"Yup," Dash replied shaking his.

"So where did you send 'em?" Johnny asked. Dash shot him a glare that could have killed a man.

"Listen fuckhead. I don't want to talk to you, make nice, or have a heart to heart chat. We were never friends. So get that through your thick skull. When this is over I don't ever want to see you again!" Dash exclaimed.

"Okay. I just wanted to know the name of the hotel so we can meet up to make a plan," Johnny said as he pulled his sawed off double barrel shotgun from its secret compartment under the desk, and then grabbed a box of rounds from one of the many boxes.

"Looks like they're hittin' the places we have been after the job. Stay away from those places. I'll call you with the info. Until then I don't give a shit what you do," Dash said angrily. Johnny loaded his shotgun and set in on the desk. Then he began the long process of loading all 10 of his clips for his Scorpion. In the background he could hear Dash doing the same for his weapons. As each bullet clicked into the place flashes of memories kept coming back. The job they pulled just yesterday, the joking and jaw jacking they did. The long night hanging out at the bar picking up chicks and the millions of races that they have had on their bikes. "He can't hate me," Johnny thought. A pit started to grow in Johnny's stomach.

"You can't hate me!" He said as a breeze whipped in through the window and was gone adding a moment a stillness to the already tense situation. "Look man, I know that savin' my life is what sent you down this path. Yeah I get it I was making a quick buck working for Fat Montey, which screwed us both over. You think I like this? You think I wanted this? I may have been raised like this, but I was getting out. I was getting enough money together to get the fuck out of Neo-Japan. I had bigger plans too. I was going to be someone…. Who that was I don't fucking know. I was 18 and didn't have a fucking clue, but I know that runnin' wasn't the job I wanted for the rest of my life. So fuck you Dash! Fuck your, 'I didn't ever want this crap' cause I didn't either. Matter of fact." Johnny threw on his helmet and jumped on his bike. He fired her up and was ready to peel out of there. Stopping for a moment outside the warehouse to look back at his friend.

"Where you going?" Dash yelled as Johnny revved his engine.

"Why do you fuckin' care we ain't friends anymore!" Johnny yelled through his helmet and squealed his tires leaving a semi-circle tread mark on the floor. As Johnny sped away the last thing he heard was Dash yelling, "I don't need you anyway!" It hurt to leave Dash like that, but if he wasn't his friend then why the hell should he help him. Johnny was on his way to El Diablo and to whisk Kate off her feet and ride off into the sunset.

Giichi strolled into the El Diablo Tavern whistling a little tune accompanied by his four best men each of them wearing dark suits and sunglasses. The jingle of the bell on the door announced their entrance. The bells brought Kate's attention to the door.

"Good evening boys, table for 5?" Kate asked as she grabbed some menus and escorted them to a table. "The special for today is the salmon burger and the soup is double bacon bean. What can I get for you to drink?" The Agents looked to Giichi for a queue as what to do.

"I'll have water with lemon," He said pretentiously as he eyed the waitress.

"I'll have that as well." His men said in unison. Kate hair caught the breeze of a nearby ceiling fan as she turned around to get the men there drinks. Shamus filled the glasses as he eyed the new customers.

Shamus whispered softly to Kate, "If they give ya any trouble you holler, okay?" Kate gave him a reassuring wink and took the glasses back to the table.

"Alright fellas, here you go. Did you have enough time to look over the menu?" Kate asked as she smiled at them.

"Excuse me. I need a new glass of water. This one is dirty," Giichi demanded.

"No problem sir, sorry about that," Kate said and took the glass and brought back a new one, but before Kate could ask what they wanted Giichi spoke up again.

"This glass is still dirty. Maybe you could have a non disease infested Alpha bring it to me this time." Giichi mocked her trying to get her to react.

She raised her arm to slap him. Her hand got dangerously close to Giichi's face before he grasped her wrist and twisted her arm behind her back. Giichi forced her down to the table and moved her hair from the back of her neck.

"Calcium patch. Filthy Echo," He said and spat on her. "You're coming with us."

"Is there a problem here boys?!" Shamus asked nervously. Shamus knew exactly who they were TCS Agents and with Shamus's connection to Fat Montey and the Irish mob he knew that they weren't in his tavern just to ask questions they were there to leave a message and TCS agents didn't leave messages without leaving a few bodies. Giichi picked Kate off the table and tossed her at one of his men. Kate struggled with them before she was pistol whipped knocking her to the ground in a daze.

"My name is Giichi. I work for TCS," He said in a thick Japanese accent as he removed sunglasses casually, he approached Shamus. "We are looking for two men that were here last night. They go by the names of Dash and Berith - also known as Dash McBragg and Johnathan Morals." Giichi thrusted his badge into Shamus's face as he began to ask his questions. Other customers' frightened by the presence of the TCS slowly began to make way for the door. The other waitress and Kate began to listen in on the conversation as people started asking for their tabs.

"Never heard of 'em," Shamus said gruffly staring Giichi in the eye. "So why don't you get your rice eating ass out of here."

"I was hoping you would say that," Giichi said as he reached over with lightning speed and slammed Shamus's head against the counter and held it there tight. "I would recommend everyone who doesn't work here leaves," Giichi announced to the bar. "It's closing time." Shamus could feel the uncomfortable pressure of Giichi pinning his head to the bar.

"We think you better leave, buddy. This is our bar," said a large biker and his friends as they began to pull knives and ready beer bottles for a brawl.

"This is sad. Men, show this south side trash why you never bring a knife to a gun fight," Giichi said as he continued to focus his attention towards Shamus. Kate, who had crawled away from the men, grabbed her co-worker and dove to the ground. Bullets and blood began to fly everywhere as the two men unloaded there Mac-10's into the bikers and the fleeing customers.

"I would say that your bar is closed for today," Giichi whispered with a vile smirk into Shamus's ear. The gun fire stopped and besides Shamus only Kate and the other waitress were left unharmed. Ten people lie dead or dying. "Tie up anyone left alive and throw the rest in the basement."

"Now it is time to get some answers. You're going to tell me where your friends are before I really get angry. Otherwise I will start killing them off one by one," Giichi threatened. Screams and moans of pain could be heard from the tavern.

"I don't know who you're talking about." Shamus grunted with his head firmly pressed against the counter.

"Grab that one." Giichi pointed at one of the wounded women that were still screaming.

"What are you doing?" Shamus asked worried for the girl.

"Teaching two lessons," Giichi said. "Boys hold him down and make him watch." Two the men grabbed either of his arms and kept him pinned to the bar.

"Lesson one. You should never lie to me. I know when you are," Giichi said holding up his index finger. Giichi grabbed a bottle of vodka and walked over to the girl.

"Set her down here, and then clear the tables and chairs," Giichi ordered. His men did what he asked. Giichi then began to pour the bottle of vodka over the woman and she moaned in pain.

"What are you doing?" The woman screamed unable to get away because of her wounds. "I won't tell anyone about what happened here."

"No you won't dear," Giichi said looking her in the eye with a diabolical grin.

"You wouldn't," Shamus said as he watched the last drops of the bottle pour out. Horror drenched his face as he could not turn away. The smell of cheap vodka filled the air.

"Perhaps it is three lessons." Giichi smirked as he lit and dropped a match on the girl and she erupted in flame. The screams were like nothing heard on this earth. "Lesson two. This is what real screaming sounds like. You will sound just like her before you die." The screams faded as Giichi walked towards Shamus. Shamus could not see but he heard the cries and screams of the other captives as he watched the woman burn. The overwhelming stench of burnt flesh pierced though the wafting scent of vodka.

"And the last lesson," Shamus said as he tried to free himself but was slammed back down to the counter. The force knocked Shamus into a haze as blood began to trickle out of a newly opened wound. Giichi got right up in his face and swiping his finger through Shamus's blood then licked his finger.

"Mmm, never had Irish before this should be a treat... oh yes where was I. Lesson three is you have no idea what I would or wouldn't do," Giichi said depraved smile that stretched from ear to ear. "Get a fire extinguisher and put her out we wouldn't want to burn the place down before we are done here."

Johnny got to the tavern and pulled his helmet off. Night
had fallen by time he got there. He barely noticed that the closed sign was flickering at him almost as if to warn him what was going on inside. He knew in his gut something was wrong. Johnny couldn't see anything through the tinted glass so he carefully opened the door, but the smell was pungent. Something he had never smelt before.

"Kate," Johnny said as he tried to sneak into the bar and was witness to a sight that he never would have expected. The smell of burnt flesh hit his nose as he entered the bar. Johnny held back the urge to vomit. He had never smelt something so vile. Two men were holding down Shamus on the bar as a third stood on the counter with one foot on Shamus's throat while he poured cheap booze down his gullet.

"Where are they Mr. O'Reily?" Giichi asked with a thick Japanese accent and a vicious grin of pure pleasure. "This will all end as soon as you tell me where they are. Do you think that Dash and Johnathan would have wanted you to waste the lives of all the people I've had to cart off to the basement?" Shamus choked as more booze was poured down his throat and Giichi enjoyed every moment of Shamus's suffering.

"You will just kill me and the others sooner if I talk," Shamus said as he choked as the last of the bottle was poured in his mouth. The bottle was set down next to four others. Most of the alcohol was spilt on the floor the rest Shamus was drenched in. Johnny could see they had been at this for some time.

"You are probably right Mr. O'Reily, but I'll make you a deal. I can just put a bullet in you," Giichi said as he bent down to be face to face with Shamus and tapped Shamus's forehead with his index finger. "Or I can burn you alive. Either way is fun for me." Shamus spit in Giichi face.

"Fuck you," Shamus replied. Giichi removed a handkerchief from his breast pocket and wiped the spit from his face.

"New plan! Bring me my knives. It's going to be a good day after all," he ordered and he rubbed his hands together with a psychotic grin stretching across his face. "I haven't done this in a while. You will have to tell me how much this hurts. I will find out where they are one way or another."

Johnny scanned the room and could see that Kate and the other waitress were bound on the floor in the corner. Johnny reached for his gun. His mind flashed to the fact that he had left it on the desk. He was about to sneak around to find something to defend himself with when the chime of the bell hanging above the door sounded out. Johnny was frozen. "How could I let the bell ring? I'm such an idiot," he thought.

"Hey fuckwad, I'm right here," Johnny said with a small gulp at the end like he didn't know if he was going to make it out of this one. The two men that were guarding Kate and the other waitress quickly turned to face Johnny, guns drawn and firing. Johnny threw his reinforced helmet striking the first agent in the face as he grabbed a glass off the closest table. The agent grabbed his nose after having it crushed by Johnny's helmet. Blood began to drain from the agent's face as Johnny threw the half empty glass of beer at the second TCS goon. The goon dodged the glass and began to fire. The first round went whizzing by Johnny's head as the thrown glass altered his aim enough to save Johnny's life.

The second round nicked Johnny's shoulder, only grazing him. Johnny shrugged off the tiny wound and with three steps was on him. Grabbing the wrist of the agent's gun hand Johnny pointing the gun to the side as rounds began to explode from the barrel. He quickly twisted the man wrist and followed with a right elbow strike to the face sending the man to the ground. Johnny ripped the pistol from his hand. Squeezing the trigger twice, he let a pair of rounds fly at the agent that he had hit in the face with the helmet. The bullets landed almost dead center puncturing his chest killing him instantly.

The agent holding Shamus left arm let go of him and picked up his Mac-10 off the counter and let out a Japanese samurai type yell before he began to open fire. The agent's yell gave Johnny a chance to take cover. Johnny jumped over the nearest table, grabbing the edge with one hand and tipping it over to use as cover.

As the crazed man began to reload his gun Johnny heard the sound of a bottle being smashed against the counter, then a shrill scream of agony. Johnny stood up to see that Shamus had broken a bottle with his free hand and stabbed Giichi in his thigh. Giichi collapsed behind the bar with the bottle still stuck in his leg. Johnny rattled off three shots into the agent that was still fumbling around with his Mac-10 as he reloaded. The bullets struck him in the leg, stomach, and chest. He slumped to his knees and fell over dead as a door nail. The disarmed TCS agent had recovered and made a move for the dead TCS agent's weapon by doing a diving slide across the floor. Johnny was able to get three more rounds off, but the bullets missed their target slamming into the wall behind the bar. This gave the agent enough time to get the dead man's gun and began firing.

Johnny knew he was in trouble if he stayed behind the table. Johnny seized the moment as the agent went to reload his weapon and moved from his cover. As the agent's clip locked into place Johnny leapt over the bar. He looked for Shamus to make sure he was alright. Johnny watched as Shamus grappled with the man that was still trying to hold him down. Shamus grabbed the goon by his hair and yanked him over to the other side of the bar slamming him to the ground. Shamus reached for his prep knives from under the counter and drove the small paring knife into the man's chest over and over again.

Giichi was still screaming on the floor, trying to crawl away, when bullets came flying over the bar counter. Johnny reached his hand over the counter and fired rounds back at the agent that was still standing. More hot lead came flying at the bar breaking what was left of Shamus's stock. Johnny heard the clicking of the empty gun, so he stood up and took aim in the direction the bullets were coming from. The agent began to duck for cover to reload once more; Johnny put his last bullet through the agent's skull sending him to his grave.

With all the TCS dead or dying Johnny went to go help untie the girls. "Hi Kate, been a pretty busy day for me. How was your day at work? Mine was very interesting to say the least." Johnny said trying to make light the seriousness of the situation. He removed the gag from her mouth and helped her up. Kate eyes lit up at the sight of Johnny and filled with tears of relief.

"Oh God! Johnny, look out!" Kate yelled point behind the bar. The man that had been stabbed in the thigh rose from behind the bar his pistol pointed at Johnny.

"You will regret the day you crossed the Takahara Corporation and me, Giichi!" He yelled firing a shot at Johnny. Johnny did the best he could to keep himself between the girls and the bullet. The bullet hit him dead center in the chest knocking him to the ground. Johnny hit the ground like a ton of bricks as a large parrying knife came flying form the other end of the bar striking the man in the throat ending his life with gurgling gasps.

"Johnny, don't die. You promised me a date," she said as she dropped to her knees and began putting pressure on the wound. "Johnny, get up."

"It's kind of hard when you're pressing on my chest," he said with a little chuckle.

"You should be bleeding more?" Kate questions as she inspected her hands. "Why aren't you bleeding?"

"I'll make sure to do that next time. Damn that fucking hurt," Johnny said with a laugh as he sat up. The very distinct howl of the TCS Agent sirens began to be faintly heard in the distance. "Well that's my queue." The other girl grabbed his helmet and handed it to him.

"Thank you for saving us," the other waitress said and bolted for the door. Moments later the squeal of tires could be heard in the parking lot as she fled the gruesome scene. Johnny rifled through the dead bodies quickly, finding a few spare clips and a pair of unfired pistols off the dead men. He put the two Glock 18 pistols in his back waistband and the clips in his jacket pocket.

"Shamus, are you ok to handle the TCS?" Johnny asked.

"Get out of here kid! I ain't sticking around," he replied and waved Johnny off.

"Johnny, where are you going?" Kate asked as she chased him to his bike.

"I have to go help Dash. If they came here they're probably hunting down every lead they have and if I'm right, then they're on their way to that hotel that he's hiding out at," he said.

"How would they know where he is?" Kate asked as Johnny got on his bike and started it.

"Cause knowing him he has visited there on a few occasion to keep an eye on her," Johnny replied. "Kate, I want you to call your roommates and stay with Shamus. He'll keep you safe."

"I don't understand. What's going on? Who's this "her" that you mentioned? Why can't I go with you?" Kate asked in a panic clasping tightly to Johnny not wanting to let go.

"Cause this is just the beginning. Until this is finished you have to hide or risk ending up dead and I can't have that. Ya need to trust me. I'll come find you when it is safe," Johnny told her.

"This is crazy. This can't be happening. All I wanted to do was meet a nice guy," Kate said with a panic. Johnny pulled her close and kissed her.

"You did meet a nice guy. It just happened to be on a bad day. I need you to calm down and stay with Shamus. I'll be back soon enough. Shamus, I'll call you when it is safe to meet," Johnny said. Kate began to calm down and released her grip on Johnny as tears began to appear in her eyes. Johnny started to take off when he heard Kate call his name.

"Johnny, Wait!" she yelled. He stopped his bike and she came running up to him. He pulled off his helmet. Kate threw her arms around him and began kissing him passionately embracing him tightly with her arms as if her life depended on it.

"Everything will be alright," Johnny said with a confident smirk.

"You better come back. I'm holding you to our date," Kate said shedding a tear and kissing him lightly again. Kate pulled away from the kiss and Johnny put on his helmet again. Kate stepped back as Johnny peeled out turn his bike around and speed off. He was headed back to the warehouse to see if Dash was still there and to pick up a few things he had left behind.

"You may not like me right now Dash and you may not want to be my friend, but I can't leave you to the wolves. Not after everything we've been through," Johnny thought and then cranked the throttle back. The wind caused by his high speeds rushed over him as he raced to his friend's aid.

Dash watched Johnny speed off. "What the hell is he thinking?" Dash thought. "He's smarter than that... You know what? To hell with him anyway, I'm taking my shit, picking up Fern, and getting the fuck out of town. I don't need his stupid ass for that!"

Dash finished packing up his bike. He made sure to pack as many rounds as he could. His Raging Bull strapped to a hidden holster in his pant leg and an UMP-45 hidden in the bag strapped to his back. He was off to the hotel. A sense of excitement filled him. This would be the first time he'd be able to talk to Fern since homecoming.

Dash had not spoken to Fern in three years, but he had been sending her letters through Jack the entire time. Each letter filled with his love and regret that he couldn't be there. As he pulled into the hotel it is was easy to spot Frankie and he parked next to the van. After making sure none of his guns were noticeable he entered the hotel lobby. It was a nice little place three stories tall and had over 300 rooms. The hotel had a bar, swimming pool, and water slide. It could compete with most major chains in Neo-Hiroshima, if it were Takahara Corp. business.

Dash went to the front desk. "I'm looking for a friend," he said to the pretty girl standing behind the desk.

Behind Dash a woman spoke, "Really, a friend, I thought you might be looking for a girl you once knew." Said a sweet voice. A voice he could never forget. Dash turned around to see Fern. She may have been in her work uniform, but she made it look good. Then again, to Dash she could be wearing a paper bag and she would turn his head. "I'll be taking Mr. McBragg to his room and I'm going to take my break... If that is ok Shelly?" Fern said to the girl behind the reception desk.

"Sure thing Fern, it's kind of slow today anyway and shouldn't be a problem. If you wanted to take off for the rest of the day I'd understand," Shelly replied with a little giggle as she checked out Dash. Fern nodded in acceptance of her co-workers gesture.

"If you would please follow me, Mr. McBragg, I'll show you to your room," Fern stated as she motioned for him to follow and started to walk to the elevator. Fern tossed her long fiery red hair as she turned around and headed for the elevator. Fern stood slender, 5'9" with milky white skin. Her hair draped down her back perfectly ending at her shoulder blades. Dash enjoyed watching her perfectly toned ass walk away. Dash couldn't help but stare, and quickly followed after. Once they were alone in the elevator he spoke.

"Fern, I missed you. I tried so hard to get to you. To leave the life I was trapped in. I just wanted to be with you. I wanted so many times to just come get you and run away, but I couldn't. I couldn't let you live the life I was living. You were always on my mind. I just had to see you at least one more time." At that, Fern glanced to the ground her red hair fell in front of her face. The doors opened and she began to walk towards the room.

"Fern please listen to me. I have to go away. I'm leaving Neo-Japan. I don't know for how long and even if I'll ever be back." Fern opened the door and went in. It was a nice room; too nice for what he gave Jack to spend.

"Fern, I love you." At that she froze in her steps. The door shut behind Dash. Dash put his bag down and walked up behind her. "Will you at least look at me?" Dash asked as he turned her around. She was still looking at the ground. He slowly lifted her head and used his other hand to move her hair out from in front of her eyes. As their eyes meet it was as if they were 18 again. Fern was overwhelmed, tearing up.

"Baby, don't cry. It is ok. I wasn't going to leave again without you," Dash said with a charming smile. Dash was so happy he didn't know what else to say. Fern could take it no longer. She wrapped her arms around the love of her life and held him tight.

Fern started with a kiss and then threw him back against the door she began to remove his vest and pulled his shirt over his head. She was just a bit shorter then Dash, which meant they fit perfectly with each other. They are like two puzzle pieces out of a billion piece puzzle locked by love. Dash picked her up and her legs wrapped around him. He moved her to the bed quickly. Their kissing became more ravenous as if they were making up for lost time. Fern began to remove her shirt revealing more of her perfectly pale skin. Her skin gave her a look of pure innocence as if she was his personal angel, but her flaming red hair revealed her fiery passion. She flipped Dash over and straddled him. Kissing him more passionately then she pulled away. She sat atop him and stared into his eyes with one hand brushed over his rippling chest and stomach muscles and the other slowly caressing his face.

"I love you," she said straddling him. Dash smiled as he pulled her close.

The three hours passed very quickly. Dash had fallen asleep holding Fern close. A deep sleep that only she could have given him.

It was a sleep that relieved all the regret that he had built over leaving her so long ago, but this relief was fleeting. Dash began to be brought back to reality at the sound of Fern getting dressed.

"Fern?" Dash asked confused.

"I have to get home," Fern responded.

"Why? We could stay here the rest of the night and we can run away together in the morning. I have it all planned out. I have some money saved from the last three years of shit I had to do to stay alive and a few friends that could get us across the border..."

"Stop it," she said softly trembling voice. "We can't."

"What? Why? I thought..." Dash said perplexed.

"Cause I have others that I have to look after," she said with newly formed tears in her eyes.

"What? I don't understand," Dash said as his heart sank as Fern finished getting dressed. "No. No. This can't be it!"

"Dash..." she said.

"Don't do this. We can be happy like we always wanted," Dash began to plead a little.

"That is not who you are anymore. That is not who I am any more. Things have changed since you left. I had to make some decisions and they broke my heart, but it was what was best for us," she said as she cried.

"Best for us, fuck that! You got my letter you knew I was coming for you. You can't do this..." Dash said fearing where the conversation was going.

"I got all your letters and they broke my heart with every word. We can't do this. I hope that you'll understand some day," Fern said as she went for the door with tears flooding from her eyes like rivers. Dash leapt from the bed still naked from the night's earlier activities and with a step caught her by wrist just as she stepped in the hallway.

"If you're leaving I want to know why now..." He yelled at Fern confused and hurt.

"It is complicated..." She started to say.

"Look out!" Dash yelled as he saw the two men at the end of the hall take aim and light up the hallway with automatic gun fire. The pitter patter of the bullets striking floor, walls, and ceiling filled the hall. Dash grabbed Fern and yanked her back through the doorway grabbed the doorknob with his other hand and slamming the door shut. Dash grabbed his pistol. "Take this and hide in the tub," Dash said in a stress filled panic as he handed her his Raging Bull. "Pull the shower curtain and if anyone but me comes to get you shot them." Fern was shaking so much when Dash handed her the gun she dropped it. She was so frightened she couldn't speak.

"Fern... Honey, I love you, everything will be alright," he said as he touched her cheek and looked into her eyes then picked up the gun and handed it back to her. Fern got into the bathroom leaving the door open just a crack; Dash flipped the bed up in front of the door and slid the dresser in front of it.

"That should hold them for a minute or two," he said as he threw on his pants, vest, and shoes. The bullets started to come in through the door. He opened his bag and pulled out his UMP-45, locked in a clip and threw a couple in his vest pockets. More bullets came pouring through the mattress and Dash flipped off the safety as he prepared himself for a shoot out.

"They will be inside in a second. Think, Dash, think," he thought. Dash shook his head in frustration. Johnny had always been there even though Dash didn't want him to be. Dash regretted the day he saved Johnny's life, but now he wanted nothing more than for him to come rushing in and pull his ass out of the fire. He still hoped Johnny would burst through the glass patio door like a SWAT team to save the day, but he knew better. Dash had run off the one person he could have counted on.

Then there was a little tap on the balcony door which startled Dash. Dash knew Johnny couldn't stay away. Dash combat rolled and took aim at the target, but it was Jack. Dash was happy to see Jack, but sad that it wasn't Johnny.

"Some back up is better than no back up," he thought knowing he would have to count on himself to get out of this mess.

Jack had crawled over from the next door balcony, panicked by the shooting, and was just in time to have to jump back over. As the TCS guards blew open the door and came flooding into the room. Dash let loose a burst of rounds catching the first one square in the chest. The bullets were absorbed by the guard's bullet proof vest, but sent him to the floor. Jack pulled Dash on to the balcony as he fired.

They were able to jump from balcony to balcony dodging bullets until they reached the corner of the building. Jack reached into his bag and pulled out a detonation switch.

"This will take care of them," Jack said as he went to press the button. Dash quickly snatched the control from him.

"Knowing you Jack, the explosive will blow up my room, your room, and almost every room on this floor. I can't let you do that. Fern is still in my room."

"Dude it's either us or her," Jack said as he reached for the control. "I ain't ready to die yet." Dash shoved Jack away pointed his gun at Jack.

"You better be ready to die if you push this button. There is no way I am letting you blow up the building, at least not yet," Dash said with a smirk. Dash didn't know what to do. There were at least fifteen Takahara Corp. Security guardsmen chasing him, and after a quick scan the parking lot many more down stairs. Dash quickly contemplated his options as more bullets smashed in to the cement balcony walls chewing away at the railing. Dash lifted his gun over the wall and fired back. His shots were hitting their mark, but the TCS vests were preventing him from doing any real damage. Dash was only slowing them down and it wouldn't be long before they were over-run.

"Jack, get in that room; get the dresser, mattress, everything you can in front of that door!" Dash yelled over the gun fire. Jack went to work. Dash took up a better position on the balcony squeezing a few shots at the security guards clipping one of them in the leg sending him down.

More bullets embedded themselves in balcony. "Thank God that Jack had taken care of the door to the room. It'll take a few pounds of explosives to break in through that direction," Dash thought to himself.

Just then he heard the most annoying, yet beautiful sound in his life -- the whining engine of a Honda CBR1000. The high pitched roar of the engine was very distinct because of the personal modifications Johnny had made to it, and then his headlink rang. This was the call he was waiting for.

"You're a hard man to reach. I have been trying to call you for a couple hours," Johnny said.

"Been a little busy," Dash answered as bits of cement fell over him and concrete dust was kicked into the air. The balcony wall wasn't going to hold for much longer.

"I can hear that. Be up in a second. What room are you in?" Johnny asked as Dash heard the revving of the bike's engine and the squeal of the bikes tires.

"End of the hall third floor. Johnny, do me a favor get Fern from room 312 she is in the bathroom and then get the fuck out of here. Jack and I have our own way out," Dash said.

"I ain't leaving anyone behind. We need to stick together or we're both going to end up dead," Johnny said with authority. Dash could hear gun fire echo through his headlink as Johnny entered the building.

"There's no time to argue. You save her and I'll owe you one and be careful, they've got armored vests this time," Dash said.

"Not happening. I'll get her then I'll come get you," Johnny stated. "Now start working on a plan to get all of us outta here."

"Listen Johnny. I don't need you to get my ass out of here. The only reason why I'm still here is because Fern is in danger and I can't leave her. Not again..." Dash yelled angrily through the link. "You get her out and it'll square a lot of things between us. And Johnny?" Dash said with a pause.

"Yeah," Johnny responded as he rode his bike through the lobby.

Gunfire could be heard over both headlinks now.

"Thanks for coming," Dash confessed. Dash could hear the thump, thump, thump of Johnny's bike heading up the staircase.

"What are friends for, if not to dive head first into crazy shit like this," Johnny replied. The smile in his voice could be heard through the phone.

Dash could hear the echo of the bike's engine as if it was in a canyon, echoing down the hallways. Gun fire and the high pitched engine of Johnny's bike could be heard coming closer. The gun fire at the balcony stopped for a moment as the bike sped down the hall.

The wide staircase made it easy for Johnny to navigate up to the third floor. Johnny had shown up in the nick of time even though he had to make a quick stop to pick up his weapons. The TCS guardsmen were about to blow open Dash's door so Johnny ripped into them with his Scorpion and made short work of the agents setting the charges. Johnny shot them anywhere they were exposed arms, legs, and head, going through three clips on full auto until they stopped moving. He holstered his Scorpion and continued down the hallway.

Johnny stopped at the intersection, reading the hallway sign showing the direction that rooms "300-325" were in. Johnny then raced down the hallway toward Fern's room. The bikes engine alerted the TCS guardsmen as he approached. Their attention was drawn away from Dash and Jack and the TCS started moving into the hallway appearing from the doorways of each room, Johnny pulled his two pistols from his waist band as his sped down the hall. Round after round he fired putting one guardsman after another down. He ran out of bullets as he reached room 312 and put the two pistols back in his waist band. Johnny removed his double barrel sawed off shot gun from its hiding spot on the bike and cautiously entered room 312. The room appeared to be empty and quite compared to the hall way.

"Fern!" Johnny yelled as he entered the room. "Fern where are you?" Johnny opened the door to the bathroom and stepped in.

"Who are you?!" She asked as Johnny pulled back the shower curtain. The red headed girl startled and fired a round into him. The round pierced through his vest into this gut. He collapsed to the floor. It was really hard for Johnny to breath. The red head crawled out of the tub keeping her shaking gun hand pointed at Johnny. She was holding Dash's Raging Bull and he always loaded it with armor piercing rounds. As Johnny gasped for air and tried to get to his feet he realized that this was Fern. "Fuckin' red heads, always too much damn trouble for what they're worth," He thought.

"I'm not going to let you kill him!" She shouted as she circled around him to get to the door. She raised the Raging Bull level with Johnny's forehead. Through his gasps for air Johnny spotted a TCS guardsman that had slowly crept into the room getting the drop Fern.

"Drop it," He said as he pressed the barrel of his weapon to her head. Fern dropped the gun and threw her hands in the air. "Now on your knees."

Johnny locked eyes with Fern, motioning to his shotgun and then towards the security guard. Fern got the picture. She dropped to her knees and rolled out of the way. The guardsman had no chance. Johnny raised his gun and unloaded both barrels point blank into his chest, making a gigantic hole and throwing him and his organs against the wall with a splattering sound. Johnny finally got his breath back, but was bleeding bad and he knew the he needed to get help fast.

Johnny flipped up his visor and spoke, "I'm Dash's friend I got a bike outside to get you out of here. Help me up." They could still hear gun fire from outside. "Help me up please." Johnny reached out for Ferns hand. Fern grabbed Dash's gun and pointed it back at Johnny.

"Help yourself. Now get up." She motioned with the point of the barrel. Fern wasn't a scared girl anymore. Johnny got up slowly. "Let's go." Fern continued to point the gun at him. Johnny peaked out into the hall way all the attention was on Dash's room down the way. As he turned his head to peer the other way his helmet was struck by a fist. Johnny stumbled back and two men stormed into the room. Johnny could tell by the punch to his helmet that these guys were different than normal TCS agents. Johnny recovered from the massive blow just in time to kick the machine gun out of first advancing attacker's hands. The second man back-handed Fern and knocked her to the ground then aimed his gun at Johnny.

"We need the Beta alive, Tatuso." One of the men said. The other lowered his weapon begrudgingly. Johnny knew his wound was dire and his adrenaline was only going to keep him up for so long. He also knew that he didn't have Dash's skills for talking his way out of a sticky situation. He had to act fast if he was going to be able to get out of this mess.

"Takeshi, the girl!" Tatuso yelled with urgency. Fern raise Dash's gun from her position on the ground. She steadied her hand and prepared herself for the recoil of the massive hand cannon. Takeshi spun around and kicked the gun up as she fired, putting the bullet into the plaster ceiling. Johnny took the opportunity and kicked the man in the back of his support leg knocking him to the ground. Tatuso struck Johnny in the back with his fist. The trauma plate from the vest absorbed most of the blow, bending the plate slightly from the force of the hit. Johnny let out a grunt of agony none-the-less.

Tatuso's hands weren't human. Tatuso swung with his other fist connecting with Johnny's head, busting the faceplate out of his helmet. The hit took Johnny to the ground, hard. Johnny rolled to the side and snatched up Dash's gun. With a fluid motion Johnny rolled up to his knees, pistol in hand and ready to fire. He knew he would only get one shot and the other would take him out, but the men stopped in their tracks at the sight of the hand cannon in the hands of someone that knew how to use it.

"Fern get to my bike in the hall. Sorry guys you'll have to catch me next time," Johnny said as they circled each other, Johnny clutching his wound with his other hand. Tatuso's hands were bloody and Johnny could see the metal under his skin. He knew why he could feel those punches through his helmet. Tatsuo's hands and probably much more of him had been cybernetic enhanced.

"He'd only be able to get one of us, Tatsuo," Takeshi said as he began to circle around behind me.

"Then I shoot you first," Johnny said as he backed his way towards the door. "Back up or this bullet will change your sex life." Johnny got on the bike and started it. The pain of his wound made him grimace with every move. Johnny handed the gun back to Fern. Fern got on behind him shoving the gun in his side. As soon as the gun was off Takeshi and Tatsuo they moved in to attack. Johnny put the bike into gear and whipped the bike around, knocking his attackers back. Johnny turned the accelerator and began his getaway. "I'd like to see Dash do that with his bike," Johnny thought.

Johnny gunned it through the turn and jumped the staircase, making their way out of the building. Johnny called Dash on his headlink as they began to fly down the stairs on his motorcycle.

"Headlink on, call Dash. " The phone rang once and was picked up, "Dash, I've been hit. I got Fern, but I can't come get you. Sorry," Johnny explained.

"We will just go back to plan A," Dash said. The call disconnected and within seconds the explosions started Johnny could see them clearly his review mirrors. He could also see Fern looking back. "He's alright. He said he had a way out. Where are we headed anyway?"

"Just drive," Fern said as she pressed the gun harder into Johnny. Johnny winced from the pain of his wound.

"You can trust me. I'm one of the good guys," Johnny replied. Fern started giving directions after a few minutes. They ended up at a nice house with a beautiful yard, white picket fence, and nicely mowed lawn. Looked like what most people would call the American dream.

"Everything Dash wanted in his life with Fern," Johnny thought as he began to feel dizzy.

"Nice place," he said his voice sounding groggy. Johnny tried to apply pressure to his wound which was a major mistake. The pain shot through him like a bolt of lightning causing his vision to blur, but he had to try to stop the bleeding somehow.

"Shut up. Get inside," Fern said jabbing him in the back with the gun.

"Okay," Johnny agreed as he took a step toward the house and stumbled. "Watch that first step." He stumbled again and then collapsed on the front porch.

Johnny faded in and out for a while. He kept hearing voices and saw flashes of images. There was a man in a surgical mask.

"He has lost a lot of blood I don't even know how he's alive at this point," The man wearing the surgical mask said.

"Why are you doing this?" Fern asked.

"Cause he saved your life," The man replied as he went back to work on Johnny as he lost consciousness again. Later he awoke to Fern dabbing his head with a cool cloth.

"I don't know how, but he's alive. No one should have lived through that," The Doctor said as Johnny passed out again. He woke up once more to see a little red headed girl playing on the floor. She watched Johnny as he lay there. Johnny reached out towards her. She couldn't have been more than two or three years old. She walked over and took hold of his hand until Fern walked in and removed her.

"No. No. Honey you mustn't play with the man he needs to sleep," he heard Fern say and then fell asleep again.

Johnny awoke groggy and in need of a drink of water. Johnny's throat was so dry he felt as if sand was poured into his mouth. He tried to sit up, but it was hard his gut was still bandaged up. Johnny slowly worked his way into a sitting position and swung his body to put his feet on the floor. He eased off the table keeping his hand on it for support. The floor was cold on Johnny's bare feet. His clothing had been removed save for his underwear which he was pretty sure wasn't his. Johnny stood for a moment looking around. There was a washer, dryer, and he could see a faucet with a large sink in what he could only assume was a laundry room.

He slowly moved over to the sink and turned it on. Scooping handfuls of water into his mouth helping the grogginess slowly fade away. His shoulder and gut had been neatly sewn up. Upon Johnny's inspection of his wounds he found they had been treated quite nicely. Better than any of the third rate back alley docs he had seen in the past. Johnny could have sworn a surgeon had done it as flashes of his consciousness came back to him. He snapped out of his thoughts as he heard the door creek. Johnny put his hands up.

"Fern don't shoot me. I've had enough of that," Johnny said as he slowly turned around. There stood the little girl a spitting image of her mother except for her eyes. They were grey and looked really familiar, but he couldn't place it. "Well hello, who are you?" Johnny asked the little girl.

She was startled and ran back out of the room and from the sound of it up the stairs. Johnny started to get dizzy again and headed back to the table. A moment later Fern walked in gun pointed at Johnny. He chuckled as he waved a finger at Fern. "You know I just told your daughter not to shoot me and she didn't, perhaps you could learn from her example."

"Get back on the table. You shouldn't move. You could tear your stitches," she said as she motioned with the gun.

"Why the hell are ya still pointin' that thing at me? Hasn't Dash filled you in yet? It's me. Come on we went to the same damn high school together. I know we never hung out, but the school wasn't that big." Johnny tried to explain through a dizzy spell. Fern looked again at Johnny.

"Johnny... Johnny Morals. Dash and you disappeared around the same time I never thought that it was you. Always figured your Southsider ass was dead in a ditch somewhere," she said as she walked over to him.

"Yeah well, I wasn't..." he began to say as Fern interrupted him with a slap across the face. The slap echoed in the basement. "What in the hell was that for?"

"Well, for a lot of things, but mostly for taking him away from me," Fern said fighting back tears.

"Yeah, I probably deserved that. Maybe next time, tell Dash not to be a god damn hero," he said as he rubbed his cheek with his hand.

"Thanks for patchin' me up," Johnny said as he rubbed his wound. The gun shot was still very tender.

"Don't thank me, thank Tommy. He was pretty sure that you were a goner, but then somehow you pulled through," Fern said as if she almost didn't want him to make it.

"Well I'll have to thank Doctor Tommy when I get a chance," he replied with a chuckle, trying to break the tense mood. Fern couldn't take the small talk any more.

"You've kept him away from me all this time, when he should have been here with me. I should have shot you more than once!" Fern said furious as hell. She turned away as if she didn't care, but Johnny could tell she was just hiding the buildup of emotions. He could see she really didn't know what to say to him and was glad they were alive.

"Well it is kind of a long story. Dash saved my life and with what happened during his rescue he couldn't exactly go home. My Uncle gave us a job... Phew, these painkillers must be wearing off this is starting to hurt again," Johnny said as his voice grew weak. "We have been trying... hey when you... got all... fuzzy." Fern turned around to see that Johnny had accidently reopened his wound and was bleeding.

"Oh no, lay down. You're bleeding again. Tommy, bring your bag. Tommy!!!" She screamed and within seconds a man appearing to be in his fifties with peppered black hair was down stairs addressing Johnny's wound.

"Damn it. He was supposed to stay in bed. The virus is still repairing his liver," Tommy said as he grabbed instruments from his bag. "Get the chloroform and knock him out." Fern ran from the room.

"Hey Doc, I was supposed to thank you but it may have been too soon," Johnny said as he voice weakened and his breathing became labored.

"You will be fine Beta. You just need rest," Tommy said.

"Beta, what the fuck? You're workin' for them!" Johnny yelled and became a little more alert as his adrenaline pumped into his veins. He tried to struggle by pushing Tommy away, but was too weak.

"We will talk about it later. Trust me you are safe here," Tommy assured him. "Now, this is going to hurt."

"I'm sure this pain is worse, Doc," Johnny replied. Tommy started to apply pressure to Johnny's wound to stop the bleeding. "Oh... fuck... just shoot me Doc." Johnny was feeling the worse pain he had ever felt. He clenched his teeth grinding them together. The original bullet wound hurt less. Just then Fern returned and used the chloroform to knock Johnny out. Johnny was no match in his state and was quickly unconscious. The last thing Johnny heard as he passed out was Tommy saying there was still a piece of bullet lodged in his liver.

The next time Johnny awoke he couldn't move. He was very groggy, but he could tell he was still in the same room. As the grogginess started to wear off Johnny felt the handcuffs around his wrist as he was strapped down to the table and had I.V.'s in his arm, heart monitoring equipment, and other necessary items for an unconscious patient. He knew he was safe even with all the tubes running in and out of him. Johnny decided it was better to stay laying down this time and just wait for Dash. He quickly fell back a sleep.

"We clear?" Jack asked as he walked up behind Dash startling him.

"Fucking shit, I could have killed you!" Dash yelled, his hand already on his weapon.

"Jesus, Sorry!" Jack said putting his hands up. "So are we clear?"

"Yeah we're clear. Go get Frankie," Dash said and Jack ran off. Dash popped the lock on the fence to the junkyard and opened the gate. Dash was so tired the bags under his eyes had bags. Jack and Dash had been running for two weeks now. Not getting more than a few hours of sleep a night if any at all. Most of their time awake was spent filling up the gas tank and finding new places to hide. They were beyond exhausted.

What was also weighing heavily on Dash was that he had not heard from Johnny the entire time. "I hope they made it out. Fern better be ok or I'm going to fucking kick Johnny's ass," Dash thought as Jack drove into the junkyard. Dash shut the gate behind him. Dash couldn't help but wince every time he saw Jack with Frankie. Dash and Johnny had torn up the van a few times, but not like this. Frankie looking like battered Swiss cheese that someone had put extra holes in, left out for a few days, and then backed over it with a lawnmower.

"I really hope your mites can work miracles," Dash said.

"They are nano bots not mites," Jack mumbled.

"What was that?" Dash asked gruffly.

"Um... nothing... She will need time, but she will be just like new in 24-48hrs," Jack said with a smile, but with worry in his voice. "I hope... maybe sooner."

"Make sure she doesn't eat the box or what's inside it," Dash mentioned.

"What is it? This box seems so important. Do you think it is really worth all our lives?" Jack questioned trying to get Dash to reveal what was in the box.

"Nope, but the Takahara Corp. thinks it is and I like being a thorn in their side since they've been such a pain in my ass."

Dash stood amazed, watching the piles of junk next to the van started to erode. "Check on Frankie I'm going to try to call Johnny again. Try catching a nap too I'll take first watch." Jack nodded and plugged his lap top into van. "Contact, Johnny," Dash said ordering his headlink to attempt to call him. His headlink started to ring, but went directly to voice mail.

"This voice mail box is full," the answering service said. Dash was really starting to worry, but the good news is that Johnny's body had not turned up in the morgue otherwise his headlink plan would have been turned off.

Dash's concern for the love of his life and his friend twisted his stomach; that and the fact that Dash and Jack hadn't really had a chance to eat in a few days. Candy bars and gas station food are all right, but when you've had them for two weeks straight they tend not to be such a tasty treat anymore. The growl of his stomach couldn't be stopped when he noticed a diner through the junkyard fence. It was just a few blocks down from their location as the scent of rain filled the air. Dash pounded on the van's back door. Frankie needed to fix itself so they had a little time to kill and Jack needed to get some food too. His incessant complain about not getting a good meal had filled most of their two week excursion.

"Jack, park Frankie around the corner out of sight and let's go..." Dash said before Jack interrupted.

"But you told me to get some sleep and I'm tired. I can barely move. Just let me rest for a little bit longer. I promise I'll go to class today." Jack yawned and whined in his half delirious state.

"Well I was going to say we could go get some grub, but I guess you're too tired to eat," Dash said with a hint of sarcasm. Jack jumped out of the van with a look on his face like a little kid on

Christmas day.

"Something to eat, where?!" Jack asked with hope in his eyes. "You'd better not be messing with me."

"Yup, I was totally messing with you. I have another candy bar if you want it," Dash said jokingly as he pulled one out of his pocket.

"I guess the candy bar is ok. Thanks," Jack said down trodden about not eating really food still he snatched up the candy bar.

"Jack, there is a diner down the block. So hurry up and hide Frankie and we'll get going," Dash said. Jack perked back up and smiled.

"Do you think it is safe?" Jack asked. "I hate to leave Frankie all by herself."

"Yeah, we haven't seen any of those ass hats for most of today. I think we've finally lost them," Dash said, pretty confident that he had given the TCS the slip. He still worried, because they had found them ten times in the last two weeks, but they needed to eat something that wasn't out of vending machine or off gas station rack. Jack hid the van and met Dash at the gate. They both scooped out the street and proceeded cautiously to the diner as it began to rain. The large neon sign said "Mama's Diner" underneath that it said "All welcome".

Dash and Jack watched the door for a moment before crossing the street and heading in. They watched as multiple Alphas came and went. After a few minutes, Dash knew that it'd be safe to grab a bite to eat. It was a well-known fact that no self respecting Alpha would work for Takahara Corp. Even if the flu vaccine wasn't the cause of the mutation, Alphas blamed Takahara Corp. for it.

Dash and Jack went in and grabbed a seat at a booth. Dash took the seat facing the door to keep watch. The waitress was an Oscar. Her pimple covered nose, over-sized canines, body builder physique, and the skin of her broad shoulders were dry and flaking were the telling signs of her affliction. The whole staff was Alphas, not a big deal for Dash, but it was definitely different to see so many in one place.

"Haven't seen you around here before, what can I get for you two pretty boys?" The waitress said with the best smile an Oscar could manage. Her massive gold plated incisors sparkled in the light like she was doing a tooth paste commercial.

"Well, Rachel," Jack said as he read her name tag. "What's good here?" The whole place went quite. The sound of the rain hitting the glass could be heard over the mass induced silence. The sliding of chairs across the floor sounded like a high school gym. Everyone was staring at their table or trying to get a better look. Even the cook letting something burn while he watched.

"What's your name?" Rachel asked really quietly as she grabbed Jack by his shirt and lifted him into the air like a rag doll.

"Jack," Jack whispered back with a gulp looking at Dash for help. Dash made the hands off motion and went back to reading the menu.

"Well Jack, would you ever ask your mother if the food was good. No you wouldn't because she's your mother. Take another look at the sign and maybe you'd like to rephrase your question," She said as she started at him intently.

"Ah. What's the special?" Jack asked with a squeak in his voice hoping not to get pummeled.

"Wrong questions! The special is special so you don't need to know what it is to have it. Go back to your own side of town. Northsider!" She said gruffly as she dropped him to the floor.

"Hey, sweet cheeks," Dash spoke up. "Please excuse my friend. His brain is fried from not eating and reading through a billion lines of computer code. He's forgotten his manors. I'm sure a beauty like you would give him another chance. I would love the special and a beer." Dash gave her his usual charming smile and she gave in to his good looks and wiles. She stood there for a moment tapping her foot and staring at Jack who was still sitting on the floor.

"Um... Two specials and two beers, please?" Jack muttered.

"Three specials and three beers coming up," Rachel said, giving a wink to Dash. About fifteen minutes later the food arrived and to their surprise it was macaroni and cheese and hot dogs for Jack and foot long spicy burrito with all the fixing on the side for Dash. Jack and Dash looked at each other as if you say, "Did you tell them?" but they didn't care they were hunger and started devouring there meal like ravenous animals almost not bothering to chew.

"Enjoy boys. Everyone loves Cookie's specials," Rachel said smiling at Dash. "The special is always what you're craving most. I don't know how he does it, but it never fails. Cookie is a marvel."

Dash and Jack barely had time to really get into their food when the waitress brought the check. "Check already Rachel? Our table manners aren't *that* bad," Dash said with a wink.

"Are you boys expecting company?" Rachel said, nodding her head in the direction of the front window.

"Mother fucker!" Dash said as he pounded his fist on the table and looked out the back. "Jack we got to go. They're on to us."

"But, I still have another dog and half a beer," he complained as he shoveled the rest of his macaroni in his mouth. Jack chugged the rest of his beer as he noticed the black Hondas pulling into the parking lot. These were no ordinary Hondas. They were top of the line with all the extras including spy gadgets. Red dot laser sights began to fill the diner. They were Takahara cars that had been chasing them for the last two weeks. Jack sprayed Dash with his beer and pointed out the window. Jack grabbed his hot dog and moved quickly out the back door. Dash followed after him. They covered the few block with a quick jog and back tracked through alleys to make sure they weren't followed.

"Home sweet home," Jack said as he set eyes on Frankie.

Dash followed the comment with a sarcastic, "Yeah."

Later, while listening to the radio, they found out why they were able to get back to Frankie without begin followed. Apparently a few Takahara Corp. guys got worked over by the Mama's diner staff. Takahara agents in a diner full of Alphas. Takahara Corp. may have never been prosecuted for the testing, but those agents were punished thoroughly. Dash and Jack laughed for a good twenty while listening to the news report and making jokes about the waitress

Rachel giving them the special where the sun doesn't shine, or Cookie handing out knuckle sandwiches for free.

As they finished joking around the rain ended and they were able to get a full nights rest in the back of the van. Dash's mind wandered during the night. He didn't know what his next step was. He could go to Fern's home to see if they had found them, or back to the warehouse to ditch the van because Frankie stuck out like a sore thumb. He didn't know if Fern and Johnny were dead in a ditch somewhere. His mind raced through the night, but eventually he fell asleep.

The next day Frankie was all but done with repairs. So Dash and Jack loaded a box of scrap metal into the back of the van so Frankie could finish up the repairs on the road. After two weeks of gun fights and car chases Dash was down to his last clip. "Must be an awful lot of guys on Takahara's payroll because I've put at least twenty in the ground" Dash mused. It was time to find out what happen to Fern and Johnny. Dash and Jack couldn't run anymore.

"Jack, we need to find Fern and Johnny." Dash had decided.

"Yeah I know. But I keep trying to look up her name and I get nothing," Jack said as he typed on his lap top.

"You can't find Fern. How did you deliver all those letters I gave you?"

"By using an email I found from your high school. I typed them up and sent them."

"You read my letters to Fern!" Dash became angry.

"Not really... I just typed the letters up and... and sent the email," Jack lied poorly, but still hoped that Dash would buy it.

"Fuck it. That isn't important right now. We need to find them, before the TCS does," Dash said as he pounded his fist on the steering wheel. Jack breathed a sigh of relief. "Sorry Frankie." Dash was too preoccupied with everything to find out if Jack was telling the truth about the letters.

"Hey, be easy with Frankie. She's got feelings too," Jack said and Dash couldn't help, but laugh at the fact he just apologized to a car with feelings.

"Ah. Dash," Jack said trying not to interrupt Dash's train of thought.

"Yeah, what is it? You find her?" Dash asked impatiently.

"Um. I think so," Jack said with at gulp. Jack turned his monitor to Dash it was a wedding picture of Fern with some Doctor Thomas Johnson. Dash was so shocked by the image. "How could this be? We just... This can't be right." Dash thought as car started to swerve. He tried to remember the conversation they had before the gun fight. Fern kept saying people were counting on her.

"Um. Dash, Dash," Jack said as he started to panic about moving into the other lane. Jack put on his seatbelt.

"It can't be. Check it again," he said as he snatched the lap top and began reading the article.

"Dash!" Jack spoke up as he grabbed the steering wheel and moved them back into the correct lane just avoiding a head on collision. Dash continued to read the article. Jack did his best to steer. "Dash, could you pull over so I could drive?"

"What!? You've got be fucking kidding me," Dash said as he read. "Ok, I won't drive, but could you at least watch the road," Jack pleaded. Dash pulled Frankie over and switched seats with Jack so he could finish reading the article. As Dash read the hole in his heart reopened anew. Fern eloped right out of high school with a doctor. Dash thought to himself, "She is married, but we...Just... Fern would never. She loves me. How... why... she would have waited. This isn't possible. This can't happen."

"No. No! NO!" Dash yelled.

He paged through the information and found her address. "Here is her address. Now drive!" They sat in silence the entire way. Dash fought back his tears that filled his eyes. Instead he filled them with rage and hate. Johnny had cost him the one thing he held most dear. Dash was going to prevent him from taking anything else from him. Dash was going to kill Johnny if he wasn't already dead.

As they arrived at Fern's house Dash jumped out of the van and removed the safety from his UMP-45 and charged to the door. As he reached the door he kicked it in.

"Where is he?!" Dash yelled. Fern rushed to pick up her child as she began to cry because of crash of the door and Dash's yelling. "That son of a bitch! Where is he?"

"Dash, stop yelling!" Fern said to him. Dash started to search the house when he ran into Tommy. "Where is he?" Dash wore his anger on his face and he glared at the doctor.

"Perhaps you better leave until you calm down," Tommy said as he pointed at the door.

"You gonna make me!" Dash said with a chuckle and stared down Tommy with his fists clenched. There was a fire in Dash's eyes that could only be put out with Johnny's blood. Jack came up to the front door, poked his head in and decided that with all the yelling he would rather stay outside.

"Dash, calm down," Fern said as she handed the little girl over to Tommy. "Why are you so angry?"

"It's all his fault," Dash said as he moved from room to room looking for Johnny. "He's cost me my life. So I'm going to take his. Where is he?!"

"I'm not going to let you. He's kept you alive all this time. He kept me alive. He's your friend Dash... He's your *friend*." Fern said emotionally as she stood in front of the basement door. Dash continued to search the rooms until he noticed that Fern stopped following him.

"Get out of the way Fern!" Dash said. "He's ruined our lives. We were the ones that were supposed to get married and live happily ever after. How can you protect him when he has cost us everything?"

"It isn't his fault I got married," Fern said, but the words fell on deaf ears. Dash shoved her aside and charged down the stairs into the basement. There Johnny was sleeping. Dash walked over to him and placed his hands around his throat and began to squeeze. Johnny woke up and looked into Dash's eye. Dash could see the question that Johnny spoke with his sadness filled eyes. "Why?" Johnny wanted to fight back but was still strapped in so he didn't reinjure himself.

"She married someone else because of you!" Dash yelled at him. Fern emerged from the stair well and rushed to stop Dash. She was not strong enough to stop him.

"Dash let him go. You're killing him," Fern pleaded as she tried to free his hands from Johnny's neck.

"That's the fucking point," Dash said coldly.

"No, Dash. It is your fault!" She screamed. Dash stopped her words finally pierced through his rage. The rage began to melt away as he repeated what Fern said.

"My fault?" Dash questioned confused by her accusation. "But he was the one that got me into this mess. You getting married to someone else *is* his fault." Dash was still struck by the words and let go slumping to the floor. Johnny gasped for air coughing and choking.

Fern collapsed around Dash holding him tight. "I wanted to tell you at Homecoming, but you were chased off. I was pregnant Dash. The little girl upstairs is yours. I was 18 and pregnant and I was scared. I needed help. Please forgive me. I didn't know what to do?" Tommy had reached the bottom of the stairs still carrying the little girl. "I'm sorry Tommy; I was young and didn't know what to do." Fern began to cry as she confessed.

"She wanted mommy. So I brought her down after the yelling stopped," Tommy said as he handed over the little girl with tears in his eye. "I... I'm going to go get some milk. I'll be back in a little while." He kissed the little girl on the forehead gave her a big hug and left. Dash stared at his hands. He had never felt some much rage or hate in his life. He thought to himself, "What was I doing?"

Dash's thoughts began to spiral. He had a little girl. It was an amazing feeling. So much of his life that was lost on the run washed away in this new knowledge that he was responsible for someone now besides himself. A new and wonderful person had just walked into his life. Dash sat on the floor, awestruck at the new turn of events that his life had just drastically taken.

"I'm so sorry," Dash said as he cried. "Never again. I'm so sorry." He had hurt the three most important people in his life. He shoved Fern, scared his little girl and damn near killed Johnny. Dash decided then and there the past was the past. He could no longer blame Johnny for what happened. They just needed to work together to fix it. Then they could go on living their lives. It was time to stop running and fight back, for all of their sakes. There is no way that the Takahara Corp. was throwing this many guys at them for a stolen box. There was more to it. Dash kissed Fern and the little girl on the forehead. He sniffed back his tears. "And who is this little one?"

"This is Scarlet, your daughter. Say hello baby," Fern said still wiping away tears.

"Hi." Scarlet said as she buried her face in her mother's chest.

"She's shy it'll take time," Fern told Dash.

"Now that you've had your family togetherness moment, can I get out of this? I don't want to chance one of you choking me or shooting me, again?" Johnny said with a raspy voice. Fern handed Dash the key to the hand cuffs. Dash got up and removed the cuffs. "I ain't stayin' pinned to that bed any more. I don't care how much I need to lie down." Johnny proceeded to remove the I.V.s form his arm. "Ouch." Dash stood up and walked over to his friend and gave him a hug.

"Thank you for keeping her safe," he said.

"Ok, ok. Will you let go of me now? That *hurts*," Johnny said as he rubbed his throat.

"Sorry. I'm just... you know," Dash said not sure of his words.

"That you're a fucking pussy who is getting all mushy on me," Johnny joked.

"Hey, language," Dash said as he gave Johnny a shot to the chest. Johnny groaned in pain as he held on to the table for balance. Dash watched as Johnny removed his shirt. There was a large bandage where over his gut. "What the hell happened to you man?'

"Ask your girl. She's the one who did it," Johnny said with a chuckle and a cough.

"He came in the bathroom and he wasn't you," Fern replied.

"I wonder who told her to do that," Johnny said sarcastically as he inspected his wound. "The stitches are still good. No worries Fern. So what do we do now?"

"I have a plan. Hey Jack. It's safe now. Get your ass down here and bring your computer!" Dash yelled up the stairs, and then looked back at Johnny confidently. "We're going to take the fight to them."

"Just so I understand what exactly happened. Please explain

to me how the Beta escaped capture and why he was wounded?!" Mr. Takahara demanded pacing in front of Takeshi and Tatuso who knelt before him in shame. The floor was decorated with two large body bags that were lying next to Takeshi and Tatuso. Dr. Maki sat quietly away from the men in the room.

"We are sorry Mr. Takahara, please forgive us. Give us one more chance," Takeshi pleaded. Tatsuo looked at Takeshi and shook his head.

"Sir, what my partner was really trying to say is that, as we engaged the subject in hand to hand combat, we lost the advantage do to a red headed woman we have yet to identify," Tatsuo tried to explain.

"So you are saying that you were bested by a woman?" Mr. Takahara said with a chuckle. "Ichiro."

"Wait sir there's more," Takeshi quickly pleaded. "We believe that the red haired woman is important to one of the men traveling with Beta. They arrived before he did and were there for several hours. While that Beta was across town at the El Diablo tavern..."

"Get to the point!" Mr. Takahara shouted and returned to pacing in front of them.

"The Beta doesn't know what he is. He was unaware when we referred to him as such during the attempt to capture him." Tatuso took over for Takeshi who was scared to response. "Also, unknown to him, we were able to acquire a blood sample of the Beta."

"A blood sample?" Doctor Maki became excited and stood up from her chair with an out-stretched hand. "Where is it?" Mr. Takahara shot a glare at her and she became silent. She began trembling.

"A blood sample you say. Where is it?" Mr. Takahara asked.

"I sent it with one our men to Maki Labs, so that it could be properly taken care of and evaluated," Tatuso responded.

"Which prompts me to ask, why are you even here Doctor Maki?" Mr. Takahara asked. The coldness had fallen from his voice, but a small amount to joy could be detected. Doctor Maki quickly left the room.

"As for you two, thank you for your assistance. You have completely failed the tasks of your mission. The Beta was not captured, the Delta drug was not recovered, and these body bags do not contain the Betas companions. However you were able to salvage part of the mission, good work. Ichiro would you come in here," Mr. Takahara ordered as he finished the debriefing.

"Wait sir wait. I thought you said we did good work." Tatuso pleaded knowing what calling Ichiro to the office meant. Ichiro walked into the room and up behind the two men.

"You did. However Takeshi here asked to be forgiven and I'm feeling inclined to be generous." Mr. Takahara explained.

"No don't. Let me continue in your service." Takeshi pleaded as Ichiro began walking towards them "Don't do this I can be useful."

"Takeshi you are..." Mr. Takahara started.

"Wait, Mr. Takahara, wait," Tatuso said. "What if you let him serve under me to restore his honor? We are a great team and it would be a tragedy to split us up."

"That is very true," Mr. Takahara responded. "I give you a sincere promise that you won't be separated after we are through here. I forgive you both." Ichiro moved fast, pulling out a pair of tasers that quickly sent enough volts into Tatsuo's and Takeshi's bodies that would have put down a horse.

"I'll have this taken care of," Ichiro said switching the taser off.

"Ichiro," Mr. Takahara called to him.

"Yes, sir," Ichiro replied.

"Have them sent down to reprocessing. Bodies like those would be a shame to throw away. Have the doctors give them a simple mind wipe and reprogram them," Mr. Takahara stated.

"It will be done," Ichiro replied with a bow. Ichiro left the room with the bodies. Mr. Takahara sat at his desk and brought up his monitors. The monitors changed every few seconds.

"Where are you Beta? Where are you hiding in my city?" Mr. Takahara said as he dimmed the lights and sat an elbow on each arm rest and his finger tips touching each other. Light from the setting sun caused a shadow from where he was sitting to stretch over the wall of monitors as he watched his city.

Johnny never liked it when Dash had that look in his eye. It always ended badly. The only thing Johnny could think of is that Dash felt he was really close to getting the life back that he had wanted all along. "Dash, we can't do this, we should run man. You've everything you need now. It's is time to disappear. Think about it man. There's no happy ending for you if we do this. We die... end of story!" Johnny tried to explain to Dash.

"Are you retarded? Do you think I was going to suggest we walk through the front door clean shaven with a grin on our faces? No, we're doing this the smart way. I guarantee there's a guy in charge ordering the hunt for us. We find out who that is and we fix our problem by eliminating his ass. Cut the head off the snake and this is over. We can live our lives," Dash stated. "Think about it. They've been after us like their lives depended on it. They aren't going to stop unless we make them, which leaves us with only one option. They aren't going to stop, Johnny. They're *never* going to stop. They've started attacking our friends and family. If we leave everyone we have ever met will be in jeopardy. This is the only real choice we have."

Johnny started to leave the room. He had heard enough and knew this wasn't going to end well.

"Where are you going? I'm going to need you on this one. And face it; you really don't have anywhere else you want to be right now or any other choices. You know I'm right," Dash said trying to get his friend to stay.

"I know," Johnny said as he paused in the doorway. "I figured that I would hit up the warehouse see if it was still standin' and collect the rest of our shit. We're gonna need it." Johnny shook his head in disbelief about what Dash was planning. "Dash. Keys. I'm gonna need the van." Dash pointed at Jack. He tossed Johnny the keys as Johnny headed out the door. Johnny thought to himself, "He better have one hell of a plan."

"Hey. Stay to the back streets. Takahara Corp. has the city wired and if they see that van they'll be all over you like flies on shit." Dash warned.

"No they won't," Jack said.

"Really, why's that? It's not like they have been chasing it around town," Dash said mockingly.

"Frankie has a new license plate number and color," Jack said proudly.

"How did that happen? You haven't had time to do that," Dash said, pondering what Jack had done to the van.

"Frankie did it. She said she was tired of being shot at -- so she disguised herself. That and I hacked the camera system and all you have to do is plug the lap top into the van and everywhere you go the camera will loop and you will never be seen," Jack said with a smile.

"Then I guess I'll need this too," Johnny said and he snatched Jack's lap top.

"Hey." Jack whined.

"Well it is either I borrow your lap top or you come with, your choice," Johnny interrupted his whining.

"Fine, just take it easy on her. It takes a lot of metal to repair her," Jack insisted.

Dash smiled at Jack, "One day you'll have to tell me everything that gal can do."

Johnny set the lap top up and went to the warehouse; sure enough it was still standing. He was sure they would have found it by now and took pause in order to think over a few different scenarios. Of all the places they could set up an ambush to kill or capture them and get the box back this would be it. Johnny thought, "Are they toying with us? This doesn't seem right." He sat in his van over a block away and let the engine idle, deciding whether he should just try somewhere else or go in.

Johnny gambled that this time was a trap. His only choice now was to head over to Uncle Dylan's and see if his stash was still there. Johnny turned Frankie around and headed back to his Uncle shop. Taking the back streets to the pawn shop extended his trip by a half an hour, but Johnny needed the time to sort out what he was going to see when he got there. Johnny parked within sight of the door as a memory of his uncle came to the front of his mind.

"Well, what do you think Johnny?" Dylan asked and waited for Johnny's response.

"Looks great, but I'm thirteen I have no fucking clue what I'm supposed to me looking for," Johnny replied only half interested in Dylan's new pawn shop.

"Well you better get a clue since you will be helping me. No one stay for free in the Morals' house." Dylan smiled as he admired his new business.

"You know that Takahara has been buying up this street. What are you going to do when they come by?"

"You relax and let Fat Montey and me worry about them," Dylan said with confidence. "Besides I would burn it down before I handed it over to them."

Johnny smiled to himself as he made sure the coast

was clear. No agents, no guards, no tape, no chalk outline. The stench of a rotten body blasted Johnny's sense of smell as he opened the back door of the shop. There he was. The TCS had left him here for the rats. Johnny clenched his fist tight as his anger grew, but pushed his emotions to the back of his mind and got back to the task at hand: the search for the stash. All Johnny had to do was find his way into the secret room in the basement. He had done it once as a kid and really pissed Uncle Dylan off. Johnny had interrupted a high stakes poker game that was attended by most of Uncle Dylan's clients and they weren't the most understanding of individuals.

He went down the stairs to the storage room. He remembered the door being in the back wall somewhere. Johnny shook his head as he recognized the switch to the back room. An Irish mobster should have known better than to use a little leprechaun as a switch. The leprechaun clicked as he pushed it and the door popped open.

Johnny knew that Dash and he had a lot of guns and ammo, but Uncle Dylan had him beat in spades. Johnny stared in awe of all the guns, ammo, and a hell of a lot more. He found a few duffle bags and started loading up.

It took Johnny a little over an hour to fill the van as he cleaned out the room completely. On his way out Johnny raid his uncle's secret liquor and cigar stash, which Dylan kept under his work bench. Johnny was surprised to find two bottles. "Uncle Dylan, you've been hitting the bottle a little hard lately." Johnny said with a laugh and a smile. He shoved the unopened bottle in his bag, and then popped the cork off the open one. Johnny took a whiff of the scotch. The strong alcoholic smell overloaded his sense of smell causing Johnny to quickly remove it from under his nose.

"How could you drink this?" Johnny joked as he took a swig. The scotch burnt as it went down which gave him an idea on how to send his uncle off properly. "Thanks for taking care of me," Johnny said, taking another drink and pouring the rest on his Uncle's desiccated corpse. "You know we wouldn't be in this mess if it weren't for you, but then again, we wouldn't be alive either."

Tears began to form under his eyes. "Thanks for the drink." Johnny took a large swallow of scotch then grabbed a cigar and his uncle's Zippo lighter from the cigar box. As he pulled the cigar out he noticed there was a false bottom on the bottom of the box. "No time to check that now. I'll have to check that out when I get it back to Fern's." He thought. He lit up the cigar and took a few puffs to get the cigar burning well. With one last nod at his Uncle Johnny tossed the cigar on the pile of papers that he had hastily assembled at the feet of his uncle, which were also drenched with the scotch. The body lit up just as his uncle would have liked it – a true Irish Funeral.

Johnny put the final bag in the van and closed it up. Smoke started to billow from the building as he drove away. Johnny wouldn't let any more tears fall from his eyes. He was done crying and it was time to let it go. Even though he was fully determined to exact revenge on Takahara Corp. he knew that those feelings had no place on the job – they'd get him killed. So he shoved his pain to the back of mind and focused on what he needed to do. Keep everyone alive.

It didn't take too long before he arrived back at Fern's. After locking the van up he went inside, cigar box in hand. As he entered the house he could hear Jack explaining some information that he had found doing some searching on Fern's home computer. Johnny handed back Jack's laptop and waved hello to everyone. After which Jack moved back to working on his laptop as soon as Johnny handed it over. "Thank God. A *REAL* computer!" exclaimed Jack. Johnny watched as Jack frantically searched through the information he had pulled up.

"... So I think I'd like to go now. Please don't make me do this anymore... can I just go home?" Jack pleaded as he stood up and started to pace.

"No Jack you can't go home. You blew it up!" Dash said grabbing him by the shoulders and sitting him back down in front of his laptop. "What have you got?"

"Well recently reported was the theft of a prototype physical enhancer called Delta enhancers and was set for testing in 2 weeks which was supposed to make Takahara Corp. billions upon billions," Jack said defeated yet again.

"That doesn't explain why they have been after us for 3 years." Johnny interjected.

"I was just getting to that. I got a news report that say that the men you killed 3 years ago were all TCS agents, and one of the men was Joseph Takahara. He *was* the son of the head of Takahara Corp here in Neo-Japan and Maki Labs is named for Dr. Akemi Maki wife of the other Mr. Takahara. Her husband is the head of the whole damn thing," Jack began to explain.

"So we killed Mr. Takahara's son and he wants us dead." Dash jumped in.

"Yes and more yeses and no." Jack continued. "Here is the short of it. Takahara brothers run Takahara Corp. Their names are Kenji and Akiyo. Kenji is the head of Takahara Corp and is also allegedly a major player in the Yakuza. Kenji is also married to Dr. Maki, as in Maki Labs -- the people responsible for the Alphas. They practiced a genetic experiment on thousands of people without any approval and got away with it due to the transition from the U.S. government to Takahara Corp. A *miiiiinor* oversight.

You killed their nephew. The guy that has been after you for so long is Akiyo Takahara. He had one son by the name of Joseph Takahara. His wife died giving birth to Joseph. Takahara's policies in Neo-Japan changed drastically after Joseph's death. When I say drastically I'm talking comparing grenades to A-Bombs. You guys are fucked beyond fucked and now I'm fucked beyond fuck. I gotta get out of here. I've GOTTA get out of here!" Jack said as he began to panic, beginning to rub his clammy palms.

"Jack calm down and let me think," Dash said.

"I don't think returning the box is going to do it," Jack cried and began to breathe frantically. "They're going to kill us all... though probably not before they torture us... I've seen the employee files. No employee has quit or been let go in three years... All of them are dead... I'm glad I got out when I did... If that's how they treat their employees, I'm sure we're in for a long painful death filled will all sorts of pointy, sharp, and all around unclean objects used on us. I'm too young to die!"

"Calm the fuck down, Jack. You're going to scare the girls," Johnny said, scared himself, but keeping his cool and forcing an awkward laugh. Their pursuit would go on forever. Johnny knew the sting of losing a loved one and knew that Takahara and his family would pursue them until they weren't breathing.

"Our only chance now is my plan. This certainly makes any other solution completely moot." Dash announced, re-iterating his solution. "Jack, get back on the computer as start working your magic. I need the blueprints of the building and Takahara's schedule,"

Dash ordered. Jack's frantic breathing began to make his head spin.

"I think he needs a paper bag, before he passed out," Johnny said, motioning to Fern to grab one for him. She quickly ran and got one. Johnny handed it over to Jack, who began to breathing in and out of it, calming him down.

"You want me to do what? No fucking way! They'll know I was there before I even get in." Jack told Dash in between breaths.

"Jack," Dash said grabbing Jack on the shoulders. "I need your help man. You're going to be the only hope I have to make this work. We can make it out of this if we all work together."

Johnny couldn't believe that Jack sat down and started working. He figured he would be out the door screaming his head off, but there he was typing away.

"Hey Fern, can you keep an eye on him. Make sure he doesn't freak out again," Johnny said as he patted Dash on the back to get his attention. "I have something to show you." He led Dash to the garage and opened the back doors of the van. Dash's jaw dropped.

"This isn't our stuff," Dash said confused.

"I know. I got it from a friend," Johnny said with a smile.

"What friend do we have left that had this? What friend do we have that would part with this. Shamus would have brought it with him. Who had to die for you to get your hands on this?" Dash asked.

"Uncle Dylan," Johnny said sorrowfully. "Yeah, no one had rifled through there yet or at least they didn't do a thorough job. So I gave him a sendoff and nabbed his gear. He even had a bottle of scotch and some cigars left over. I have the bottle in the bag over there and the cigars right here." Johnny patted the box of cigars he was carrying as Dash pulled the bottle from the bag.

"Looks like it'll be a good night when we are done with this," Dash said with a confident smile.

"Dash, man... I don't know about this. This cat is running out of lives." Johnny leaned up against the van and set the box of cigars down in the rear. He pulled his pack of cigarettes from his jacket pocket and popped one into to his month. Using his Uncle's Zippo he lit it and took a drag easing his nerves. "Fuck man, I shouldn't have made it out of the Diablo or survived the bullet the Doc pulled out of my chest. There *has* to be another way."

"The fact that you made it out of there and everywhere else where we've been in a jam, is what I'm counting on. The fact you lived when no man should have. I talked to Fern she told me how bad it was. The bullet was lodged in your liver and you should have bleed out, but you didn't. We can do this and we will never have to run again."

Johnny couldn't take that away from his friend. Dash's freedom and happiness was within grasp and Johnny couldn't take that away for a second time.

"What if we fail? We're dead and there's no one to protect them." Johnny pointed at the house cigarette in hand. "We can keep them safe if we run." Johnny continued.

"It's all or nothing time buddy; time to put our chips in the middle. If we want to do right by the girls, Jack, and Shamus we have to do this. We got them into this mess. Only finishing what we started will get them out of it." Dash said laying all his cards on the table.

"Well Dash, this is probably a new level of stupid, but I'm with you," Johnny said, taking a last drag off his half-finished smoke and flicking it into the street. He then extended his hand to his friend.

"Never had a doubt you wouldn't be. You *are* a sucker," Dash said as he took his hand and they shared a man hug. Johnny's eyes began to water a little. He had his friend back. He shoved Dash away.

"You are *such* a woman!" He said as he shook off the tears.

"What? *You're* the one crying and you call *me* the woman," Dash joked. "Go change your tampon you big girl."

"Fucker," he replied as he wiped his eyes. Johnny finally knew that his friend was back in his corner. It was a good feeling. "I'm going to do an inventory in the garage, if that's ok with Fern. You'd better get back to Jack before he explodes."

"Yeah. Once we have something figured out I'll come get you,"

Dash said.

"If you have a plan figured out by time I'm done with this we're redoing it," Johnny said as he shook his head. Dash chuckled.

"My plans are never *that* bad," Dash said as he ran back into the house.

"Hey Dash, wait." Johnny stopped Dash before he went inside.

"What are you gonna do about the Doc?" he asked. "I know he went for milk hours ago, but he'll be back." Dash looked at him for a long second.

"I don't know. That's Fern's decision. I love her. I know she loves me. Scarlet is my child. I know she lied to him, but that's a discussion she has to have with him," Dash said.

"Dash, I just want you to be prepared. She did marry the guy." Johnny brought up the painful truth.

"So what? She only did it because she was pregnant and scared about taking care of a baby by herself." Dash started to become a little irate. "We just had a good laugh. You really don't want to push this button right now."

"Just don't kill him I need to talk to him. He might have some information for me," Johnny said. Dash nodded with an intrigued look on his face.

"Is there something we need to talk about?" Dash asked very puzzled by the Johnny's comment.

"Not yet. It depends on what the Doc says," Johnny replied.

"All right but you better not hold out if it's important," Dash responded and then went inside.

It didn't take Johnny as long as he thought it would to do the inventory. Lots of repeat items will do that. The inventory was quite grand and even included a box of grenades, some flash bangs, and enough ammo to occupy a small third world country. He thought to himself, "If we have to use all this somethin' has gone terribly wrong."

Johnny was in a good mood and decided to have a little fun. He strapped as many weapons as he could to his body and began moving around the garage. Figuring that no matter whatever plan Dash cooked, up he would have to strap on a lot of fire power. Johnny began doing tumbles and diving over things like he was preparing for a fight. It was not a pretty sight. The little giggles of Scarlet, who was peeking through the slightly open garage door, interrupted his less-than-graceful tumbling.

"Hey, ya shouldn't be out here," Johnny said as she tried to shoo her away, but she just came in a sat down to watch him as if it was a game. He tried different set ups on his weapons and again tumbled and dove around the garage. Scarlet would clap and giggle. After a few minutes Fern began to call her name.

"There you are don't scare mommy like that," Fern said as Johnny handed Scarlet off to her.

"She was out in the garage with me." Johnny let her know.

"Doing what? Learning how to field strip a rifle," Fern said taking a look a Johnny. "Can you even move with all that on?"

"Not really," Johnny replied adjusting the holsters and firearms. "And it kind of chaffs."

"So were you teaching her what *not* to do?" Fern said with a smirk. "Scarlet it's lunch time."

Lunch was prepared. It wasn't much, just a bunch of sandwiches, but as Johnny sat down to eat with everyone he was filled with happiness. For the moment everyone was smiling and eating. As they joked and laughed, Dash and Johnny took turn catching Fern up on the last 3 years. Fern in turn shared some pictures of Scarlet and her. As Dash kept flipping through the pictures, over and over again Johnny realized that something was missing. He saw Dash and Fern and how much in love they were. His thoughts drifted to Kate. The only thing close to a solid relationship that he'd had for a long time. He needed to bring Kate here. Fern's house was honestly the safest place to be and they hadn't seen any TCS agents or guards for a while so Johnny decided to make a phone call.

"Hey, Fern I need to use your phone," Johnny said.

"What for?" She asked.

"To make a phone call," Johnny said sarcastically. "Or is there something else I'm supposed to do with it."

"Do you think that's safe? Why don't you use your head link?" Fern asked. Jack waived his hand in the air and he tried to quickly swallow the bite of sandwich he just took.

"Making the phone call will be fine. I have erased her so she won't show up on Takahara's systems. All the bills are now going through a fake name and we should be safe here for a while. I also cleared your headlinks. So we won't have to worry about Takahara hacking our calls and finding us," Jack said, taking another bite of his sandwich.

"Huh, I guess I don't need it then," Johnny replied.

"He can do that with his computer?" Fern asked completely boggled by the thought of what Jack had just done. Johnny nodded yes to Fern's question. He contacted Shamus's cell with his headlink. The call went to voice mail.

"Hey it's me. Call me back for the address." Johnny hung up the phone. A few seconds later his headlink rung.

"Hey there Johnny; thought you boys were dead," Shamus said sounding shocked to get the call.

"Came pretty close, you want to grab everyone and head over to 103 Blue Park Ave. Everything is clear for now. Better get over here quick. I'll be outside so you can find the place," he said.

"Ya I'd like to get these girls off my hands. See you in 30 to 45 minutes," Shamus replied.

"See ya then," Johnny said and ended the call. Johnny went out to the garage and took off his gun holsters and reinforced vest, then put them in the back of the van. Johnny picked up the box of cigars and went back in the house. "Fern I'm going to use your shower and there will be some people here soon. They're in the same trouble we are."

"Why'd you invite them here then?" Fern demanded to know.

"Ya, Johnny. That was a pretty fucking stupid move actually," Dash said, scolding Johnny like a two-year-old.

"Well, right now the TCS doesn't know we're here and it would be the safest place for them. They need our help and since we caused this mess," Johnny explained.

"What if they are followed?" Fern said sounding scared.

"They won't be. Shamus is better than that. He's old school," Johnny explained.

"I really don't know what that means, but you'd better be right. Shower is up stairs on the right," she told him.

"Thanks," Johnny said and bolted up the stairs cigar box in hand. He shut the door, locked it, and started the water. He took all the cigars out and put them on the counter and removed the false bottom. Inside there were only a few things. The first was news clippings about a fire at a Takahara Corp. owned laboratory that claimed the lives of twenty children 18 years ago. Johnny quickly read the article, but the article was excusing all the blame from the laboratory saying there was no way it could have been prevented. "What a bunch of shit," Johnny muttered. The picture of the laboratory resembled that of Maki Labs.

"Could the two labs be one in the same?" Johnny thought. There was an older article from a tabloid magazine stating that Maki Labs and Takahara Corp. were poisoning the public with the free flu vaccine they were offering. The article was about 30 years old and was attached to another article dated a few months later. It was an obituary of the man that wrote the tabloid article. Johnny looked into the mirror.

"What does this all mean? What the hell is going on here?" Johnny thought knowing that he had something to do with why Takahara Corp was after them, but wasn't entirely sure what. In the bottom of the box was a medical bracelet. It was slightly melted and soot cover most of it, but from what he could make out it said.

B E R ITH

Johnny couldn't make out the rest, but he knew then why his

uncle's nickname for him was Berith. His uncle had kept him in hiding and raised him as his own. Johnny wanted to know more, but Maki Labs was the only way to find out. "Maybe someday I'll find out," He thought to himself. Johnny turned on the faucet and splashed some cold water on his face. He stared at himself in the mirror for a moment and noticed a small amount of water had landed on the band revealing another letter. Johnny held the bracelet under the water trying to scrub off the soot reveling more of the puzzle.

BET EX ER ENT: ITH 20

Johnny had no clue what it meant but hoped to figure it out in time. He quickly put everything back in the box shaking the doubt from his head and hopped in the shower.

He hadn't taken a shower in a while due to being strapped down to a table for a few weeks. He pulled the bandage off his wound, it was still a little tender, but it was almost gone. It would still need another bandage when he was done. Johnny entered the shower and turned on the hot water. The hot water poured over him like a warm summer rain. It felt good and was such a comfort that he lost track of time as the water flowed over his skin.

When he stepped out of the shower it had been 40 minutes and he could hear yelling. Johnny thought he should perhaps wait it out considering what he was hearing though the door. The extra time allowed Johnny to grab a new bandage for his wound but noticed it had completely healed and the stitches had fallen out. "What the hell?" Johnny thought, slightly panicking. "This isn't normal."

Johnny covered himself with a towel and began to look for the Doc's clothes. Tommy was pretty close to his size. His luck just seemed to be abundant. By the time he was done the yelling started to come up stairs.

"I can't believe you cheated on me!" Fern yelled.

"Me, you got married. I think you hit a whole new level of cheating." Dash yelled. Johnny made a quick bee-line out of Fern's room. As he left Fern bumped into him just outside the room. She took one look at him and screamed in frustration, pushing him aside and went into the room, slamming the door behind her. Dash followed after, stopping to look at Johnny.

"Thanks a lot dumbass," Dash said as he followed her into the room and slammed the door behind him as well, locking. The arguing continued.

"What'd I do?" Johnny pondered as he walked down the stairs very puzzled. He saw Jack holding Scarlet and she was pitching a fit. Jack looked squeamish and uncertain of how to handle a child. He was completely out of his element. Johnny smiled a bit to himself as he went to investigate some voices coming from the dining room. As he entered he saw Shamus, who was drinking a beer and chuckling at the girls. Johnny then recognized the other girls; they were Kate's roommates. Johnny had spaced the fact that they were with Shamus too. Kate looked up from the chatting girls to see him. He gave a little wave. She scowled at him pushed through the two girls. Johnny prepared for a hug and got the glare of death. The look that was just as bad as getting slapped across the face.

"Hi, Kate. What's going on?" Johnny asked.

"You tell me?" she asked with a scornful look on her face.

"Ummmm," Johnny said, trying to find the words, when she slapped him across the face.

"Son of a bitch! What the hell was that for?" Johnny asked.

"For leading me on!" Kate screamed at him.

"What *the hell* are you talking about?" Johnny asked even more confused.

"Oh so you really *don't* have a whore hiding around here somewhere like your asshole of a friend? You think you can play games. Well I can play games too. Where is she? I want to meet her and tell her was a scumbag you are. That you like to trick women into falling in love with you and then break their hearts!" Kate yelled at him with tears in her eyes.

"You're off-the-wall crazy you know that," Johnny said with a smile, as he rubbed the side of his face. "You should really get your facts straight before you slap a guy. Dash's old flame lives here with his kid. You can hear her in the other room. I don't have a girl on the side. Ask Dash. I'm terrible with women. I'm lucky enough to find one girl to put up with me," Johnny said a little confused by the Kate's statement, but happy to hear it.

"So there's *really* no one else?" Kate asked, warming up to Johnny a little.

"No. There's no one else," Johnny stated when Kate smothered his lips with hers. "Well, here's to hoping that all of our arguments will end like this," Johnny thought to himself. Kate's two roommates awed at the kiss. The sounds of arguing up stairs turned into giggles and moaning after about 5 minutes. Johnny shook his head and could thought, "Boys 2 girls 0."

Although he wondered what would happen when Dash and Fern came back down stairs. There's a lot they needed to talk about and they couldn't just avoid it by having sex, which is what Johnny was pretty sure they were doing. Dash would also have to deal with the fact that Fern had chosen him. When the Doc came back it wasn't going to be pretty.

"I'm gonna grab another beer you want one Johnny?" Shamus asked to break up the silence.

"Ya," Johnny said, rubbing his cheek that still stung from Kate's slap.

"Dink," Scarlet said as she wandered into the room.

"Hey Jack, would you grab Scarlet something to drink?" He asked.

"I really don't think a little girl should have a beer," Jack said curiously.

"Come *onnnnnn*... I figured ya put a couple of beers in her a she'd pass right out..." Johnny said mockingly. "No dumbass. I meant a sippy cup or something like little kids drink," Johnny replied.

"Oh, yeah. Sorry," Jack said and ran in the kitchen he was back in a flash with a sippy cup in hand.

"Ok Scarlet here you go," Johnny said to her as he handed her the sippy cup and put her back in her play pen. She started singing along with a kids movie that was on the television and sipped her juice contently.

"Let's go outside to talk," he ordered softly as he signaled everyone to be quite.

Johnny enjoyed the fresh air and it got them away from Scarlet and the escapades that were going on upstairs.

"Johnny?" said one of the girls, "Um... what's going on?"

"Well," Johnny answered with a chuckle and cracked open the beer that Jack brought to him. "That's kind of complicated and a rather long story. In a nut shell -- we took a job that needed us to.... a*cquire,* some property from the Takahara Corporation. The Takahara Corporation is after you to get to Dash and me. If you leave they will find you and torture you until you tell them where we are, and then probably kill you. This place is safe so we brought you here. Dash, Jack, and I are working on a plan to fix this. If you can be patient we should have this wrapped up in no time." Johnny smiled at them when he finished his speech.

"Seems like you've got everything figured out," Shamus said with doubt in his voice as he smacked Johnny on the back of the head. Johnny expected it. He could always expect a reality check from Shamus when he was over confident.

One of the girls crossed over to Johnny and slapped him. Her slap was harder then Kate's and caused the inside of Johnny's check to bleed. Johnny rubbed the side of his face, but the pain was quickly gone.

"She packs a hell of a swing," Johnny thought. He pondered for a second how a little thing like her could pack such a wallop. Johnny attributed it to her bow.

"This is nothing to joke at! We could end up dead because of you," said the other girl and she began to cry. Kate pulled her close and gave her a hug.

"You're going to fix everything right Johnny?" Kate said as she comforted her friend. She looked Johnny in the eye trying to judge his response. She was looking for something to hope for. She wanted to know that everything would be alright.

"I promise," Johnny said looking back in Kate's eyes. Johnny was so certain that he could fix everything for them, for her. Even with Johnny's promise it wasn't long before the three girls all burst into tears.

"We'll get you home...don't cry. It is okay. I want to go home too," Jack said as he patted them on their backs very lightly.

"Perhaps we should find a room for you girls to clean up. I'm sure Fern has some clothes that you can wear," Shamus said as he led them inside. Dash came out a few minutes later.

"That didn't take long." Johnny chuckled.

"Make up sex never does," Dash replied as he finished putting on a shirt. "Fern is taking care of Kara, Sara, and Kate."

"Is that really wise?" Johnny asked.

"She offered. Besides you were the one that made them cry so, I'm in the clear for now," Dash joked.

"You can't pin that on me," Johnny said with a little shock in his voice.

"But I just did," Dash responded with a laugh.

"Great, another thing I'm never going to live down," Johnny said with a sigh. "Well how did the planning go so far?"

"Good, but not great. We need uniforms, access cards. For the higher level, we need to fake a voice recognition and retinal scan. Not to mention the 30 or 40 highly trained guards armed with assorted weaponry. He's normally in his office on the 120th floor. Getting back down after the job is done will be damn near impossible without any alarms going off," Dash said.

"Jack anything you can do to help?" Johnny asked.

"Well I got the building blue prints and they're very detailed. I'll try to find something. His schedule was easy enough to find, he isn't leaving the building for the next month. They run a tight ship around him and unless you learn to fly, I'm going to need some time to figure out how to get you out of there. I can try to hack the alarm system, but I'm sure that I'll only be able to do little things otherwise they'll get suspicious and it could ruin your chance to take him out. I might be able to reroute the alarms so that if you trip one it will sound off in a different part of the building. This would send the guards in the wrong directions, but that will only work as long as you don't get spotted. After you take out Takahara it's going to be hard, but it's possible to cause issues with the doors since they lock electronically. Then as long as I could get access to their mainframe..." Jack began to ramble.

"Jack," Dash said.

"As long as I piggy back through perhaps... The camera system they have all over town it would be harder for them to dig my code out of there system. Getting through there firewalls is going to be the tricky part especially unnoticed," Jack continued on.

"Jack!" both Johnny and Dash yelled.

"Huh. What?" Jack asked.

"You were yakking up a storm. Why don't you grab your laptop and see what you can do?" Dash suggested.

"Before you go and work your magic. You find anything out about Maki Labs?" Johnny asked.

"No, why?" Jack asked.

"Yeah, why?" Dash followed, figuring it might have to do with what Johnny wanted to talk to Tommy about.

"Well they made Delta and since that's what they are after, finding out what it can do might be important," he answered.

"It's a physical enhancement drug, but I said that earlier," Jack said. "So you know that. What are you looking for? Maybe if I know what I'm looking for I can find more." Jack sat down at his computer.

"Yeah, what are you looking for Johnny?" Dash asked.

"Nothing. Just look up the history of Delta. It may be important," Johnny said.

"I can try but it's going to take some time since I don't know what I'm looking for. Perhaps if I had more to go on," Jack said with a sigh in Johnny direction.

"That is the one thing that you don't have and you're probably not going to get. Do your best Jack. Try to come up with something," Dash said. Jack went back inside to his computer.

"This is getting better and better," Johnny said.

"Could be worse, at least we're alive to be able to plan it," Dash said.

"How many floors was it?" Johnny asked.

"150," Dash answered.

"Well 150 floors, 40 guards, 40 different ways this could go wrong and about 40 different ways we could die. Not to mention that we know that they have more men that they'll be able to bring in if we take too long," Johnny said as he shook his head. "After this I'm not taking any job more difficult than walking dogs." Johnny sighed and then Dash and he began to chuckle.

They continued planning until dinner which, after a good meal and a couple of beers, everyone seemed to be getting along like a big family. Johnny, Dash, and Jack kept planning while the girls ran the house. The girls, including Kate, slept in the guest rooms and Shamus took the couch. Dash and Fern slept together and Scarlet's bed was moved in with them. Jack slept in Scarlet's room in a sleeping bag. Johnny had gotten used to the cot in the basement so he just kept sleeping there.

Tommy hadn't been back yet and it was starting to bother Johnny. Tommy hadn't even made a phone call to the house. Johnny feared that he might have been grabbed by TCS and with what happened earlier there is no telling what he would do. Johnny thought, "If I were him I would rat us out." Johnny made preparation for an alternate escape route just in case.

Johnny fell asleep and had trouble dreams. What did Beta stand for? And why did his wound heal so fast? Johnny guessed that Tommy had some answers, but there was no way for him to get Tommy to come home and reveal what he knew. Not only had Dash stole his life, but we invaded his house. How was Johnny going to convince the Doc to talk with him after that?

"I have finished my report on the blood that was collected and the results were very interesting." Doctor Maki said as she approached Mr. Takahara's desk. Mr. Takahara put up his hand making the signal for her to wait a moment. His chair turned around to face her and she noticed that he didn't look well. The bags under his eyes were dark. Mr. Takahara had spent hour after hour watching his monitors over the past few days clearly obsessed with the stream of information being streamed to him. His paranoia was getting the better of him.

"What do you have to report Doctor?" Mr. Takahara rasped, his voice cracking with exhaustion.

"Sir we were able to conclude that he was part of Beta Experiment: Birth 20, Blood type AB+, and created in Maki Labs site 1. The child was given an injection of Beta H. During the first few days of testing the child became very ill and remained ill for the first year of his life. Beta H destroyed his immune system. Shortly after year one, the child reportedly died to massive heart failure caused by the diseases that had plagued the boy. The child was dead for twenty minutes." Paused Dr. Maki.

Mr. Takahara motioned for her to continue.

"The physicians working on Beta 20 detected his heart beating again. Beta 20 began to recover. His brain function and motor skills were all intact if not better than they were before. The reports say that Beta's recovery didn't take but a month when most children would have taken at least a year if they recovered at all, but afterward Beta 20 had no signs of any disease for the next two years." Dr. Maki began.

"Get on with the important part. Why is he still alive?!" The anger in his voice rose as he slammed his fist down on his desk. "All the other Beta children were dead within three years. If they weren't dead they were given a sedative and left in the building as part of the cover up."

"You did what? While I was in Japan I was told all the children had died." Dr. Maki said in response to what she had just heard.

"We burned down the lab to cover up what had happened. Naturally anyone inside would have died. What makes this child so special?" Mr. Takahara said continued as if Dr. Maki had said nothing.

"You bastard! They were innocent children!" she screamed to get his attention.

"They were not children. They were an investment that went south. They were grown in a lab. We created them. They were acceptable loses," Mr. Takahara replied in a calculating tone. "Now continue with your report before *you* become an acceptable loss. I have plenty more researchers on my payroll and NONE that I give lee-way in talking with me like I do with you." Dr. Maki had heard the rumors and was not willing to test her brother in-law at this time. "Now. Continue."

"Beta 20 was the only AB+ child created and injected with Beta H. Due the rarity of the blood it was thought to be impractical to create more than one," The Doctor replied quickly.

"After all the mutations that occurred why would you test so few AB? Wouldn't you want a larger test group? It was the only blood type that created Echoes. Shouldn't more testing have been done?" Mr. Takahara questioned as he clenched his fist tightly.

"The Alpha experiment created what are referred to now as: Echoes, Oscars, and Tangos. They were altered according to their blood type. Alpha did create stronger and faster individuals; however, the side effect corrupted their blood and was worthless to continue testing on. As for the Beta Children, the AB blood type was too rare to create more. It was not cost efficient. Most AB children died within the first year if they made it through gestation. However, the Betas did give us insight in order to proceed to the Gamma and Delta strains," she explained.

"One more question. If all the children died or were destroyed how do you explain this one?" Mr. Takahara relaxed waited for an answer.

"I don't know sir; all the children were accounted for according to the guard on duty. There is a very slim chance that one of them got past the guards. However, with what I have seen so far, while it would have been very unlikely the child lived through it; there is still a possibility that it happened," Dr. Maki said in her defense, fearing that she would most likely be dead by the end of the conversation.

"That is ridiculous. There is no possible way that he lived through the fire. No living thing could have," Mr. Takahara insisted.

"I'm only offering a potential solution as to how the child could have lived from the data I have collected. That is all," She replied, and then attempted to steer the conversation in a direction more to her favor. "I have found something in my investigation of the Beta's blood that was not filed in the old reports. The Beta strain has surpassed all expectations in this case. The Beta Strain has replaced all his regenerative processes. Comparing the blood work from the Beta subject from our past research, to the new strain the results show that the virus has evolved. If the subject were to be brought in I would be able to do more testing." She explained. "Have you been able to capture him yet?" she asked mockingly.

"If you were not my brother's wife I would have you killed slowly for that condescending comment," he said as he stood with force slamming both hands down on his desk. Just then the door to his office door opened.

"Uncle?" Said a figure at the entry to the office. Standing at the door was a young and extremely lovely Japanese girl. She stood approximately 5'2" with jet black hair -- trimmed fashionably short, with bangs that hung down to her dark brown, almond-shaped eyes. Her skin was lightly tanned and without blemish. The scent of lilacs followed her into the room.

"I apologize sir. She slipped by me," Ichiro said, rushing in behind her.

"It is all right Ichiro. You're dismissed," Mr. Takahara said, rubbing his temples.

"Mother. Uncle. It's so very good to see the both of you," said Takahara's niece, in precise and un-accented English. She approached her mother with grace taught by the most expensive finishing schools Neo-Hiroshima could offer and gave her a hug. The girl then bowed deeply to her uncle, before saying in Japanese, "You look tired Uncle. You really should take some time off from the office. Why don't you go down to your retreat at the coast and relax for the weekend?" Her smile lit up the room and eased the tense situation.

"Juni, we're in the middle of a meeting perhaps you should wait outside," Dr. Maki said.

"Nonsense Akemi, I always have time for my favorite niece. Now what can I do for you Juni?" he asked.

"I was just wondering how the plans for my 18th birthday were coming?" Juni asked with a hint of a smile tugging at the corner of her mouth. "I sent you the guest list, the menu, the entertainment, and a request to have a dress made and you have not responded. With just a little over a week left I want to ensure that everything goes perfectly. It will be the party of the year."

"Don't you worry about anything. I'll have everything ready and will make sure that everything goes according to plan. Not to mention the gift that you'll be receiving." Mr. Takahara smiled, showing a softer side only those truly close to him were able to see.

"Oh, Uncle," Juni said, running around the desk and hugging him.

"Akiyo, you spoil her too much. Now run along Juni," her mother ordered. Juni left with a joyful smile.

"The innocence of youth... Dr. Maki you will have the Beta given to you once he is captured, but try my patience one more time and her 18th birthday will be the last you see. Now leave," Mr. Takahara said returning to his frozen tone. Dr. Maki left quickly knowing that Akiyo never made threats that he didn't follow through with. His shrewd financial skills combined with his slowly developing psychotic tendencies were slowly turning him into a monster. She had to find a way to get her husband a message.

Mr. Takahara returned to watching the monitors. He was as still as a statue as Ichiro entered the room.

"Sir, Delta 1 has been released and is on his way back to Beta and his friend, a Mr. Dash McBragg," Ichiro said with a confident smile. "He had one request; to allow him time to get his wife and daughter out of the building before we went in."

"And what was your response?"

"I gave him fifteen minutes."

Mr. Takahara sighed, "Ichiro... Kill them all except for Beta. If you can, re-acquire the Delta though it isn't a necessity. Dr. Maki can make more," Mr. Takahara ordered with a devilish grin and Ichiro left the room to attend to his duties. "You can't hide anymore Beta." Mr. Takahara began to laugh sinisterly.

It had been a week and they hadn't found anything that could help them. The girls and Shamus tried to keep their spirits up, but the pressure of fixing everything was taking its toll. Johnny was awake most nights just trying to figure it out, which tore him up inside and kept him from sleeping. Nothing ever seemed to pan out according to the plan that Dash had crafted. Kate could see that Johnny was frustrated and getting moody. Johnny was sitting in his cot when the creek of the stair told him someone was trying to sneak down the stairs.

"Johnny," Kate whispered.

"Kate. What are you doing down here?" Johnny asked.

"Couldn't sleep," she replied. "All this talk of plans and exit strategies has got my mind spinning."

"Me neither. I keep trying to figure this crap out in order to get us all out of this mess alive," Johnny said as he turned towards her.

"Johnny you're putting too much pressure on yourself. People are getting concerned... *I* am getting concerned," Kate said trying to alleviate his worry. She began to run her hand through his shaggy hair.

"Is that all?" Johnny grumbled, focusing his attention back to the building blueprints folded out in front of him. "I got way too much shit on my mind."

"Well I..." Kate began, shocked at his brutish tone. "I came down here to make you feel better and you snap at me?!" Kate spun on her heel and began to head back upstairs.

"I didn't mean it that way Kate!" Johnny said reaching out to her. "I'm sorry. I'm just tired and not thinking straight. I know you're worried about me, but we'll get out of this. We'll make things right. I trust my partners. Dash may seem like an asshole, but he's very smart when it comes to this sort of stuff. And Jack is so far out of our league mentally that it boggles the mind how he does what he does. We're all in this together and I'm going to make sure nothing happens to us, and especially to you." Kate moved to stand in front of him. She wrapped her arms around his head and hugged his head against her body. Johnny's head was held tightly to her warm breasts.

"You're right. I have nothing to worry about because I have you here to protect me," she said releasing him from the hug. Johnny placed one of his hands on each of her hips and pushed his head away from her body.

"I will always keep you safe. I promise," Johnny sincerely said.

"I know," she said as she kissed him and straddled his lap. "That's why I keep you around," she joked with a girlish giggle. Johnny smiled and used his hand to brush her hair out from in front of her eyes. She kissed him again and pushed him down onto the cot. She continued kissing him. The kisses began to get deeper and longer as she began to grind her hips against his. Johnny became aroused from Kate's quivering movements. Johnny pried his lips from her just for a moment.

"Wait, wait a minute. Weren't we supposed to go on a date first?" he asked jokingly.

"Shut up," she said and began to kiss him again. They made love that night and this time Johnny remembered it. The next morning Johnny awoke spooning with Kate. How they were able to sleep together on the cot Johnny couldn't explain to himself, but they did. Johnny awoke to Dash standing at the bottom of the stairs in his underwear knocking on the wall.

Dash clear his throat, "I was going to ask how much sugar you wanted in your coffee, but it appears that you might already have enough." Johnny flip Dash the bird. Dash headed back up stairs. "I found Kate." He yelled on his way up. Kate began to stir with Dash's yelling.

"Hey babe," Johnny said with a grin.

"Hey," Kate replied. "We should probably go upstairs for breakfast and I need to take my calcium."

"Yeah," He replied as he pull Kate close. "I'll take you on a proper date when this is over." Johnny kissed her.

"Promises, promises," Kate replied back to him with a wink and a smile. They both dressed quickly and went upstairs.

Everyone sat and ate breakfast. The bacon, pancakes and syrup were all amazing. The day was brighter and he just had the feeling that everything was going to be ok. Suddenly, Jack stood up from his computer and yelled, "I got it!"

"Got what Jack?" Dash asked as he tipped back in his chair, leering at Fern's ass with a wolfish look on his face, as she walked back into the kitchen.

"I know how we get in. We are going to use Juni Takahara's birthday party. They have been keeping it hush, hush for weeks and I was only able to find it just now on the news releases. She's turning eighteen and is having a huuuge party. Must be nice being that rich, when I turned eighteen all I got was potatoes," Jack started to confess as Johnny and Dash gave him a "get on with it" glare.

"Her list of guests is a who's, who list of Japan and Neo-Japan.

Now here's the smart bit. They're having outside catering! Oh gross they are having sushi. I fucking hate sushi, how can you eat something raw? I mean seriously you could catch something. My Uncle on my father's side once caught a bug that way and couldn't use his tongue for a week. He didn't use it much after that either, he ended up biting the thing off in his sleep. That is why I never touch the stuff and did I mention it is gross," Jack rambled on until he heard Johnny tapping his foot and Dash clearing his throat. "We just need some badges and a few other things and we are ready to storm the castle. We should probably get her something... but what to get an eighteen year old who has everything," Jack continued. "What if we get caught and we didn't bring a gift. We don't want to be rude."

"Jack for Christ sake man!" Johnny blurted becoming weary of Jack's ravings.

"Ok, ok... I have to say that I've probably out done myself. I think? Wait what if the party is a trap?" Jack hypothesized.

Something stuck in Johnny's gut on this. Like Takahara wanted them to come, but if they were going to give them an opportunity like this, why not take it. Dash and Johnny exchanged glances and they both knew that this was it the only chance they would get to pull this off. It was time to start getting their shit together.

"Okay this shouldn't be too hard... just need to get a name of one of the caterers, jump a couple of their guys, and sneak in. We should be able to get in and out without a problem." Dash said as the front door opened and shut.

"Tommy," Fern said spotting him entering the room.

"Tommy?!" Kate, Kara, and Sara echoed. The room grew quite as Tommy stared at Fern.

"Fern. You only get one chance at this. I'm leaving and I want you and Scarlet to come with me. We can get out of here alive and leave this all behind and never speak of it again. I love you Fern and you love me too. Admit it," Tommy said as he reached his hand out to her.

Fern took his hand in both of her's, "Tommy, you've been great to Scarlet and I. A great father and I couldn't have taken care of

Scarlet without you. But... I can't go with you. I love Dash. I've always loved him. Now that I have him back I can't let him go again," Fern said as she squeezed Tommy's hand one last time and let it go. Tommy turned away from her and hung his head. After a moment the sorrow that had once filled Tommy had turned to anger.

"You stupid bitch, after all I have done for you and Scarlet!" Tommy yelled and began to clench his fists.

"Tommy," Dash said as he entered the room.

"Only Fern calls me Tommy. It's Doctor Johnson to you. What the hell do you want?!" Tommy yelled as he ran his hand through his slicked back hair.

"Well, it sounded like you were about to get violent, and if you are looking to get violent you should point that in my direction," Dash said.

"Perhaps you're right, but why would I waste my talents on you." Tommy scoffed and turned away. "Fern, I'm going to take Scarlet away from this travesty of a life that you're creating for her."

"Tommy, don't. She's my daughter and you can't just take her. Look I'm sure we can work something out," Fern pleaded as Tommy began to walk towards the play pen where Scarlet was beginning to awaken due to the shouting.

"Fern she's coming with me. You can come with if you wish, but whether you like it or not she's coming with me!" Tommy demanded as he picked up the Scarlet. Johnny heard all the commotion and began to move through the house to get on the other side of Tommy.

"Daddy," she said and rested her sleepy head on his shoulder.

"Shhh...baby," Tommy said trying to comfort Scarlet.

"Put her down you're not taking her. She's *my* baby," Fern said as she reached for Scarlet.

"No," Tommy said and a small ball of blue light emerged from his hand. The ball hit Fern in the chest throwing her against the cabinets lining the wall. As she slid down motionless the girls screamed and ran into the other room to hide.

"Fern!" Dash yelled as he ran to her side. She was still breathing.

"You son of a bitch..." Dash growled, getting ready to rush at Tommy. Johnny pulled his Glock 18 from his hip holster aiming it in Tommy's direction. "No guns!" Dash shouted. "You might hit Scarlet."

Tommy began to back away towards the doorway as Shamus stepped out of the bathroom adjoining the kitchen. "What the hell's going on out here?"

Tommy released another blast into the old man's gut, sending him to the floor in a crumpled heap. Dash and Johnny sprang forwards during the distraction. Tommy turned back towards the action and, just as Dash was about to release a haymaker from his cock-backed arm, unloaded another blue pulse into Dash's chest. The impact of the blow threw Dash through the drywall and studs, into the next room

Johnny took advantage of the situation and threw a chop into the carotid artery in Tommy's neck, stunning him and loosening his grip on Scarlet. Johnny pulled her from Tommy's clutches, turned and sprinted into the other room. As he crossed the threshold he took a blast to the back that sent him spinning and knocked the air from his lungs. Scarlet crawled out from under Johnny's slack body, unharmed, but crying at the top of her lungs. Looking up Johnny caught sight of the terrified girls, peeking out from a closet. He waved one over to get Scarlet and stood shakily, turning to go back into the kitchen.

Tommy had composed himself, and was massaging his neck as he noticed Johnny re-enter the room. "Not bad Beta. Though not likely to happen a second time, even with your enhancements."

"Who... No. *What* are you?" Johnny asked, assuming a fighters stance though weary of his opponent's abilities.

"Takahara Corp. took care of me so that I could take care of you. I have been given their new Delta drug," Tommy said, glancing at his watch. "And I'm going to make this quick. No time to play this little game you see."

"Expecting company?"

"You could say that."

Johnny dreaded to hear that, knowing now that Tommy was in league with Takahara and that reinforcements were on the way. With Dash and Shamus down he knew the only thing between his friends and an untimely death was him.

"You really shouldn't have gotten up. It'd all be so much simpler if you would have let me walk out the front door with my daughter. You might have even had time to have your friends run away before the rest of Takahara's men show up."

"She's *not* your daughter," Johnny said, getting angrier by the second.

"What?"

"I said she's not your daughter. She never will be. She's Dash's. Look in her eyes and you will see the truth," Johnny said, and then Tommy charged at him wildly.

The two fought like a pair of rabid animals, both caught in the same snare: Johnny, in order to save the life of his friends; and Tommy, knowing that if he didn't get out soon, he'd be shot dead with the lot of them by a Takahara hit squad. There could only be one outcome.

The two exchanged bows with Tommy's bio-electrical blasts proving to be a telling factor in tipping the balance of power. Midway through the fight Tommy stood over Johnny's body, which had just been caught in a blast so strong that it blew the windows out of the kitchen. His left arm hung limp and crooked at his side, being broken in two places by Johnny.

"This ends here Beta. Scarlet honey, come to daddy. It's time to go." Tommy panted, leaning over Johnny and lifting his fist high in the air. His right fist glowed with a nimbus of power that was amplifying with every tick of the clock.

Ka-booom!! The distinct roar of Dash's Raging Bull pierced the air. Dash lay belly to the floor, propped up on his elbows and looking much worse for wear. A cascade of blood was disgorged over Johnny as the bullet ripped through Tommy's guts. Johnny kicked upwards with the last reserves of his strength directly into the stomach of his assailant, knocking him backwards into the kitchen furniture, and toppled over the table.

Johnny leapt up, grabbed Tommy by his lapels and rammed him downwards upon one of the broken legs of the recumbent table. The leg pierced through Tommy's chest and protruded four or five inches above his flesh. Bubbles of bloody froth oozed from Tommy's lips.

"When are they coming Tommy?" Johnny shouted, shaking Tommy by his lapels.

It looked as if Tommy wanted to say something as more bloody bubbles spurted out from his mouth intermittently. Johnny leaned in close trying to make out the words.

"Fucking Beta.... Didn't.... Know you... Had it in you..." Tommy wheezed. "Get my.... Get my daughter out of here."

"But she's..." Johnny began.

"Quiet." Tommy was clearly straining now in order to finish what he had to say. "I love her.... Just get... her out of here before..." Tommy continued to wheeze through the blood oozing from his mouth.

"Before what? How much time do we have?" Johnny screamed. Automatic gunfire began pouring into, and through the front of the house. "Oh shit they're here!" Johnny said as he dropped to the floor. "Everyone get down!"

"*Who's* here?" Jack yelled.

"People that are fuckin' shootin' guns at us you mental melt-head. Get everyone loaded into the van we're gonna make a break for it." Johnny looked about the place. Shamus and Fern were down and Dash wasn't looking up for any sort of physical activity, leaving just himself, Jack and the girls to get everyone out safely. The odds were stacked against them. "Jack, get Frankie started in the garage and get ready to get us the hell out of here. We're gonna make a break for it and it might get messy."

"Can't be any messier than this. Consider it done!"

"Kate."

"Yeah." She said crawling out from the living room.

"Where are Kara and Sara?" he asked.

"Still in the closet with Scarlet."

"Good have them grab her and get in the van when it's ready. Then run down stairs and get the Doc's bag," Johnny said with a wink. Kate scampered down stairs. The girls grabbed Scarlet ran for the garage. Bullets spattered all around them. Kara released her bow from its wrist holster. She quickly notched an arrow and let it fly. The arrow flew true striking her target and ending his life. Kara smiled for a moment until the thundering clap of .50 caliber sniper rifle opened up hitting her in the head, popping it like a tomato. Sara and Scarlet were covered in blood. She began to scream as Scarlet began to cry. She set Scarlet on the ground as the second thunder clap was heard ending Sara's cries. Kate came back with the bag and Johnny caught her attention before she was able to see what happened to her friends. "Now go through the back way to the van. They have a sniper so keep low."

"What about the Scarlet? She's crying," Kate asked.

"Kate don't argue. The girls are taking care of her," Johnny lied, knowing the awful truth.

"Ok," She replied as she headed for the garage. Johnny pulled out his Glock and emptied his clip out the window at the TCS members that had gathered outside, preparing to rush the house.

"What happened?" Jack asked, looking green and sick. He had returned from bringing Dash, Fern, and Shamus to the van and now had Scarlet and was holding her down in a low profile despite her shrill cries of terror.

"Now is not the time, get going," Johnny said quietly to Jack. Jack nodded and ran back to the van, hopping in the driver's seat.

"Let's get out of here!" Jack yelled franticly as bullets destroyed Fern's home, sending debris everywhere.

"Go ahead. I'll be right behind you!" Johnny yelled, running back inside. Johnny ran over to Tommy and pulled his body off of the table leg.

"Why?" Wheezed Tommy.

"Because I don't leave people for dead if I think they even have one redeeming quality.... Even *if* they're an asshat that deserves it," Johnny said, dragging Tommy towards the garage.

"Leave me! I'll only slow you down. Go and help protect my... Dash's... *Our* daughter," Tommy said, looking and sounding better. "Get out of here!"

Johnny looked at the wounds of Tommy and they appeared to be knitting together on their own. Bullets began to pour into the house again and he took that as his cue to leave. He ran into the garage and jumped on his bike.

"How are we gonna get out of here? Using the door is a death trap!" Jack yelled over the gun fire that was going on outside.

"Go through the wall. Frankie's tough as nails right?"

Jack threw the van in drive and crashed through the back wall of the garage. The back yard led through more and more back yards running over crashed through the white picket fence and emerged into the alley. Johnny was following closely after on his bike. They got to the corner without any one in pursuit and ducked into a parking garage at the end of the street and got out of the vehicle so that everyone could get checked over for any serious injuries.

"Atta girl Frankie. You knew where to go, didn't you?" Jack said, praising his van.

"What the hell happened back there?" Dash questioned. "Is everyone one okay?"

"You and Fern got knocked out. I got the shit kicked out of me. Shamus is a bit winded. Everyone else is fine," Johnny replied.

"This isn't everyone. Where are the other two?" Dash asked. Johnny didn't want to answer, but knew that everyone would want to know.

"They didn't make it," Johnny answered quietly try not to alert Kate, but she was listening and wondering where her friends were. The news gripped her by the heart and she let out a scream of anguish over the loss of her friends.

"Noooooo!" She collapsed and cried louder. "Why them? This

wasn't their fault. It's yours!" She began pointing at Dash and Johnny. Fern moved Kate inside the van and began to comfort her. Her crying could be heard clear from outside the van. Johnny moved up beside the van.

"Kate, I'm sorry. There was nothing I could do. Kate!" Johnny yelled at the van.

"Johnny. Come on man," Dash said and he pulled Johnny away.

"Kate you've gotta believe me!" Johnny yelled again.

"Knock it off; you're going to get us caught," Dash said as he threw Johnny to the ground.

"So what? We just lost two people that had nothing to do with this. It would serve us right!" Johnny shouted.

"Then we'd have more bodies on our hands! Do you want that?" Dash asked with frustration as Jack handed Scarlet over to him. Johnny looked at Scarlet and quieted down. The crying was muffled but could still be heard coming from the van. Finally after about ten minutes the crying stopped and then Fern stepped out of the van.

"She cried herself to sleep. Dash what happened?" She asked as she had a family hug between Dash, her, and Scarlet.

"Your husband happened. He ratted us out and came to take you and Scarlet away. I guess Takahara had a different plan." Johnny interjected and slid down to the floor defeated. Fern turned away.

"Don't blame her for this," Dash said.

"I don't, I blame you," Johnny said with anger and frustration.

"Let's not forget who started all of this," Dash stated.

"Blaming everyone will get us nowhere," Jack said.

"Shut up Jack!" Johnny and Dash yelled simultaneously.

"So what happened? I was in and out of it the entire time," Dash asked.

"Tommy came back and whooped our asses. We lucked out and barely got out of there alive," Johnny said not really paying attention to the conversation. He was still worried about Kate.

"Yeah I got that. I mean all the glowing and blue sparks," Dash clarified.

"Oh, that. Beats me. He was calling himself a Delta? Whatever the fuck that really means? He's a tough son o' bitch though. Fern will you go check on Kate," Johnny replied and Fern went back into the van.

"Delta?" Dash asked curiously.

"Now that I think about it though, it reminds me of a job we did." Johnny said. "You remember that kid..." Johnny said and Dash began to ponder.

"Yea. I remember now," said Dash. "It was our first big job. You and I broke that kid out of a training facility just north of town. I think the boy's name was... Jaster. We were almost out when we got trapped in that elevator shaft. They would have had us for sure, but Jaster thanked us for trying and then we were magically at the warehouse. Never saw the kid again." Dash finished the story as Jack, Shamus, and Johnny listened.

"I think he was on the Delta Drug or something similar. If Takahara has been experimenting on people it was first with the Alpha virus then Beta and then.... Delta?" Johnny began to question. "That doesn't make sense. Gamma is after Beta."

"What da ya mean?" Shamus asked.

"In the Greek alphabet it goes; Alpha, Beta, Gamma, Delta," Jack said jumping into the conversation.

"And they call the alpha infected Echoes, Oscars, and Tangos. What the fuck are you getting at, Johnny?" Dash asked.

"I don't even know myself, but there has to be some connection," As Johnny spoke he realized that if he was going to get any answers they needed to get to the labs where this all began, but that would have to wait for another day.

"So what's the next step?" Jack asked.

"We finish this," Dash said as he walked up behind them. "We have a week to prepare and no time to lose... Let's end this."

"What do you think our shot of doin' this and comin' out a live are," Johnny asked with a smirk.

"Probably, fifty-fifty," Dash guessed.

"Got a coin?" Johnny asked. Dash handed him a coin. He flipped it off the edge of the parking garage. A breeze rolled through the parking lot cast the coin further away from the structure.

"Why did you flip it off the edge?" Dash asked who was confused.

"Cause if we don't know whether it is heads or tails we can still pull it off," He answered with a smirk.

"That's the dumbest thing I've ever heard of," Dash scoffed. "And now you own me 100 yen."

"You're just mad you didn't think of it first," he proclaimed.

"How about you wander your ass down there and retrieve my coin then," Dash ordered.

"No way, the coin would be impossible to find," Johnny complained.

"Should've thought about that before you tossed my money off the edge of a building," Dash said.

"Fuck that. I'll pay for your next bar tab before I go lookin' for that coin," Johnny responded.

"Excellent. I'll hold you to that." Dash grinned.

Johnny and Dash left it at that. With one week to plan and acquire all the items they needed for the job they needed to get to work right away, especially since funds were low. First though, they needed somewhere they could set up shop until they it was time. Shamus volunteered to scout out a few places but he was unable to come up with any place secure enough to fit their needs.

"What are we gonna do now? I think we're out of fuckin' options," Johnny said.

"We could set up at a camp site," Dash suggested.

"Hey guys," Jack tried to interrupt.

"That won't work. It's still too public," Johnny said. "How about using an abandoned building?"

"Hey guys," Jack said again.

"I'm not taking my kid to an abandon building. She could get hurt," Dash said.

"Um, guys," Jack interrupted again.

"What Jack?!" They both yelled at him.

"I have hacked a local apartment complex and have control of their video feeds. We could use one of the vacant apartments in the building on the left. We just need some food to hold up with," Jack said.

"I knew there was a reason Dash wanted to pick you up," Johnny said with excitement that something was finally going their way. "You've out done yourself Jack. Get the girls over there and then have Shamus go pick up food."

"Shamus, make sure to get a list form Fern. She'll know what Scarlet needs," Dash added, making his first, cautious steps into fatherhood. Shamus nodded as he went over to the girls to get the list made. They moved the girls and their gear over to the building and Jack played with the cameras so no one would see them go in.

"I picked a furnished apartment on the third floor. I hope that is ok? Who is getting food? I'm starving," Jack asked wanting approval.

"That will be fine, but I'm sure Shamus will hate you for havin' to haul all the food he has to buy up the stairs," Johnny joked. Jack got a worried look on his face.

"Jack calm down Johnny was only busting your balls. I'm sure that Shamus won't care…much," Dash said. Jack looked worried but went back to work on the building plan. Finding the best ins and outs of the Takahara Tower was a daunting task and Jack would need all the time he had to work his hacking skills.

While Jack worked out the layout of the building, the girls and Shamus laid low, and Johnny and Dash began to work on some projects of their own. Johnny was distracted trying to talk to Kate, but she shied away from him, never letting him get close enough to start a conversation. She would always start talking with Fern, helping Scarlet, or become busy doing something.

Jack and his undisputed hacking skills found out that the catering companies would have to bring in large freezer and ovens to help with the preparations. That information fueled an idea for Johnny and Dash. They knew if they could get a hold of one of the catering trucks they could easily slip in unnoticed. They were able to get a hold of a similar fridge owned by one of the companies serving hors devours and, with the help of Jack and Frankie, they were able to create secret compartments and after adding additional insulation the scanners wouldn't be able to pick up anything except for what Johnny and Dash wanted the scanners to pick up.

The week came and went quickly, but they were ready. Jack spent the week twisted in wires and building sub routines and viruses to hack into Takahara's mainframe in order to take it over. Jack downed energy drinks like it was vital for his survival, and didn't sleep for more than a few hours a day. Johnny and Dash made him get a full night's sleep before the day of the party. Jack continued to mention everything he had to do the next day. His check list was over a hundred items long and he recited them like they were engraved in his mind. Jack was ready to run video and communication ops from Frankie.

Shamus spent the week staking out the catering business to learn how we were going to commandeer their catering truck. One of the cooks always took the shops leftovers to a local homeless hangout. If there wasn't an opportunity to just club him over the head they had a back-up plan. It wasn't the greatest idea, but it would work.

When Shamus wasn't watching the caterer he was working on the fridge. He was able to trick scanners with a little reflective material and normal freezer parts. The additions to the fridge allowed for the storage of Dash's AK-47, Raging Bull, and his Springfield pistols along with Johnny's Scorpion, a modified Glock 18 with automatic fire and extended clips, and his shotgun. Any time that Shamus wasn't working he was trying to get a hold of armor piercing rounds. With them Johnny and Dash stood a chance even if it was a long shot.

The week was long for Fern, Kate, and Scarlet. Kate spent most of the time in bed. While Fern tried to help, but didn't know what to do. She took care of Scarlet and Kate, but wanted to do more. Dash did his best to show her a few things when Scarlet was sleeping. By the end of the week Fern could take apart, clean, and load Dash's Springfield pistols. If it were possible to take her out to practice shooting the weapon they would have. Johnny joked every time he saw Fern handle the pistols saying that he didn't want a repeat incident.

Dash made sure his weapons were clean. He made sure that they didn't show up on any scanner. Dash needed everything thing to go right and didn't accept any subpar work from anyone. He made sure the parachutes were in working order by double checking them at least 10 times. Jumping off the roof wasn't the best plan, but it was a good fall back. Dash kept Fern calm by showing her how to handle a weapon. Teaching her how to handle herself gave Dash a piece of mind as well. He knew if their plan failed that she would be able to defend herself and at least put up a fight.

Johnny had a similar routine to Dash, cleaning weapons and helping with the fridge, but most of the time his mind was time thinking about Kate. She kept herself away barely taking time to eat and shower. If it weren't for Fern, Kate would have probably stayed in bed for the rest of her life. Johnny thanked Fern every time he saw her. Jack had downloaded a flight simulator for the model helicopters that Takahara used. Johnny spent what time he could, learning to fly -- another back up plan if they couldn't take the helicopter with the pilot alive.

The week went by faster than they would have liked, but even with a month of preparation they couldn't have been more prepared then they were. It was time to leave. Everyone had gathered outside to say their goodbyes just in case, even Kate joined them.

Johnny tried one last time to speak with Kate before they left.

"Kate," he said. "Can we talk for a moment?" He waited patiently for her answer.

"I've a lot to do. What is it?" She responded not making eye contact.

"Well this is the last day you have to hide you'll be able to go home after this," Johnny said, his eyes begging for her to give him some kind of reaction. Kate stopped preparing lunch and looked at him. Her eyes still puffy and blood shot from all the crying.

"Good luck and come back. I don't think they could make it without you," Kate said forcing a smile. Johnny could almost feel the pain as he looked her in the eyes.

"I'll be back for you. I love you, Kate," Johnny barely said as a lump started to form in his throat. Before she could say anything else Johnny headed for the door. Dash and Johnny had their fake id cards and chef outfits on. All they needed to do now was wait for the caterer to make a pit stop take out the two inside and they were on their way.

Dash reached into the one of the secret compartments of the fridge removing his Springfield pistols, checking to make sure the safety was on, and handed it over to Fern.

"Here, hang on to this..." Dash said as Fern injected.

"I don't want any goodbye mementos..." She said as she began to raise her voice. Dash placed a finger to her lips to shhh her. She scowled at him for doing so, but became quite.

"I want you to have it just in case they find you while we're gone. You spent the week working with the weapon. I just figured it would be handy to have around. Don't get me wrong, I want it back. That pistol is part of a match set and very hard to come by," Dash began to ramble.

"Liar," Fern said and kissed him. "You'd better come back for it."

"You know I will," Dash said with a cocky smile. Dash kissed and hugged both Fern and Scarlet and got into the van. Before Johnny could make any smart ass remarks about how cute his good bye was Dash asked about Kate, "So is she finally talking to you?"

"I don't want to talk about it. How did Fern take you leaving?" Johnny asked changing the subject.

"It was...difficult and I don't want to talk about it either," Dash answered, thinking about the last thing that Fern said to him.

Phillip Wallace / Tyler Anderson

It was the night before and Kate's cries of sorrow could be heard through the door. Johnny sat outside her door ready for her to call to him, but she never did. Jack and Shamus where in the other room, tucked into a pair of bunk beds, passed out from the week of relentless work. Fern and Dash sat on the couch with little Scarlet asleep in their laps.

"Dash," she said quietly, trying not to wake anyone. Johnny had passed out asleep on the floor.

"Yeah baby?" He responded.

"I love you," Fern said as she kissed him lightly. "I'm scared."

"I love you too. Don't be scared," Dash replied. "Don't worry, everything will go fine."

"How do you know? I mean… anything could happen. I lost you for three years. I don't want to lose you forever," she confessed with tears forming in eyes.

"I'm not going to lie. This is a bit dangerous but we're not on some fools crusade. We're fighting for us and for our future. After this there will be no more hiding. No more running. No more dying. We will be free to do what we want and raise our baby in peace. Life will fix itself and we'll never be apart again," Dash said. "All I can promise you is this; we've taken every precaution there is. I'll be as safe as possible."

"There's one thing I want you to keep in mind though Dash. No matter what, your perfect life doesn't work without *you*. So the one thing I want on your mind is; no matter what you have to do, just come back to us. If it comes between your life and his you choose yours every time. I know that sounds selfish, but if you asked him. I'm sure he has already made that decision. He wants to come back just as bad as you. Now that he has something to comeback for…" She quietly preached to Dash before he interrupted.

"Stop it. You don't know him like do. I love you, but I have to get some sleep," Dash said ending the conversation. Dash reached over for a blanket and covered him and Fern and they both slept with Scarlet lying next to them.

"They've been stuck in traffic for an hour. They gotta pull over some time," Johnny said, worrying that they should have taken the vehicle back at the caterer's shop. Dash ignored this latest distraction and began to focus on the job at hand.

"Well, it looks like they're stopping. Wait... they're going again; they're turning left and pulling into a gas station. Wonder why they'd do that?" Jack asked.

"Jack, take two seconds and look up from your computer and you'll see what they are doing." Dash chuckled. One of the two men ran inside while the other was getting gas.

"Oh... well at least we know the program works," Jack said a little embarrassed. Jack had hacked into the trucks low jack and had been tracking it for the past hour. Jack provided turn by turn directions when Johnny and Dash could see the vehicle the whole time. Jack was lucky they had other things on their minds otherwise he would have got an ear-full of back handed comments.

"It's okay man. Thanks for looking out for us. Dash, do you want the one on the inside or out?" Johnny asked.

"Rock paper scissor for inside?" Dash said. "One Two Three!" Dash threw rock and Johnny through scissors.

"Fucking ass you always get the easy ones," he said as he begrudgingly got out of the van.

"The force is not strong with this one," Dash said. Jack broke into an unrelenting laughter.

"Star Wars jokes I love 'em." Jack started making lightsaber sounds and laughed so hard he had to wipe a tear from his eye. Dash got out of the truck and headed inside, while Johnny walked up to the guy pumping gas. Not sure what to say to draw his attention. He walked back and forth for a moment.

"Hey man, your back tire looks little flat," Johnny said.

"Thanks man I'll get it with the air hose," The driver said.

"That didn't work," He thought.

"Oops," Johnny said as he pretended to trip and fell on the ground and still got nothing from the guy. Johnny dusked himself off.

"So what you hauling?" he said as he walked up to the guy.

"I've been to this truck stop a thousand times and I'll probably be a thousand times more. Tell your buddies to knock it off," he said. The driver went back to pumping gas.

"Wait what do you think I'm trying to do here?" Johnny asked.

"You're trying to get free food. I come here all the time and you ochikobores are always looking for hand outs. Did Parnel` send you?" The driver responded.

"What... no. no. no," Johnny said a little confused then came up with a plan. "Well actually... Parnel` said you probably wouldn't be able to help me anyway."

"Every fucking time I come here I get this. I swear Parnel` is always tried to get me fucked out of a job. Get in the cab. I don't have time to feed everyone and if they see you. Who knows how many will come pouring out of the wood work. I'll be in there in a second. I'll take care of you, but it has to be quick. Bill will be back after his phone call," The driver said in an annoyed tone. Johnny hopped in the cab and waited for the driver. Johnny heard the opening and closing of the trucks rear door. It wasn't long then the driver entered. Johnny felt really bad for what he was about to do to the guy. Who knew he would run into someone that helps the unfortunate. Still didn't change what he had to do.

"I grabbed a few things you can have," The driver said as he hopped into the cab.

"Remember what you said about Parnel' getting you fucked out of a job?" Johnny asked.

"Yeah," The driver replied.

"Well, you might want to start lookin' for a new one," Johnny said slide up to the guy and put a pistol in his side. "Make this easy and you don't have to die."

"You're fucking kidding right?" questioned the driver, as he slapped his forehead with the palm of his hand.

"Not this time buddy."

"Shit," Pouted the driver. "I swear every gas station in this town either someone is trying to screw you or someone is trying to fuck you," The diver said. Johnny laughed a little. The driver put his hands to his side and they exited the cab. Johnny took the driver to the back of the van and they both got in. Johnny wacked him on the back of the head with the pistol and knocked him out.

"Jack, tie him up and gag him," Johnny ordered as he tossed a roll of duct tape at him.

"OK, get the truck going. I have to drive around back and pick up the other guy. Dash is shoving him out the back window. He'll be out in a second," Jack said.

"What... How do you know that?" Johnny asked.

"The program is working really well. I can access any video feed within 10 miles," Jack said with an excited smile.

"Any?...I don't know if that is a good thing or a bad thing," Johnny said with a smirk.

"Yep..." Jack said as he flipped his lap top around showing what appeared to be a handheld video camera peering over the top of a wall in the women's dressing room in a department store near the Takahara building.

"Damn dude you got some mad skills," Johnny said giving Jack a fist pound. Jack flinched at Johnny raising his fist, but returned the fist pound once he figured out what Johnny was doing. "Alright get going." Jack drove over behind the gas station and Dash made his way out front.

"Well first part's done; now let's get the fridges switched," Dash said as he took a swig of his soda he bought in the gas station.

"Thanks for gettin' me one. Asshat," Johnny complained.

"It sure is tasty too." Dash smirked.

"Taunt me again and I'll throw it across the parking lot," Johnny joked.

"I've shot men for less." Dash returned sarcastically as he took another swig of the cool refreshing beverage. They drove over to a secluded parking garage and switched out the fridges and some of the food inside in order to hide their arsenal. Johnny thought he would get back at Dash for not grabbing him a soda and made a sandwich from some of the food they weren't able to fit in to their modified fridge. As they got back in the truck and began to drive to Takahara Tower, Johnny started to munch on the sandwich -- a giant stack of turkey, Swiss chess, pickles, lettuce, tomatoes, and onions, all topped with mustard. It crunched while he ate it.

"Wow, I out did myself on this one. It is delicious." Johnny smirked at Dash as he took another bite.

"Where did you get that?" Dash asked as he licked his chops, stopping himself from grabbing the sandwich.

"I made it with the stuff form the fridge and boy is it *tasty*," Johnny said, putting emphasis on tasty, and took a bite. It was the best sandwich in the world right at that moment and it was all his.

"Trade you half my soda for the rest of the sandwich," Dash pleaded.

"Okay," he agreed as he took a huge bite almost finished the sandwich. "The rest is yours," he mumbled through the monstrous bite as he handed offer the sandwich. Dash seeing this grabbed the sandwich and began to chug his soda and finished it 2 large gulps.

"Aaahhhhh," Dash said after finishing the soda taunting Johnny.

"What the fuck man?" Johnny mumbled still chewing the enormous bites of sandwich.

"What? My half was at the bottom," Dash said as he started in on his part of the sandwich. "Wait another few minutes and I can get you the first half."

"Huge fuckin' asshat is what you are." Johnny forced out through the large pieces of sandwich.

"You guys are funny," Jack said as he took a drink from a soda and starting his packed lunch. They both sat back for a second as Dash came to a stop light and then they couldn't hold it for any longer. They began to uncontrollably laugh. Johnny was just barely able to get the rest of his sandwich down before he choked on it.

"You brought a bag lunch on a job," Dash said trying to hold back his laughter.

"Knowing Jack, the bag is probably rigged to explode as well," Johnny joked.

"No, but the van is," Jack said with a straight face. Johnny and Dash immediately stopped laughing.

"Please tell me you are joking," Dash said as he as looked as he turned around to look at Jack.

"Ha ha, got you guys. Like I would rig this van to explode. I certainly wouldn't do that. I love this van. I couldn't do anything to hurt the van. No way, no how." Jack proclaimed but with the tone in his voice both Dash and Johnny knew better. They both let out a heavy sigh and when the light turned, they continued towards the tower. The tower cast a shadow over everything in the city at the right time of the day. Even the space needle cowered in the dark shade of Takahara Tower. The closer they got the more and more intimidated they became. They more they realized that this wasn't just a bunch of guys with guns they are trying to take down. They were trying to take down Neo-Japan itself.

"Let's do a mic check before we head in there," Jack suggested breaking the ominous silence.

"Ok." Johnny said as he flipped on his headlink. "Check 1, Check 2." Dash's head link and Jack's computer rang.

"Check, Check," they all said.

"Sounds good on this end. Keep the volume low until the shooting starts," Jack said.

"Will do," Johnny replied. "We're going to keep them linked from now until this is over." Johnny finished as he took a depth breath.

"You ready?" Dash asked with a sigh.

"No. You?" Johnny asked with a smirk.

"Nope."

"I suppose this will be it when we're done here. You go on with your life with Fern. Get a real job, raise Scarlet, and probably have another baby or three. Oh and more one thing, since you are going to be busy and all. I call dibs on Jack."

"You're going to replace me with Jack?" Dash scoffed.

"Guys, I'm sitting right here," Jack said, but went unnoticed, then spoke softly, "Jerks."

"He has his uses and can be kind of funny in that, 'I spend too much time in front of my computer so I really don't get the world outside' kind of way. And I'm sure you haven't missed the fact that he's in love with his van. I'm sure I'll get hours of entertainment from him," Johnny said jokingly.

"There will always a place at my family's table for you. But you're right... this is it. Here's to the last job." Dash raised his fist in a mock toast.

"See you on the roof then," Johnny said as the shadow of the service entrance crept over the van, as if devouring it.

Akiyo Takahara sat at his desk staring at his son's picture. Tears began to form at the edge of his eyes but quickly dried up. He placed the picture back on his desk and turned to face the monitors.

"Please send in Shinobu from the party security," Mr. Takahara requested. Not a few moments later Shinobu entered the room. He was well dressed, wearing a fancy two tailed white tuxedo, white shirt, white bow tie, and a hidden holster that could barely be seen when he walked.

"Mr. Takahara, Sir. How may I be of assistance?" Shinobu asked with respect.

"How is security for the party?" Mr. Takahara asked.

"Excellent Sir, We did background checks on all the outside staff to include retinal scans and finger prints. Their food has been tested along with all their containers. Special badges were made for them and delivered secretly to prevent possible theft. I have two helicopters on standby, if needed, along with the one parked on the roof. There are over one hundred Takahara Security Officers and Guardsmen to keep the event safe and sound." Shinobu said with pride.

"Good work, Shinobu. I have been disappointed by many of many men lately. Perhaps it is time that I send you out in the field after the Beta," Mr. Takahara stated.

"It would be a great honor," Shinobu responded.

"Then consider the job yours if tonight goes well." Mr. Takahara made Shinobu an offer he could not refuse.

"After tonight's event I will prepare my men. We will leave no stone unturned looking for the Beta," Shinobu announced.

"You will need this file, Shinobu," Mr. Takahara stated as he turned around and opened his desk drawer. He pulled out a large file and pushed it to the edge of his desk. Shinobu retrieved the file and began to flip through it.

"Sir, most of this file is death certificates of the men who went after the Beta. There must be more than thirty certificates here." Shinobu said as his tone became a little more uncertain.

"Is this more then you are prepared for?" Mr. Takahara asked in an inquisitive voice as he turned back towards the monitors.

"It appears that the last team had also lost track of them. Is that correct sir?" Shinobu asked. Shinobu knew of the many co-workers he had lost recently and did not want to join them.

"Yes. The last team failed and has been recycled." Mr. Takahara said as he folded his hands together. "Shinobu, I feel that perhaps you aren't ready for such a task. There would be no shame in saying so." Takahara said sinisterly.

"Mr. Takahara, sir, I will have no problem apprehending the Beta and his associates. Again, it is an honor that you have chosen me," Shinobu said with a bow.

"Very well, I hope that you are able to do what your counter parts could not. It would be sad to have to let you go," Mr. Takahara stated. "Please continue with the party preparation."

"Yes, Sir," Shinobu said with a bow.

"And Shinobu; this is a very special day for my niece. Nothing had better go wrong," Mr. Takahara said sternly.

"Everything will be perfect Mr. Takahara." Shinobu said intimidated by the chill in Mr. Takahara's voice. Shinobu left and began double checking with his people to make sure nothing would go wrong. Mr. Takahara continued to stare at his screen until his desk intercom chirped.

"Yes," Mr. Takahara stated.

"Dr. Maki is here with her results. Shall I send her in?" His secretary said.

"Please do so, thank you," He responded. Dr. Maki came in carrying a data pad.

"Mr. Takahara, the test results from the Deltas are amazing. They surpassed almost all my predictions," She stated with excitement.

"Good work Doctor. Now can you explain to me, what went wrong?" Mr. Takahara demanded.

"Sir, there was no way to foresee what happened with Doctor Johnson. Due to the Delta drug regimen, his regenerative abilities have kicked into overdrive. However, the new drug is highly addictive and will wear out in roughly a week's time. Delta one peaked too early," Dr. Maki said as she pondered what might have gone wrong. "This possibly was an attributing factor in these complications that we are seeing. I would, however, like to perform some more tests on the Dr. Thomas in order to see if we can stabilize him in order to return him to field work."

"Well then Dr. Maki; let's see if we can use this knowledge to avoid the loss of any other Deltas," Mr. Takahara stated and pulled a piece of paper from his desk and slid it toward Dr. Maki. "On another note... My brother is taking an interest in the results that we are producing here in Neo-Japan." Mr. Takahara smiled. Dr. Maki examined the paper. The two page document stated that Juni was to take part in cyber enhancements within the next year. As Dr. Maki reached the end of the list her mouth dropped in horror. Juni was also slated to take part in the Delta trials once the drug was completed and considered to be safe. Dr. Maki was aghast at what her husband had approved, noticing his signature graced the bottom of the page.

"My husband would have never have approved this. Why? Why does he want to do this to our little girl? Hasn't he experimented on our family enough." Dr. Maki said in shock.

"In my brother's own words he said that she could be Takahara Corps finest accomplishment. She's... the *future*."

"But, the Delta drug isn't even close to being perfected yet. We're still in quality testing protocols. Delta is still very dangerous and very addictive. It could hurt her! That's why we tested it on Doctor Johnson," Dr. Maki said frantically. "We need more results from the Doctor before you could continue with Juni."

"I see that you leave me no choice," Mr. Takahara said as he pressed the intercom button. "Ichiro, go with Dr. Maki and help Doctor Johnson along with the trials. Use force and your special ways of coercion if you must."

"Yes Sir," Ichiro replied through the intercom.

"Well Dr. Maki, you get to play mom and keep Juni a little girl for bit longer. I expect you to keep working on Delta until the addiction is no longer part of the side effects. Am I understood?"

"Very well sir," she replied. Dr. Maki didn't know what to do with both her husband and her brother in-law back this proposal she was limited to her options.

"You are dismissed. Go and enjoy the party with Juni. This time in her life is quite precious," Mr. Takahara said with a smile. Dr. Maki left quickly to not show her brother in-law her tears. Ichiro entered as she left.

"Sir. Delta: One is not being cooperative with us. How should I proceed?" Ichiro asked.

"Break his addiction and then proceed to break his mind. We need to know what happened inside the house. Other than that I could care less," Mr. Takahara said. Ichiro turn and began for the door. As he opened the door Mr. Takahara spoke hesitantly, "But leave him alive. He may still have uses. I'm giving you fifteen minutes. Inform me upon his progress before the party starts. I do not wish to be disturbed."

"Very well Sir," he responded with a confident smile in his voice.

"Hello. We're here for the party," Dash said, handing the delivery paper work to the rear guard. The guard looked over the paper work, stamped it, and handed it back.

"Pull ahead. Follow the red line around to the side and you will come to the service elevator to the kitchen. You are to head to the 100th floor."

"Got it, thanks." Dash took back the paper work and pulled away, following the red line through the parking structure. The place looked like it had taken on extra security for the party, as if all the TCS guardsmen had been pulled off of border patrol and put at each exit of the building.

"Jack. It looks like they have fingerprint and retinal scanners like we thought," Johnny said as he glanced at the guard station. The guards were checking people in as they drove by and led them to a parking stop by other guardsmen. "You got us in the system, right?"

Johnny asked as they drove through the parking lot. Jack remained silent as he went through his list.

"We planned for them. Jack you got anything?" Dash whispered through his headlink.

"Um... I thought I checked it off my list but it's not. I can fix that though. Give me a second," Jack said as he began to hack into the Takahara Corp data base. Johnny and Dash parked the truck, took the fridge out of the back, and began pushing the fridge toward the elevator.

"Do you have it yet?" Dash whispered.

"Not yet," Jack said back.

"You got about 30 seconds," Johnny informed Jack they approached the check in. They were next in line and things weren't looking good. Johnny knew he could get to his guns if the flipped the fridge around, but doing so would look suspicious. He hated being unarmed. Especially since everyone one here wanted to put a bullet in them.

"Just push slower," Jack replied.

"Just hurry," Dash mumbled through his head link and reached down to "tie his shoe".

"You know; you could have dropped off the fridge and then parked the truck," One of the guards said at the elevator door as he peaked into the fridge.

"Thanks should've thought of that. I'm just a little nervous; our boss said we'd be fired if we screwed this up," Johnny said as elevator doors opened.

"Understandably so, we'll need a thumb print and then step over to the retinal scanner," The guard ordered.

"Sure just let me put the brake on the fridge here," Dash said as he let go of the fridge and it began to roll backwards.

"I can't hold it," Johnny said and the fridge began to roll backwards. The fridge rolled backward for about ten feet before the guards and Johnny stopped it. They helped push the fridge to the elevator doors and put the brake on the fridge.

"That was a close one," Johnny said.

"Sure was. That is the heaviest one yet," The guard replied as he began to inspect the fridge. It was a tense moment, but the fridge cleared inspection.

"Yeah, it's a new fridge packed with all sorts of goodies," Johnny began.

"So where's this scanner? I've heard your boss doesn't like delays so we'd really like to get the merchandise upstairs in order to retain maximum freshness." Dash cut in.

"Just put your right thumb here and then step over to the retinal scanner," another guard said.

"Sure thing," Dash said as he put his left thumb to the scanner.

"No, no, your right thumb sir," The guard restated.

"Oh. Sorry," Dash said as he placed his right thumb to the scanner. The scanner flashed green. They both cleared the retinal and finger print scanner.

"Well we'd best get moving. The party is almost ready to go," the guard said as Johnny and Dash entered the elevator pushing the fridge. Dash hit the button for the 100th floor. That last button in the elevator. The elevator doors shut.

"This one must not go all the way to the top," Johnny said.

"Ya, think?" Dash replied sarcastically. Johnny shook his head because he should have known better than to say that around Dash.

"Glad we put the food in the fridge," Johnny said.

"Yeah." Dash reached in a grabbed deviled egg of a tray and scarfed it down. "I thought you were going to start swapping life stories there for a while back there with the guards. Damn this is good."

"Good job Jack. That would have ended our day rather quickly if we would have been nabbed at the door," Johnny said.

"Yeah I got you and I got the cameras too. It's working like a charm. You should be on the 100th floor soon, only 50 more to go," Jack said with a bit of pride creeping into his voice.

"Jack, is everything set past this point?" Dash asked.

"Yup, Frankie and I talked it out. She will be ready to go," Jack said.

"What do you mean you talked it out?" Dash said, raising an eyebrow.

"Don't ask. She was the one that decided that we should discuss it," Jack said.

"Ok. Maybe you're right Johnny." Dash laughed. "He really *loves* that van."

"Maybe I'll let you keep Jack, wouldn't want to be a third wheel with that couple." Johnny chuckled.

"Don't you mean fifth." Dash scoffed.

"It's more like a sixth wheel. We can't forget the spare." Johnny laughed loudly.

"What's that supposed to mean?" Jack asked.

"Nothing Jack, you ready for this," Dash said.

"Yeah Frankie and I are right where you need us to be," Jack replied.

"Well then see you when we're done. Just keep us posted on their movements," Dash said as the ding of the elevator finally chimed. The elevator doors opened into a huge kitchen. Hundreds of cooks lined the floor along with ten armed guards. The aroma of all the dishes filled the room and made their mouths water. Johnny and Dash hurriedly pushed their fridge where it could be plugged in and started pulling food out of the fridge, carefully as to not expose all the extras that were inside of it. He then slipped a gun under his waiter's jacket where it couldn't be seen.

"You guys are late. The party has started so get your first course out there," a guard said as Johnny grabbed a tray.

"Sorry. Traffic was a bitch and we wanted to make sure everything was perfect for the evening," Johnny replied.

"Just get out there or you're going to make the boss look bad. If he looks bad you'll look worse – splattered all over the pavement after over a hundred story drop," another guard said gruffly.

A man with a clip board came into the room. He was dressed

very finely with a white two tailed tuxedo jacket, fancy white shirt, and white bow tie. "You're here. Thank god. Why the hell are you late?"

"Because of endless questions like yours," Dash said with some flare in his voice. Dash nudged him aside with his elbow and strode past into the party with a tray of hors devours.

"Sorry sir. He's a bit of a perfectionist when it comes to events like this and we," Started Johnny.

"Nobody treats Shinobu like that!" Sneered the obviously irritated Shinobu. "Just get out there. And tell your friend to see me afterwards for some *discipline*." Shinobu shooed Johnny away.

Yes sir," Johnny said and gave Shinobu a salute. He lifted his tray of appetizers on one hand and carried them out like a snobby waiter. Once he was out the door began to serve the guests, keeping an eye out for their target.

Johnny was soon swarmed by teenagers yelling, "You got to try this!" as they scooped up handfuls of snacks. Johnny was just tall enough to see over their heads when he locked eyes on the man that Johnny believed was Mr. Takahara. He was at the head table sitting next to what Johnny could only assume was Juni; the purple birthday girl sash and two-hundred and fifty-thousand-yen dress gave it away. Johnny wiped his mind of impure thoughts of her.

"Mr. Takahara is an older Japanese man.... Probably in his fifties.... Wearing a nice black suit... Complete with all the accessories. Including a bulge at his side where most would normally carry a gun," reported Johnny, as he whispered into his mic. The man's eyes were cold and calculating and there was no doubt about who he was. Mr. Takahara was taking no chances even with the party being on the 100th floor of his building. He had over twenty armed guards in the room. They were stationed at each exit, at the bathroom doors, and a few mingling with the guests.

Johnny hoped that this would end it all -- give Dash a chance to live a normal life with his girl and his kid, and maybe give him a chance at starting a life with Kate. Johnny thought about sending a bullet downrange into Mr. Takahara's head, right then and there, but had second thoughts with the man's niece sitting so closely to him. They would have to wait until he went to the bathroom or she went out to dance. Johnny went back to the kitchen, noticing his tray was getting low on snacks. Dash took his cue and began his circuit.

"He's at the head table on the left in the front," Johnny whispered as he walked by. Johnny set down his tray and grabbed another one. As he turned around he came face to face with a finely dressed woman.

"I know who you are. Come with me or I'll end your little escapade," she said as she walked out of the kitchen, flashing her badge to the guards. "I need to speak to this caterer privately. They made such a delightful treat that I must have the recipe." Johnny followed her out into the hall and into a private room.

"Who are you?" Johnny asked as he readied himself to jump her and take her out quietly.

"I'm Akemi Maki. You may know of me as, Dr. Maki, head of Maki Labs. I created you," she stated.

"Created me? What the hell are you talkin' about?" He asked full of confusion and shock.

"You any many others, your brothers and sisters, were created and then injected with the Beta Virus. The Virus was an attempt to create a better regeneration and immune system in human. It was thought that all of you died, but somehow you lived. From the tests I have run on some of your blood it appears that Beta has taken over both systems. Without more tests I won't know for sure what the virus has done to your body, but I can tell you this, you are a very special case," She confessed to him.

"The others? You mean people like Jaster and the Doc?" Johnny asked, unsure of everything he was hearing, his mind reeling.

"Jaster? He was part of the Gamma trials and your Doctor friend is our first Delta test. They are completely different cases," she explained.

"You're responsible for the Alpha's and then you continued to make more. You have to be some kind of monster," Johnny said with shock and anger in his voice. He looked upon her as if she were pure evil.

"After the Alphas, I was forced to continue my work by the head of the corporation here in Neo-Japan. I had no choice," she said with sorrow in her voice.

"If you know who I am you have probably guessed why I'm here or at least have some vague idea," Johnny said relaxing a little. If he was going to be detained by the guards it would have already happened by now. Dr. Maki was up to something.

"Yes. You're here to kill the man that's had you chased all over the city... and I want to help," she explained.

"What? Why would you help me? What's in it for you?" Johnny asked trying to dig out the real reason she offered to assist him.

"He's left nothing but a trail of blood and bodies in his path to power. He's become detached from reality... And he's planning on using *my daughter* as a guinea pig to see the effects of a combination of cybernetics and the Delta drug.... I'm not letting that happen.... " She explained.

"And you think you can trust me because?" Questioned Johnny.

"I don't have to trust you. I just have to use you. But if it matters at all, the Delta, Dr. Johnson as you know him, had a change of heart. After having his mind shattered by one of Takahara's operatives I was able to see him, briefly. During our quick chat I was able to glean a sense of your own conscious... as he described your actions in saving his life, as well as the concern for your friends, in the face of immense danger," she said as she looking him up and down.

"Tell me more about the Beta experiment." Johnny blurted out.

"And during the first three years of your life I was only person in your life that raised you. Your mind programmed yourself to believe I am a person you can trust -- a maternal figure. All the Beta children began to see me as such before the fire. I was the only female on the project," she began to confess. It was true. Johnny knew even if he tried he couldn't hurt her. Johnny was confused but uplifted by her words.

"I'll help you, but after this I have more questions for you to answer." Johnny began to bargain with her.

"Beta. Just trust me. You and I want the same end to this madness, albeit for differing reasons," she said. There was joy hidden within her calculating tone. Flashes of a younger Akemi Maki's face popped into his mind.

"Call me Johnny." He smiled. "Here's what I need you to do, wait in the hall I'll gather the kids out there, bring them to you, and you'll get them out of the building," Johnny said, peaking into the hall to check on the positions of the guard team.

"Thank you Beta… Johnny," she replied softly and led him out. Johnny went back to the kitchen and started to put together a tray of food.

Dash was working his way to Mr. Takahara's table, slowly progressing from table to table trying to avoid running into any snot nosed, panty waste, brats who were having, what an appeared to be, the time of their lives. Dash thought to himself, "I *hope* I wasn't *this* naive when I was in high school. These kids have no clue what they're in for." Dash reached into his waistband with his freehand and gripped his Springfield pistol. Getting closer to the table he noticed a painted portrait behind the table of honor at which the Takahara Family was seated. In intricate detail was painted the image of the man whose neck he had broken that fateful day three years ago. But he also noticed something else; the young man bore a striking resemblance to their primary target, the same chin, the same nose… then it all came together. They had killed Mr. Takahara's son.

He remembered Jack explaining to them earlier that they had killed Mr. Takahara's son, but it really did hit him until now. The uncanny family resemblance reminded him of how much Scarlet looked like Fern. He understood what he had taken away from Mr. Takahara, but Dash wasn't going to let this aristocratic megalomaniac take it from him. There was no doubt about it. Dash hadn't really put any thought into what had happened three years ago. He did what he had to do because they would have killed Johnny if he hadn't. And now that Fern and Scarlet were in his life it only strengthened his resolve.

Dash stood there staring vacantly at Mr. Takahara while he weighed the consequences of what was about to happen. He now understood why Takahara had them chased for so long. If anything would have happened to Scarlet he would have done the same, but now was the time to act.

"Can I help you son?" Mr. Takahara asked, drawing the attention of the guard's to Dash. Dash's thoughts were interrupted by the question so he decided to keep up the rouse for a little longer, hoping that the attention of the guards would be drawn elsewhere.

"Would you care to try something from this tray perhaps Mr. Takahara?" Dash asked, presenting the tray.

"It depends. What is in them?" Mr. Takahara asked menacingly.

"They are a simple...fish rollup," Dash said as he blanked on what the food was.

"A Fish Rollup?" Mr. Takahara inquired, raising an eyebrow.

"Yeah, fish roll up. I can't remember what exactly goes in them. I make the pigs in a blanket, the kids love'em." Dash gulped, hoping he bought it. Mr. Takahara took one delicately and ate it. Chewing it slowly he stared at Dash and swallowed before answering.

"Very delectable... my compliments to the chef," he said.

"I'll make sure he knows," Dash said as he turned to walk away.

"What is your name?" Interrupted Mr. Takahara.

"Bill," Dash replied quickly pointing to the name tag.

"How long have you been working for the catering service, Bill?" Mr. Takahara asked, sipping a small glass of sake.

"Not too long, started about a month ago," Dash said as a bead of sweat ran down the side of his face. He knew that he could take out Takahara right now, but there was no way that he would live through it. He tried to play it out in his head as they spoke -- each approach he took always ended with him dead.

"You like the work?" Mr. Takahara asked.

"It's all right, though it keeps me away from my family. I really wish I could find some other work," Dash responded subtlety referring to what Mr. Takahara had done to him.

"Why haven't you?" he asked.

"Well there's some trouble at work between some of the psychotic management running things around there. If I outright quit this job I'll probably have a bounty out for my head. I'm pretty sure they'd try to hunt me down and kill me," Dash said hinting at the situation.

"That's too bad. You have been running around for... excuse me... for this company for a month and you're already that indispensible. You must be a hard worker," Mr. Takahara joked.

"It may have been only a month but it's felt like 3 years," Dash said with a little anger in his voice.

"I'm glad you were able to have this little chat with me, even if it was for just for a moment," Mr. Takahara said as he offered his hand. Dash shook his hand and began to walk away.

Shinobu came up to Mr. Takahara and whispered in his ear, "It has been confirmed."

"Waiter... one more thing," Mr. Takahara said.

"Yes sir," Dash said as he turned around.

"You would have been better off trying to poison me, with your, "fish rollup." It would've been the wiser plan. I'd be dead right now." Mr. Takahara scoffed in his usual cold tone. "Though with you and your friends daring attitudes I'm guessing that you wanted to come in here and blaze away with your guns instead. Guards!" Mr. Takahara yelled. The five men standing around Takahara stepped towards Dash. "Please show Mr. McBragg out. It was nice chatting with you." Mr. Takahara folded his hands together and smiled mischievously.

The five men approached Dash with their hands inside their jackets; their hands were obviously on the grips of their pistols. There was no way Dash could draw his gun and get all of them before they got him.

"Be on the lookout for the Beta too. He is never far behind," Mr. Takahara said as he waved them off and went back to watching his niece enjoy the party on the dance floor.

"Unless you want this whole floor and every guest in it blown-the-fuck-up you'd better call off your trained monkeys. So just back... the fuck... off," Dash stated as he stepped a few paces away from the guards.

"Get my niece out of here!" Mr. Takahara yelled as he pointed to her dancing with one of the waiters.

"Exit plan A, repeat exit plan A!" One of the guards shouted in to his wrist microphone. Dash took the opportunity to grab one of the nearby chairs and chuck it at the guards, and then drew his pistol from his waistband. He dove to his right and threw a table over for cover. Dash knew his cover would not last long, but that didn't matter, he could see that Johnny had already made his move.

Johnny watched
Dash head for the master table. He knew that when shit went down the kids needed to get out of there. He hoped that what he was about to do wasn't the stupidest thing he had ever done, but in his mind he knew it was at least in the top ten. As he walked out on the dance floor a slow song began. He tapped a young man dancing with Takahara's niece on the shoulder, "Can I cut in?" It might have been the fact that Johnny was older or just the fact he twisted the kids arm to near breaking, but he stepped aside. He offered his hand to Juni and they began to dance.

"Hello, my name is Johnny. What's yours?" Johnny asked trying to break the ice. The lilac smell of her perfume caught Johnny's attention. It was a very adult scent for such a young girl, but it smelled wonderful.

"My name is Juni. If you were a guest you should have known that. I'm also going to gather that, while you said that your name is Johnny and your nametag says it's Matt, that you also aren't a caterer. So who are you Mr. man-of-mystery?" she said with a giggle. "You know my uncle would be very upset that I'm dancing with a stranger. But since this is my favorite song I think I'll give you a bit of time before I start screaming my head off. If you're convincing, or at the very least, entertaining; maybe I'll let you out of here without my uncle knowing. He has such a temper sometimes."

"Well I'm glad such a beautiful girl would take the time to dance with me," Johnny said putting on what little charm he had.

"Flattery will get you nowhere. Time is wasting away while you try to tap-dance around my questions," Juni said with a playful smile. She was a beautiful girl and if Johnny had been younger and not trying to kill her uncle he probably would have made a move, but he kept the conversation on her.

"So if that is your uncle where are your Dad and Mom?" Johnny asked.

"Oh, my dad is in Japan. I'm studying here for a semester. My dad said it would do me some good to be away from home. My Uncle did all of this for me and mom is around here somewhere. So it's not *all* that bad."

"It is nice to have an Uncle that looks after you," Johnny said thinking about his dead kin.

"Yeah it is," she replied as the song ended. Johnny was about to reveal his plan to her when she broke his train of thought.

"So now I think it's time you turn into a pumpkin? Isn't that how the story goes?" Juni mocked him.

"Listen Juni. I need you to listen to me and do exactly what I tell you," he said sternly. "Things are about to get very dangerous around here. You and your friends need to get out of here so they don't get hurt. Your mother is waiting outside in the hall to help you. So do something, anything to get these kids out of here." However it was too late. Gun shots rang out and people began to panic. Johnny turned around and saw Dash flip up a table for cover.

"Beta is here!" A guard yelled pointing his gun at Johnny and pulling the trigger. The bullet ripped into his vest, but the vest held strong. He stumbled to the ground on top of Juni.

"Juni get your friends out of here. Find your mother she is waiting for you in the hall," Johnny said as he slowly got up and pulling a gun from his back waistband with one hand and helping Juni up with the other. He took aim at the primary target at the head table.

"Juni!" yelled

Mr. Takahara. He pulled his gun and shot the guard who had shot in his niece's direction - one hell of a shot for anyone and even more impressive for the older man. The guard slumped to the floor, dead. Johnny got up and pulled his gun, pointing it at Mr. Takahara pulling the trigger once. The spray of bullets from the modified Glock peppered the windows behind Mr. Takahara. Dash took the opportunity to put some more lead into it with his modified .40 Caliber Springfield pistol. Send a full clip through the window with its automatic fire, the combined effect was devastating. The main window blew out the behind Mr. Takahara. A strong gust of wind started sucking guests out the 100th floor as the area quickly began to depressurize. Johnny began to feel sick to his stomach as he watched people fly out the window.

Mr. Takahara's eyes were wide as he grasped for anything within arms-reach that could anchor him inside. He madly gripped onto his chair and the two of them were slowly drug backwards, and then out into the night. His shrieks pierced the moment as he spiraled into thin air, still holding the chair like a pair of dancers before he dropped to the street below. Juni reached out to her uncle as he was blown from the building but was hauled away by guards as Johnny made a sprint towards Dash. They took advantage of the chaos and confusion to make their way back towards the kitchen entrance together, taking turns covering each other on the way.

Johnny reached the door first and gave Dash covering fire as he bulled through the kitchen door, smashing a guard that was taking cover on the opposite side with the door. Johnny followed closely behind. He watched as Juni was hauled off. Hopefully her mother would be able to get her out in time. Johnny and Juni caught a glimpse of each before she was hauled out of the room. There was a look in her eyes that he wasn't able to make out. The glance was fleeting and Johnny quickly ducked into the kitchen.

Johnny and Dash took cover near their fridge to allow them a quick breather in the deserted kitchen. The guards in the ball room were busy getting people out and dealing with the constant gust of wind caused by the climate control and the height of the floor they were on. Three guards meandered on in from another service entrance, looking panicky and not noticing Johnny and Dash until it was too late.

"What are we going to do now that the boss is dead?" A guard fretted nervously to his companions.

"This is going to end up as a blood bath if the other clans get news of this. This could create a power vacuum. Maybe we should return to Japan," The second of the three said.

"What will Kenji Takahara do when he hears of this fiasco? Lord, help us all when that news arrives," The third said.

"Pretty sure you boys won't have to worry about that," Dash muttered, firing his pistol into the cranium of the nearest one. Johnny sprayed bullets into the guts of the remaining two, their innards messily spilling to the floor, some blood spraying on Dash.

Dash wiped himself off with a towel that was lying on the counter as Johnny checked the ball room door. Luck was on their side due to the fact that it was such a large party the guards were still busy dealing with guests and treating the injured. Dash threw the towel on the ground and went back to the fridge to load up.

The chance to catch their breath has passed as bullets passed though the wall next to Johnny's head.

"That was close," Johnny said. "Let's get a move on."

"Almost done. I wonder what was going through Takahara's mind during the last seconds of his life?" Dash smirked. "I'll bet they'll still be scraping his carcass off the cement months from now." Dash opened the hidden panels on the fridge they brought in.

"Hurry up, will ya. Those guards aren't gonna stay busy out there forever. Grab me some spare clips though. I'm almost out." Johnny said as he double checked his ammo count. Dash handed Johnny a few spare clips and finished loading up. Johnny ejected his clip and slapped in the new one. The empty one clattered on the ground.

"Your turn," Dash said as he took Johnny's position watching the door. Besides his parachute, Dash looked like jungle partisan with two crossed bandoliers of clips, an AK-47, his Springfield was now in his chest holster, and his Raging Bull hand cannon on his hip. "Let's go Rambo." Johnny chuckled as a bullet whizzed by his head.

"Shit! Hurry up! It looks like we just ran out of time. We needed to be on our way to the roof by now." Dash said, unloading into a TCS guardsman that tried to make it through the kitchen access door he was guarding. After getting his parachute on, Johnny took no time getting ready to move. Glock 18 in one hand and his Scorpion machine pistol in the other, extra clips were strapped on his legs and in chest pockets. His shotgun holstered on his back with a ring of shells attached to his leg and a backpack holding some 'odds and ends.'

"Jack. Are you ready with the exit route, because we could really use it right about now!" Dash yelled into the headlink over the gun fire.

"They're moving around a lot. You will need to take the elevator up a floor," Jack suggested. Johnny and Dash pushed the fridge in front of the kitchen door and made a brake for the maintenance elevator. As the doors to the elevator slid open, four guards stood in front of Dash and Johnny. Surprise was complete on both sides; Johnny and Dash were caught in a full sprint and the guards were caught jaw-jacking. Dash ducked left and Johnny ducked right in order to get out of the line of fire. Shots rang out from the direction of the elevator. The guards had recovered first. Bullets whizzed over their heads as Johnny and Dash slid deeper into cover behind some of the metal cooking appliances.

Shots also started coming from behind them. Johnny took a quick glance back to see if they were going to be surrounded. One of the TCS guardsmen had shifted the fridge that was barring the door enough in order to squeeze his machine gun through the crack. The fire wasn't very accurate but it was enough of a threat that it had to be dealt with. Dash rolled over a counter top in order to get a clear shot without losing his head.

Bullets fired blindly from the machine gun ripped through the air. The indiscriminate fire was doing more harm to friend than foe and three of the four guards in the elevator were down and bleeding. The fourth gave up, throwing his gun to the ground, and ran out another exit. Johnny and Dash made their way to the elevator using cover against the machine gun, poked their heads into the elevator and looked at the carnage. Three dead – they looked at each-other and shrugged before quickly entering the elevator. More bullets were fired at their direction and Johnny yanked the bodies out of the way of the door and it finally closed.

"I'm going to make the assumption that we are climbing through the roof," Dash said remembering that the elevator only went up to the 100th floor.

"Yeah. You have to crawl out the roof and get in the air duct," Jack replied.

"Jack," Dash said with a sigh.

"Yeah," Jack responded

"Remind me to punch you when this is over," Dash said as the elevator began to move. Dash opened the access hatch on the top of the elevator and pulled himself up and through. Dash reached down and grabbed Johnny's hand and helped him up. Johnny shot out the controls after he was pulled up and pulled out a couple small blobs of C4 which he pressed to the elevators cables. Johnny and Dash grabbed the ladder in the shaft, and ascended up to an air duct. At the top of the ladder Johnny pulled out a remote detonator and blew the cables, sending it crashing down to the bottom of the building.

"Nice work Johnny," Dash said impressed.

"Thanks though I hate these fucking air ducts. I would have tried to make it to the stairs if I knew we were going to have to crawl around in these damn things," Johnny said complained.

"Sorry, it's better than being dead," Jack responded timidly.

"I like breathing and if you want to keep breathing you'll get in the fucking air duct in about two seconds," Dash said. As Johnny climbed in he followed. After 30 yards of crawling they were able to exit the duct.

"Which way now?" Johnny asked as they dropped into an empty hallway, guns at the ready.

"You should be able to take the west staircase at the end of the hallway to the left, up to the 130th floor."

"29 stories on the stairs. Good times," Johnny joked and started to run down the hallway.

"You said you wanted to take the stairs... ladies first," Dash said as he motioned with his hand. Johnny didn't mind the jokes it kept his mind off all the bullets, blood, and bodies. He took the lead and continued up the stairs still being cautious up each flight.

"Jack, you got that surprise ready?" Johnny asked.

"I need another 5 minutes and it will be right where it needs to be," Jack replied.

"How are the alarm decoys working?" Johnny asked.

"Good. Right now they think you are on the 90th floor," Jack responded.

"What the hell are you two talking about? What surprise?" Dash questioned.

"Jack and I didn't want to tell you, figured that you'd think it was a dumb idea," Johnny replied as they continued their trek up the stairs.

"You know what I really think are dumb? Surprises," Dash said as he fired rounds at a man entering the stair well from behind them. The round hit him in his groin and the man fell. Dash took better aim and made sure he didn't get up or radio for help.

"Well the fridge..." Johnny began to explain over the gunfire.

"Yeah," Dash said implying he should continue as he and Johnny traded fire with a few guards coming up the after them.

"It's a bomb," Johnny admitted.

"A what?!" Dash yelled.

"A bomb," Johnny said again.

"Yeah I heard you the first time. How big of a bomb?" Dash said demanding an answer.

"Big enough to take out a floor," Johnny replied.

"Where is it headed?" Dash said wanting to know what floor not to be on.

"That depends. Jack is going to blow it up where ever he can take out the most guys," Johnny said. "10 more floors to go."

"What if it takes out the building? Jack is known for being excessive!" Dash yelled as he rattled off a few more shots as more men started to enter the stair well.

"Also figured if we had to use it we were dead anyway," Johnny confessed clipping one of the guys charging up the stairs after them.

"Oh, Good point." Dash shrugged.

"Thought you might like that," Johnny said. "Five more to go."

"Guys the alarms aren't working any more. I just picked up a radio message calling people to your stair case," Jack informed them.

As they reached the 130th floor two men came through the door. Dash caught the first with his right fist. The man was dazed from the hit. The other pointed his pistol at Dash and was about to fire. Johnny quickly grabbed the guards hand and twisted the weapons aim at the guard's partner. He squeezed the trigger firing a shot which struck the other guard in the back of the head, killing him. Johnny and the man began to fight over the pistol. As they neared the edge of the stair railing Dash kicked the struggling man over the rail. The man plummeted down 30 flights screaming all the way down until he head clipped the railing ending his screams.

"Did you hear that?" Dash asked as he looked over the railing.

"Hear what?" Johnny said confused.

"He sounded like all those cartoon characters when they fall off cliffs," Dash said with a chuckle that was cut short by guns firing up at them. More TCS guardsmen and agents entered the stairwell. Johnny and Dash returned fire slowing their movement up the stairs.

"Ready?" Johnny asked as he grabbed the door handle.

"Hey before we go in there. I have to know something," Dash said.

"What's that?" He asked.

"Where did you come up with the name Berith?" Dash asked. "Face it man it's kind of dumb."

"Ha!" Johnny laughed. "Guess it's suiting to tell you now. It's what my uncle used to call me when I was little. I found out why when I went back to his shop. There was a medical wrist band that was melted, but was you could make out on it spelled BERITH. I find out from Tommy and Dr. Maki that I'm part of some Beta experiment and they want me alive to run some tests..."

"Huh. Well, this a longer story then we have time for," Dash interrupted. "You'll have to explain later." Dash fired a few rounds over the edge to make the TCS guardsmen take cover.

"You ready?" Johnny asked as he reloaded each of his weapons and holstered them. Johnny grabbed one of his grenades and Dash readied one of his own. They quickly opened the door pulled the grenade pins and chucked the grenades in the hallway. Johnny slammed the door shut before the blast went off. Screams of, "Grenade!" Could be heard from behind the door. The two thunderous claps of the grenades silenced the screams.

"Let's rock," Dash said as he put the butt of his rifle tight into his shoulder. Johnny drew his Scorpion and nodded he was ready. He opened the door and Dash went in. Johnny quickly followed looking for the nearest cover, but was stopped. Dash had not taking cover. He was just standing there. Johnny then saw what Dash was staring at. They both were dumbfounded as a gust of wind struck them in the face. There had to be twenty plus men lying in the hall way either dead or dying. The moans of the living filled the hallway.

"Thank God for grenades," Dash said, crossing himself.

Johnny tugged on Dash's arm. "Take watch I'm going to set up a little surprise for the guys following us. Dash took up over watch down the hallway. Johnny pulled the pin from another grenade and pinned it between the door hinges so it wouldn't go off. Johnny positioned the grenade to fall when the door was opened.

"It's set, let's go," Johnny said as he finished setting the trap. They ran for the stair case on the east side of the building. Just as they got the door open the sounds of an echoing explosion went off at the other end of the hallway. "Guess it worked. We need to move faster though, they're catching up."

"Ah... guys," Jack said through the com. A small tremble could be heard in his voice.

"What's up Jack?" Dash asked.

"It's not my fault...The roof... well... There are a lot of them...and it's not my fault," Jack said with hesitation.

"How did they get to the roof without passing us?" Johnny asked.

"Um. Helicopters... Just dropped them off. I got... four squads of ten each. Again not my fault." Jack reluctantly announced, "Although the garden up there has a very beautiful design. It is very red... personally I would have gone with purple..."

"Forty!" Dash interrupted.

"What if we went back down the stairs? How many are we looking at that way?" Johnny asked, panicked by the sheer number of guys.

"Oh...uh... more... At least three times that amount. Give or take a few," Jack replied softly.

"Well, I guess telling them we're sorry isn't going to work," Johnny joked to help calm himself down.

They both laughed briefly through their labored breath and continued up the final ten flights of stairs, preparing for the firefight that was coming. Dash was down to half a clip in his AK-47, five speed loaders for his Raging Bull, and was down to the last clip for his Springfield .40. Johnny wasn't doing much better on ammo, but this was it and they both knew it. Their boss was dead and many of their comrades were wounded, dead, or dying. These TCS agents weren't going to be pulling any punches. Getting off the roof with forty fully-armed and well-trained men in the way would be a feat all on its own.

"Jack, get the bomb up to the 149th floor. I think this qualifies as an "emergency situation" that we had planned for," Johnny barked through the mike.

"How long will it take to get the fridge bomb up here Jack?" Dash asked. "Because we're in a bit of a hurry."

"You don't seriously want me to blow it on that floor. That would easily cause the roof to collapse and kill everyone," Jack screamed though the links.

"No shit!" Dash said bluntly.

"Well. It should take 10 minutes on the elevator. Isn't there a better way with less "everyone being dead?" Jack pleaded.

"Jack, I need you to do something for me. I need you to take care of Fern and Scarlet if we don't make it out of this," Dash stated.

"This is ridiculous, you can't be serious. I don't know how to take care of a kid! There's got to be another way! Something I haven't thought of yet. Let me check a few things. I can figure something out!" Jack shouted back through at them.

"Jack. This isn't negotiable. If Johnny and I don't make it out of this it is your job to make sure that nothing happens to Fern and Scarlet. Do I make myself clear?" Dash demanded. There was a moment of silence. "And I'm sure Johnny wants you to get Kate out as well." Dash said, looking in Johnny's direction.

"Ok... I'll take care of the girls," Jack finally agreed when he knew his words were falling on deaf ears.

"Thanks Jack, I'll give you the signal to blow the fridge," Johnny said. "So be ready." Johnny nodded in Dash's direction and gave him a slap on the shoulder. "Got your back. Anytime."

Dash finished checking his guns all fully loaded as they could be and ready to go. He mentally prepared himself for what was ahead and had to focus on the job at hand in order to give Jack enough time to get the bomb up and ready to go.

"Think we can make it through this?" Dash asked as he watched Johnny change clips on his Scorpion.

"I give us 10 minutes, tops, to get to a chopper on the roof," Johnny said with a smile. "Or we get to use plan B." he said as he tapped his backpack."

"You know how to fly a chopper?" Dash asked as they entered the 150th floor.

"What do you think I was doing all week?!"

"That was a fucking computer game!"

"But how hard could it be." Johnny chuckled as he opened the door to the 150th floor. Bullets poured into the door as it swung open. He and Dash were still in the stairwell, safe from the incoming fire. The door, however, was not so lucky. The door took what had to be over sixty rounds and fell off its hinges.

"Let's see what they got," Johnny said. He poked his head quickly around the corner as the gunfire subsided. There were too many targets to count and nearest cover was ten feet away. "That doesn't look promising. "

"I got a pair of flash bangs and three smoke grenades left," Dash said as he unclipped the flash bangs and tossed one to Johnny.

"I'll roll this one out and you give that one a little distance," Johnny said as he pulled the pin on his flashbang.

"Ready," Dash said as he pulled the pin to his flashbang.

"Do it to it," Johnny said as he rolled his flashbang out the door while Dash threw his further on to the roof. The double bang of the devices sounded and they sprinted through the door. Guns were firing every which way as they ran forward. The roof was styled as a Japanese garden, complete with ornate rock and stone half walls, a small stream and a helicopter pad. The garden was set up in squares-within-squares; with entrances in the middle of each wall and bushes and shrubs decorating the top of each sculpted barrier. Stone benches could be found throughout the massive garden. The helipad itself was raised above the garden off to one corner in order to prevent the wind from the helicopter propeller from damaging the plants. It was serviceable by either a twin set of stairs or a small private elevator.

Dash reached the garden wall first using what bullets he had left in his AK-47 to provide some covering fire. As he took cover he pulled out his Raging Bull and prepared to give Johnny some support. Johnny followed Dash once he was ready, but wasn't as lucky. Rounds flew in his direction and he wasn't able to avoid them all. He caught a round in the chest knocking him to the ground. Johnny was close enough to finish crawling to a turned over bench for cover.

"You all right?" Dash yelled over the bullets and glass.

"I'm fine, but we should really think about buying our vests from a wholesaler if this keeps up. Damn that hurt." Johnny said jokingly as he rubbed the impact point as rounds continued to fly in their direction. Johnny realized that he probably shouldn't joke so much in this situation, but it was the only thing keeping him from panicking and could tell that it was helping Dash as well every time he laughed.

Dash chuckled at the response and knew his friend was alright. The stunning affect was beginning to wear off on the firing squad that they had charged into. It was only a matter of time before they were gunned down if they stay put. Johnny peeked out from the edge of his cover to see TCS guards moving into flanking positions.

"Dash, how does it look on your side?" Johnny said through the headlink.

"They're trying to flank me over here," Dash said as he leaned out and fired his hand cannon three times leaving their numbers two less. "You?"

"The same." Johnny replied trying to figure a way for them to get out of their death trap. He knew he had to act fast. He adjusted his Scorpion to full auto and combat rolled over to the adjacent flower bed unharmed. He leaned out on his side seeing three guards who had not adjusted their aim toward his new position. The rip of the bullets leaving the Scorpion and the casings hitting the ground came to a halt as Johnny emptied his clip into the unlucky guards. The men were like puppets' dancing on strings one after the other they fell to the ground dead.

"Move left." Johnny yelled as he provided covering fire with his Glock. Dash ran and dove behind a marble bench. Hot lead ripped into his back destroying the usefulness of his parachute. Dash quickly discarded it before Johnny and Dash again skirted the edge of a garden bed dispatching a few more TCS goons. Dash would have to depend on Johnny's chute carrying two if it came down to it.

Johnny let loose the rest of his clip making the TCS guardsmen and agents duck and take cover. Dash and Johnny were starting to become desperate as the bullets began to run dry. They began to scavenge weapons off the dead.

The sound of automatic fire filled the air with a thousand drum beats as their rounds chewed up the garden walls filling the air with concrete dust and bits of rock. The blast of 12 gauge shotguns filled the air like the pounding of a bass drum and decorated the roof in blood and entrails. The screams of dying and wounded souls deafened the ears of the men on the roof top. It was as if Hell's marching band and choir were performing on top of Takahara Tower.

They continued firing all around the roof top garden, which chipped, broke, or added bullet size holes to every wall, pot, and plant. Dash sat down next to Johnny and picked up a Mac-10, cocking it, and checking to see if it was loaded. He popped the empty clip out.

"Fuck, I *knew* I picked this gun up before," Dash said and quickly stood up as a guardsman stepped around the corner. The guardsman was a little shocked, but Dash wasn't going to wait for him to recover and used Mac-10 like a hammer on his head. Striking him, it made a sound like hitting a melon. It knocked him to the ground as limp as a rag doll.

Dash hit him two more times to make sure he wasn't getting up. He was breathing heavy after the assault and threw the gun down, taking cover next to Johnny. Johnny was staring into the empty breech of his double barrel sawed off shotgun and with a flick of his wrist, snapped it together.

"Well then. It's probably time for those smoke grenades," Johnny said as he dropped his empty weapon. Dash pulled out the smoke grenades and started heaving them out. He then slid out his army issue k-bar knife.

"Don't suppose you got one for me?" Johnny asked as the gun shots died down.

"Aren't you a kung fu master?" Dash responded sarcastically.

"Seriously, do you have another?" Johnny asked again.

"No I don't. I'll remember to get you one for next time," Dash said, still sarcastically. "How much time we got left?"

"Too much time," Johnny replied.

"The one time we don't need more time and we get it." Dash scoffed. Dash began to strategically chuck the grenades around the roof trying to fill it with smoke. The smoke was beginning to billow on the roof top. Coughing could be heard from the men caught in the smoke. The smoke grenades were more effective than either Johnny or Dash had thought they would.

The smoke was so dense you could barely make out shadows. The shouting in Japanese became more intense as the roof filled with smoke, which made it easy to pick out targets. A TCS guardsman ran right by Johnny without even noticing him. As the man stumbled around in the smoke Johnny closed lined him knocking him to the ground and planted his foot on his throat, crushing his windpipe.

Johnny ducked down taking cover and rifled through the dead man's gear. In the guardsman's hip holster was a beauty of a pistol. Johnny pulled it from the holster; it felt as if it was made for him. The gun was a Colt forty-five caliber Dragon XSE. The gun was made of black metal and had a red dragon etched into the handle of the gun.

Johnny would have sat in awe of the gun but more gun fire erupted at Johnny, snapping him out of his thoughts. Johnny holstered the pistol and quickly picked up the torso of the man and used him as a shield. Bullets embed themselves into the dead man as Johnny moved to cover. A scream erupted from the other side of the roof top, "No, I no want to die!" The man yelled, but his scream was cut short. Dash claimed the man's life and it wouldn't be the last.

The cries for life brought attention Dash's way and the bullets began to fly. Johnny took that time to liberate a spare clip from the dead man. The roof had become a symphony of gun fire, ricocheting bullets, shell casing hitting the ground, and cries of the wounded.

"Good timing," Johnny thought as he began to move out of cover dodging in between flower beds and bamboo trees. Dash's attack couldn't have come at a better moment. He drew his new pistol and made use of the three rounds that were left in the original clip. Johnny fed the Dragon the spare clip he had swiped earlier and took down another agent in short order.

Johnny could now see Dash on the other side of the garden. Ripping the pistol from the hands TCS guardsman and turning it on him. Dash squeezed the trigger several times, but only one round fired. The final round in the pistol was enough to slay the man, but the firearm was empty.

"Jack we could really use Frankie right about now," Johnny said through the headlink.

"There was an elevator issue and I have to use the stairs," Jack said. Dash moved from his potion and jumped behind what was left of an ornate lion statue. "Click, click, click." The sound of the empty TCS guns filled the roof top. The firing from the TCS Agents began to trickle off and then stop all-together.

"Is it possible they're out of ammo?" Johnny asked himself out loud.

"What was that? It didn't come through," Jack asked impatiently.

"Nothing. Just keep doing what you're doing," Dash answered, trying to catch his breath.

"What's the ETA?" Johnny asked.

Dash rose from his cover knife in hand. "It's time to dance Johnny get your ass up."

Johnny moved from cover and prepared himself. The remaining guards split up and starting to moving towards them. Dash invited them to him, his blade held reverse grip in his right hand.

"I need about ten more minutes," Jack said.

"Didn't you say that about ten minutes ago?" Dash said.

"I'll keep you posted," Jack said as if there was no pressure. Johnny pistol whipped the first guy knocking him to the ground, then drew and fired his final rounds from his pistol into the man's head. Johnny lifted his eyes to meet his next opponents and unsteadily exhaled at the sight. Fourteen men were bearing down on him with fury in their eyes.

As he surveyed the scene he knew that they no longer wanted to take him alive. They wanted revenge for their fallen friends. He knew that he had to keep on the move. They both had a chance if they could fight them one at a time. Letting them surround them would end the fight quickly.

Johnny began to move counter clockwise around the garden trying to separate them. Dash caught glimpse of his movements and did the same. Dash was covered in blood from the guard he had just caught in the throat. He was an intimidating vision to see. His knife was making short work of the guards easily hitting the TCS men in unprotected areas of their bodies.

Johnny moved quickly jumping over the decorative half walls filled with exotic plants. He stopped moving and turned to fight. The first man swung a potted plant at Johnny, missing him. Johnny grabbed his forearm with his left hand and struck him in the back of his elbow with his right. The cracking of bone and the popping of the joint made the man scream. Johnny swept the guardsman's leg out from under him then followed his kick with a swift punch to the guards head knocking him unconscious.

Johnny turned to face the next man but was too late to avoid his assault. The shot gun blast hit him in the square in the back. Johnny stumbled forward from the force tripping over the man he just put to the ground, tumbling over him. His vest absorbed the round. Johnny used his momentum to fall to his back. Reacting quickly Johnny rolled out of the way of the butt of the shotgun now being wielded by a guardsman like a bat and sprung to his feet. Three agents still dress in their uniforms were able to get into striking distance and began to attack him with others moving into position.

Johnny caught the arm of the first punch from the agent in front of him. He gripped his arm tightly and swung him into the oncoming kicks of the 2 men behind him. The men hit ground hard, but were not out of the fight. Using the momentum of the throw he swung around to face two others who were getting in behind him. He grabbed a handful of dirt from a nearby planter, throwing it in their eyes, giving him some breathing room once again.

"Dash, you dead yet?" Johnny yelled.

"Not yet." Dash yelled back still fending off blows. Dash was using his knife to the best of his ability. Dash had perfected the stab and twist over his three years of running. He had killed seven of the men and two more were down but refusing to die. Dash took a kick to the back of the head which knocked him to the ground. Dash shook his head trying to clear the stars from his eyes. The remaining men came rushing at their prone target, a mistake that one of them would never get a chance to make again. Dash threw his knife hitting one of the last me in the chest. Aghast at how quickly Dash was able to recover the two remaining men stopped dead in their tracks and began to approach cautiously.

Their eyes betrayed their thoughts to Dash. The realization that Dash was a man you really didn't want to fuck with was easy to see in their actions. The slowly crept forward as they approached Dash giving him enough time to get to his feet. Dash balled up his fists and prepared to feed these goons a can of whoop ass. He slid one foot back a bit, settling into a fighter's stance, not noticing that he had moved so close to the edge of the building. As he peered over the ledge Dash had a quick bout of vertigo and felt his legs turn to jelly.

"Aw fuck!" Dash said, walking shakily away from the ledge. The two men had decided their lives were more important than trying to catch this savage tiger and ran towards the rooftop exit. Dash swiftly hurried to aid Johnny who seemed to be having a hell of a time with the remaining six men.

Johnny was beginning to slow down; he was good, but not the best. He took a kick to the arm then another to the leg. The kicks were followed by a pair of punches catching him in each of his pectoral muscles, then a kick to the back. Hand to hand combat with so many opponents was impossible to keep up with.

Dash ran into the swirling melee and horse collar tackled one of them to the ground. He slammed his foot down on the back of the agents head, taking him out of the fight. Dash followed the surprise attack by slitting another's throat from behind. Johnny kept the final guards attention while one by one Dash picked them off. With three men left and Johnny barely able to stand, Dash let his presence be known as he stabbed a guardsman in the back and let him scream in pain. The two men left were horrified to see that their backup had been ambushed.

Johnny used their fear to take advantage and went of the offensive. He struck quickly with a jab breaking the nose of the closest man. While Dash grabbed the other from behind and began to choke him out. He squirmed and tried to wriggle free, but was no match for Dash's strength. He held the choke hold until the guardsman passed out and then let his limp body hit the floor.

Beta: The Scorpion and The Bull

Johnny and Dash were battered, bruised, and all around exhausted from the fight and sat for a moment to catch their breath. They could hear a clunking noise coming from the stairwell. They were relieved as the fridge waddled around through the door way and breathed a sigh of relief.

"Time to blow up the roof. Jack, get the fridge to the center of the building," Johnny ordered.

"Wait a second. Look at the condition of the chopper on the roof. *That's* not going to fly *anywhere!*" Johnny looked over to see the bullet ridden machine. "How are we supposed to get down?!" Dash yelled.

"Our chutes should hold us, AKA plan B." He motioned to the bag on his back. "Jack have Frankie arm the bomb."

"Wait. I don't have a parachute. You don't expect me to run back down the stairs," Dash argued. "Plus I fucking hate heights!"

"Get over it," Johnny said as he latched himself to Dash. "We should be fine with just this one."

"What are you doing? Don't hook me to that death trap. You're fucking nuts! Your pack is full of holes!" Dash yelled, fending off Johnny's arm. The shotgun blast to the back that Johnny's bullet proof vest absorbed not a few moments had ripped his main chute to shreds. Removed his pack to see if the chute was still useable, but the cantaloupe size hole through the pack ended his hope to salvage the easy get away.

"Shit. Well there goes plan B," Johnny said with a dead look in his eyes as he through the parachute to the ground.

"Tell me you have another plan," Dash said.

"Unless you can grow a set of wings I think we're royally fucked," Johnny said as he started to take off the emergency shoot from its clips. He hooked it on to Dash.

"What are you doing?" Dash asked. "Is this some kind of joke?"

"The backup shoot is protected by a Kevlar cover... But it's only rated for one person the weight of 2 bodies will snap the clips like a pretzel. You can get out of here," he said as he moved closer to the edge with Dash.

"Guys..." Jack said through the headlink.

"I ain't leaving you up here. We started this together we are going to end it together," Dash said determined to finish this with his friend.

Johnny looked Dash in the eyes. He had decided one of them was getting off the roof and Johnny remembered Fern's words that had woke him from his sleep the night before. Johnny wasn't going to let Dash give his life when there was a way out for one of them. Dash knew from the look that his friend was about to do something stupid.

"See you around Dash," he said.

"I ain't leaving you here to die!" Dash yelled. Johnny grabbed the emergency chute pin and pushed Dash as hard as he could. Dash went flying off the building edge as the chute began to open.

"Yes you are," he said to himself as he gave a small wave to Dash as he fell and the chute opened.

"Fuck, fuck, fuck, fuck, FUUUUUUCCCCKKKKKK..." Dash repeated as he sailed over the edge of the building.

"Guys, tell me you didn't do something stupid," Jack said.

"What do you mean, Jack?" Johnny asked as he ducked behind some cover. Bullets started flying his direction as agents began pouring onto the rooftop.

"Frankie has found a way out. At least one with a slight probability of success," Jack said.

"Why the fuck didn't you say anything? We could have used the information a few moments sooner!" Johnny shouted through the headlink.

"Way to go dumbass," Dash said to Johnny through the link. "Now you have to do it alone."

"Jack, why didn't you tell us?" He asked again through the headlink.

"Well, your plan was good and I didn't want you to second guess yourself after my suggestion. So I just didn't mention it. How was I supposed to know you were going to push Dash off the roof? I figured you would let me know if your plan failed. So that is why I was mentioning it now," Jack said trying not to ruffle any feathers further then they already were.

"Well... Jack," Johnny said waiting for his escape route.

"Well what?" Jack asked.

"How do we get Frankie to tell me how to get the fuck out of here?" Johnny asked with a sigh.

"Oh right... ah I don't know... I guess just let her lead the way," Jack said the shrug in his voice was obvious.

"Frankie is a fucking fridge with a bomb in it right now. You can't be serious that I'm supposed to follow a fridge out of here!" Johnny exclaimed while taking cover. "And there's another chopper here! What the hell! I didn't even hear it!"

"Could be a special Takahara Black Ops chopper," muttered Jack.

Johnny took a quick peek at the landing helicopter from his cover. There were six men stepping off the skids and their uniforms were not normal TCS uniforms; they looked like full riot gear. Johnny ducked back down as the bullets started to rain down at him. Johnny knew that what little ammo he had scrounged wasn't going to puncture that armor. As Johnny lay there clinging to what little cover he had left a small metallic ball about the size of an orange rolled up to Johnny and stopped.

"Frankie says just to follow her and she will lead you out," Jack said over the link.

"You have gotta be kidding me," Johnny said as the metallic ball roll toward an air duct.

"Frankie says to keep up," Jack said. Johnny stood up and fired a round. The bullet clipped one of the heavily armored men near the throat a kill shot any other time but now. The men were moving quickly down the twin staircases of the helipad, headed in his direction. Johnny followed Frankie as he made his escape from the roof.

Bullets chased Johnny as he ran from one piece of cover to the next. Johnny fired his last remaining rounds over his cover. Johnny lay prone behind the thickest piece of wall left as bullets began to chew through the half cement wall that he was hiding behind.

"Get off the roof the bomb is about to go off and Frankie says that you need to be down at least 2 floors not to get hurt." Johnny heard Jack screaming over the headlink. Johnny watched as Frankie literally ate her way through the metal grate barring the entrance to the duct.

"Jack, how much time I got left?!" Johnny yelled as he jumped in, following Frankie.

"You have 10 seconds."

Johnny slid down and burst through an access point, two floors down.

"3, 2..." Jack counted down. Johnny landed wrong, spraining his ankle. "1."

The 150th floor of the building exploded sending Johnny tumbling down to the 147th floor. The shock wave shook the building.

"I think you used a little too much this time." Dash chuckled over the link. "How do you steer this thing... oh no."

"Dash, you there?" Johnny asked.

"He is probably out of range of the three way link... I hope...I'm heading out to see if I can find him." Jack said trying not to worry Johnny, but doing a bad job of it.

"Make sure he's okay. I'll meet you at the docks. I got another 147 floors to go," Johnny replied.

"Frankie says just be sure to follow her and she will get you outta there," Jack replied.

"Don't worry Frankie I'll follow your lead," Johnny said and the metal ball rolled up to him. "Lead the way pinball."

"Frankie doesn't like that nick name," Jack replied, more seriously than Johnny had ever heard before.

"I'm sure that isn't the only thing that Frankie doesn't like," Johnny said jokingly. Frankie rolled to a stairwell access point and proceeded downwards. Johnny followed closely. They were down to the 140th floor very quickly. Franking bumped against the door. Johnny looked out the floor exit door and made sure the coast was clear before letting Frankie through. Frankie rolled down the hall to the elevator.

"You can't be serious," Johnny said to the ball. Frankie rolled up and banged against the door. "Alright." Johnny replied and pressed the button to call the elevator. The doors dinged, but the elevator didn't open. The metal ball rolled up and banged against the door again. Johnny wedged his fingers in between the doors and opened them. There was no elevator just hanging cables and building supports.

"Okay now what?" Johnny asked impatiently. The metal ball rolled up to his leg and coiled around it. "What the fuck? Hey you're supposed to get me out of here not latch on for the ride." Johnny looked into the elevator shaft. There was a ladder that he could take down quite a few floors without being seen, but it was near impossible to get there. He would have to jump to one of the beams and then use the elevator cables to swing across like a monkey.

Johnny looked down at his leg, "You've gotta be fucking kidding me. This was your way out? I just sprained my ankle..." Johnny said to Frankie as he wiggled his foot to try to assess how bad of a sprain it was. At that point he noticed the pain was gone. Johnny was a little shocked, but without a sprained ankle he knew he could make it. The jump to the beam wasn't too far, but without a lot of running room it was going to be difficult. Johnny prepared himself with a deep breath, stepped back a few paces, and sprinted toward the elevator shaft. Johnny leapt toward the support beam. He grasped the beam with both hands. His right hand slipped but his left held firm to the beam. Dangling from one hand Johnny couldn't help but look down into the abyss that was the shaft. He gulped in fear at the sight.

"The more and more I go along with your plan. The better off I was with just blowing up with the bomb," Johnny said as he lifted himself up to grab on the beam with his right hand. He pulled himself up and swung his right leg on to the beam. He gripped the beam tightly as he maneuvered himself on top of the beam. Beads of sweat formed on Johnny's brow as he stood up. Johnny was now firmly planted on the beam and was a little relieved, but that joy was short lived. He now had to swing like a monkey on steel cables, a thought that did not thrill him.

Johnny heard the ding of the elevator doors as it ground against the frame, shutting and removing his primary light source. Only dim emergency lights were left to illuminate his path. The emergency lights were effective but as the elevator cables swung freely back and forth they vanished from the light making the timing of his next jump very important. Johnny counted the time from when it swung into view, until it returned to view. It took five seconds for it to swing in and out of view. Johnny's heart raced and he hoped he wouldn't slip.

Johnny counted down, " 1, 2, 3, 4." Johnny leapt into the air as the cable came towards him. His out stretched hand wrapped around then cable attaching him to it. Johnny didn't take time to celebrate this small victory. He would have to swing to one more cable and then swing over to the ladder before he would be able to take another easy breath. Johnny began to swing on the cable to move himself closer to the severed steel cable. The cable began to groan with weakness. Johnny looked up to where the cable was attached. One of the emergency lights now revealed that the system holding the cable to the support beam had been wrecked by the explosion and was about to give way.

Johnny had one shot at getting the other cable. Johnny swung back and forth once and it still held. He did it again. A nut the size of Johnny's fist slammed in to Johnny's shoulder as it fell from the support. The impact jarred him, knocking one of Johnny's hands free, but he slapped his hand back on to the cable and kept the rhythm.

The cable was fraying loose as Johnny swung all the way back. It was hanging by its last thread when Johnny jumped to the ladder. The first cable snapped and whipped down the elevator shaft slicing into the wall as it plummeted. It could have easily cut a man in half as it fell. Johnny held tight to the ladder, looking to see if he could avoid the cable, and hoped for the best. He breathed a sigh of relief after steel cable of death passed by.

Johnny proceeded down the ladder to the 100th floor. Johnny sighed at what had happed to it. The ladder had been ripped down by the falling cables making it impossible to take the ladder the rest of way.

"Well isn't this perfect. Thanks a lot," Johnny said to Frankie who was still wrapped around his leg. Johnny looked for his next move and sighed at the sight of an air duct. Johnny moved along the structural beams to the closest air duct and climbed in.

Frankie rolled up into a ball again and led the way. The metallic ball moved quickly and easily through the ducts. Rolling left and right and falling down where needed. Stopping and shifting into a puddle that looked like mercury if it needed to climb up. The nano bots took the air duct like a walk in the park, but it was hard for Johnny to keep up. Johnny looked through the grates as he went by hoping to perhaps see an easy way out.

Frankie led Johnny to the freight elevator shaft where they had originally come up with Dash. If he could get to the bottom without being notice he would be home free. Johnny smiled to himself thinking that he just might get out of this alive.

"This is the last fuckin' time I'm doing this. After this I'm never using an elevator again, never using the stairs again... a one story building that's it," Johnny said to himself. Just as Johnny was about to start heading down the shaft he heard a familiar voice.

"It's okay Juni. We'll get out of here," Dr. Maki said. A thought passed through Johnny's mind. He needed to talk to Dr. Maki more. He needed to find out about himself and what they did to him. Johnny needed answers. He stopped in his tracks.

"Frankie. We've one more stop to make. Grab on," Johnny said and Frankie reattached to his leg. Johnny waited silently, listening carefully to pick up where he had heard the voice from.

"Mom, let's just leave. We can take the stairs," Juni said. Her echo caught Johnny's attention. They were a few flights lower. Johnny began to climb down the ladder in the freight elevator shaft.

"We're safer in here. The guards will protect us and get us out when it's safe." The echoes of Dr. Maki's voice lead him down another floor and to an air duct. Johnny climbed in and began to travel through it, following their voices.

Dr. Maki and Juni were sitting on a white love seat in what appeared to be a small office complete with desk, book case, and other assorted office furniture. There was a guard standing at the door. Johnny could easily take him out with one shot, but knew that would bring more guards. He didn't have the ammo for that.

Then the guard spoke as he put his hand to his ear, "We have a path to an exit. We will be moving out shortly."

"Thank you. Do you know what happened to the men that killed Mr. Takahara?" She asked.

"It is unconfirmed, but it is believed that they were blown up when the roof exploded. There has been no sign of them since," the guard replied. "I will be right back. There are two guards outside if you need them."

"Thank you," she said. The guard left the room. Johnny positioned his body so he would be able to kick the vent open and exit it quickly. Johnny was a flash as he jumped out of the vent as its cover clattered on the ground. Johnny pushed the book case in front of the door while the girls screamed. The first thumps began to hit the door.

"Dr. Maki, Ms. Takahara, are you alright?" Johnny asked as yells came from the other side of the door. Johnny then pushed the desk length-wise in front of the door. The size of the office made it so that the book case and the desk made a tight fit against the door. Dr. Maki stood up and moved toward Johnny. Johnny was quick to pull his gun.

"I'd sit down if I were you," Johnny said as he made sure the desk and book case would hold. Dr. Maki cautiously sat back down.

"Relax. I was just startled," Dr. Maki said.

"Mom, who is that?" Juni asked as she held close to her mother, but as she glimpsed at Johnny through her tears she identified who he was. "Wait, you're the waiter from the party that danced with me."

"Juni, be quite let me handle this," Dr. Maki said, hushing her daughter.

"You should listen, Juni," Johnny said over the thumps of the guards banging against the door. Juni remained quiet on the small couch, her eyes red from crying. Her anger at Johnny was evident to the world. "I don't have a lot of time I need to know more."

"I will explain what I can with what time that we have," Dr. Maki began. "Johnny, you were created to have the Beta virus tested on you. You were thought to be dead when the building was burned down. I was told you died in the fired." She explained.

"What do you mean created?" Johnny asked confused.

"From the combination of male and female DNA you were born from a surrogate machine," she started again.

"Surrogate machines are illegal," Johnny replied. "It was in the news they were all destroyed and outlawed. And what do you mean by a combination of both male *and* female? What the fuck did you do to me?"

"This was before Washington became Neo-Japan... before Japan and the Takahara Corporation took over. The Takahara Corporation was able to keep the surrogate machine going until the end of the Beta Experiment. Then all of the machines were destroyed," Dr. Maki explained.

"You can't be serious," Johnny replied.

"Most of the children died in the days leading up to the fire. I believe it's because of your AB blood type that you were able to survive. I can only hypothesize that the Beta virus has not only replaced your immune system, but your body's natural regenerative processes. Have you ever been sick?" Dr. Maki continued.

"Not that I remember," Johnny replied.

"Injuries?" She questioned.

"Tons," Johnny answered. "But Uncle Dylan always said that I was a fast healer."

"You aren't a fast healer. The virus is a fast healer," She replied. Johnny was a little shocked by this information. He stood there as she explained that after Beta project failed, they made Dr. Maki continue with the Gamma project. This time they used surrogate mothers instead of machines. Takahara Corp found it more cost effective rather than the cost of using more surrogate machines. Feeding and properly taking care of a woman for nine months was much cheaper than maintaining the machine.

She explained that the Gamma's were very close to a success. The Gammas were able to draw energy from their surroundings and focus it. The Gamma children were a leap forward, but when they injected the Gamma virus into an older person they died their bodies could not handle the change. That's why she was made to continue manipulating the virus, which was perfected with the Delta trials. The Delta drug was going to Japan for one last test before it was mass produced. Delta would turn people into super humans with a wide range of power and abilities. However, at its current state the Delta drug his highly addictive and unstable.

Johnny was in shock at the details that he was hearing. These people were playing with fire and Uncle Dylan lied to him. He wasn't the son of Bryan and Maggie Morals. He wasn't the nephew of Dylan Morals. He was a lab rat, a test tube baby. He couldn't believe this nonsense. Why would his Uncle have taken care of him if they weren't related? A man like him had too many things going on to take care of a child unless they were blood. Johnny felt like a fraud and was destroyed inside.

As Dr. Maki continued Johnny became lost in thought. His mind wandered through his past ripping all his memories in half, including recent events like the look in Dash's eyes as Johnny shoved him off the building; a look that for once showed concern for his friend.

Johnny began to remember what really mattered. The past relived itself in his head and filled Johnny with warmth. Jokes once forgotten, lesson taught, and happiness shared between him and his friends.

Johnny came back from his thoughts as Dr. Maki began to explain that Dr. Thomas Johnson was her first Delta test subject and she was amazed at the results, but Mr. Takahara had sent him after Johnny. While the pounding on the door continued Johnny explained to Dr. Maki what happened during Johnny and Thomas's fight.

"You are one of kind, Beta... Johnny. None of the others ever developed like you did," she said with excitement as the door began to crack and thumps began on the right wall.

Johnny looked over to the wall, "Shit, I hoped it would take them longer to figure that out. Well I've got to go Doc, unless you feel like coming with? I could get you to safety and..." A sledge hammer head came through the wall when it was removed the barrel of a gun poked through. Hot lead began to pour into the room like it was raining bullets. Johnny jumped out of the way, but the bullets found a different mark. Dr. Maki blood spattered all over Juni and the white love seat. Juni screamed as her mother fell to the ground.

"You idiot, Dr. Maki and Ms. Takahara are in there!" A man shouted from the other side of the wall. The sound of one other bullet was fired on the other side of the wall and the gun barrel was removed. Johnny rushed to Dr. Maki's side.

"No. I just wanted answers. You can't die," Johnny said as Dr. Maki gasped for air and choked on blood. Johnny had let his guard down setting his pistol on the ground next to him. Juni unharmed by the gun fire rushed over to her mother weeping. Johnny looked at her with shame.

"This is your fault! You should have never come here!" She shouted with unstoppable rage and sorrow growing in her eyes.

"Juni calm down," Johnny replied to the shout as he tried his best to put pressure on the wounds. "Help me stop the bleeding -- I can't do it myself." Johnny tried to apply pressure to the wounds, but there was no hope.

"She's dead and it's your fault," Juni continued to shout as the tears were dried up by the heat of rage and anger. Johnny tried his best to stop the bleeding but there were too many wounds.

"Johnny...." Dr. Maki whispered. "Find the Gammas... they are like you. They... are hidden in the city..." Dr. Maki coughed up more blood. "Don't let...them release the Delta drug. It could cause an epidemic." Dr. Maki began to seize in Johnny's arms and exhaled her last breath.

Juni slowly dropped to her knees next to her mother hand folded in her lap. "Mother......" She wept as she removed wiped the blood from her face. Placing her mother's head in her lap she collapsed on to her weeping. "You're responsible... *YOU KILLED MY MOTHER*!!!" Juni began.

Johnny couldn't stay any longer Takahara's men would be through the wall in moments. He spun away from the scene and with three quick steps and a leap he reached the air vent and pulled himself into it. Johnny crawled as quickly as possible through the vent back to the freight elevator ladder.

"You're responsible for her *death*!" Juni screamed after him. "I'll have you hunted down like a dog!"

The echoes of Juni's screams chased him through the vents. Johnny felt terrible, even if it was her mother and uncle that caused all this pain for him and Dash, it wasn't her fault.

Johnny scrambled through the vents to the ladder
and began his decent. One hundred stories on a ladder was no easy task, especially for a man that had been beaten and shot repeatedly, but it wasn't long before he felt the pain subside. The Beta virus was doing its job. Johnny slid down the side of the ladder for the final ten

feet and did a crash landing through the top of the elevator, landing on top of a solitary guard standing in the elevator, breaking his neck with the landing. Shards of glass and debris rained down on Johnny.

He stood up, brushing the detritus off of him, grabbed the man's pistol, and hit the button to open the doors. The lobby was mostly deserted and had been turned into a hasty command center. A few agents and staff were milling about, looking lost and shaken by the events of the evening. Weapons were drawn and aimed towards Johnny as he stepped out a few feet from the elevator.

"You really think you can take me," Johnny said with a cocky laugh. "There are over a hundred dead men that would disagree. Besides your boss is dead -- aren't you unemployed." Johnny tried his best to convince them not to fire, but it had no effect. Johnny dove behind the nearest cover, which happen to be the guard station by the elevator door. Bullets rained into the small building for ten straight seconds when Johnny heard the sound of them reloading.

He had to make a run for better cover or he was dead. Johnny tumbled for cover behind a cement pillar as bullets began their pursuit of his life. Johnny quickly peeked around the corner of the pillar firing a few rounds to keep his attackers in check.

Johnny took a bullet to his calf which was left a little too exposed and stopped firing to put pressure on this leg wound. Frankie wrapped around it like a bandage and applied the needed pressure the wound. Johnny looked confused as the metal wrapped around his leg. "Thanks...I think." Johnny said, a little confused that Frankie knew how to do that.

The gunfire stopped for the moment and a man with a bullhorn began barking orders. "Stop firing," the man ordered. He continued to speak. "Put down your gun and keep your hands above your head. I give you my word that you'll live." Johnny peaked around the corner. The man was Shinobu, the chief of staff for the party that was sporting a white tuxedo earlier. Now, he was wearing a flak vest and looked like a general at war.

"Give it up Beta. There is no way out!" Shinobu yelled. "My

honor keeps me here to do my duty though my Shogun is dead. Come peacefully and we will sort this all out."

Johnny paused and did the math. There were still over a dozen agents covering his position and numerous other support staff in the area. Plus who knew what Shinobu was capable of. "And what if I do? What then?"

During the negotiation a man appeared, walking through the main entrance to the building, walking towards Shinobu. He was armed with a chrome plated .50 caliber Desert Eagle in one hand and a sword strapped to his back. The Desert Eagle was drawn and pointed casually at the ground.

Shinobu took no notice of the man and continued. "We can work this all out but *only* if you turn yourself over to us." The other man walked past Shinobu. He became silent and bowed to the man who began to speak.

"You were in charge of security today," he stated.

"Yes, sir but I can explain..." Shinobu started.

"Resignation accepted," the man said callously and in one swift motion drew his sword and cut Shinobu's head clean from his shoulders. What had happened hadn't even registered in Shinobu's dead eyes.

The support staff panicked and ran from the building. TCS Agents turned towards the new-comer and bowed, offering their fealty as loyal soldiers.

The man stood a little taller than Johnny. He was dressed in a black suit. His eyes were covered by red sunglasses and his hair was cut into a Mohawk. Two agents were carrying a bound and gagged body, its head slumped to its chest. They deposited it on the floor next to Shinobu's headless corpse.

Johnny was worried that it was Dash. He hadn't heard from him since he pushed him off the roof.

The man waved away the remaining Agents and personnel – banishing them from the tower.

"Mr. Morals, you have become more of a problem then you are

worth," Ichiro said.

"If my friend is dead you will pay for it with your life," Johnny said as he stepped closer cautiously.

"Mr. Morals, this man is not your friend," Ichiro said and nudged the man, revealing his face. It was the Doc. "I was quite surprised how easy he was to bend to my will. I always thought the Delta's were supposed to be the next coming. Guess the Delta drug won't replace cybernetics after all."

"Quit that Mr. Morals shit and let him go," Johnny insisted.

"Or what? You're going to kill me. I'm sorry but neither of you will be leaving," Ichiro said stoic voice.

"What makes you think that you can do that?" Johnny asked with a smug grin. He was bluffing he was in no shape for another fight. Ichiro cocked the hammer on his Desert Eagle and pointed it at Tommy.

"Because Mr. Morals I'm not trying to capture you," Ichiro said as he fired a round into Tommy's head. Blood splattered all over Ichiro's suit. Johnny was shocked by the sudden death of the Doc but it gave him the second he needed to act.

Johnny pulled his gun from his back waist band and simultaneously Ichiro lifted his gun and aimed it at Johnny. They both raised their guns quickly, and time seemed to slow as they reached the firing point. Both bullets fired at the same time. The path of each bullet was set and the projectiles nearly missed each other as they passed through the air. Ichiro's bullet struck Johnny in the left shoulder, spinning him backwards, and knocking him to the ground. The pain was intense. The bullet went through his vest. His arm was limp and useless. Johnny half expected that Ichiro would have fired a second round to end his life, but it never came.

"You are a lucky one Johnny," Ichiro said as he looked at his gun. Johnny's last bullet had collided with Ichiro's pistol and rendered it useless. Johnny grunted through the pain in his shoulder and stood up, despite the ache in his leg as well. Johnny felt like a crippled animal from the damage he had sustained. He turned to face Ichiro as upright as possible.

"Wouldn't suppose you'd call it a draw after that?" Johnny asked with halfhearted laugh.

"You should know the name of the man that's going to kill you," Ichiro replied.

"I take that as a no," Johnny said with a sigh.

"My name is Ichiro. I am first son of Kenji Takahara, the true head of Takahara Corporation. I will honor you with a swift death," he said, drawing sword, gripping it tightly with two hands.

"Uncle Dylan always said "don't get killed by a stranger". Glad you introduced yourself. I would hate for this to be impersonal," Johnny mocked him, as Ichiro moved in to attack Johnny. Ichiro was almost as quick as Tommy. Johnny only had time to try to deflect the sword with his pistol. The blade cut right through his weapon but the action saved Johnny's life.

Ichiro quickly drew back his blade and came in for another strike. Johnny stepped out of the way just in time. Ichiro deafly slashed again at him. The blade came swiping across Johnny's gut for the third strike. The blade sliced through his vest slightly nicking Johnny's stomach. Johnny took a chance and struck back.

Johnny swung at Ichiro's chin with his right fist, which was still clenching what was left of his pistol. He connected cleanly smashing Ichiro in the face with his pistol grip. This gave Johnny a moment to step back from Ichiro to recover. He reached for his gut and checked his wound. It was just a scratch, but any closer and he would have been holding his guts in.

Ichiro shook off the hit and regained his stance treating Johnny's attack like it had done nothing. Johnny sighed in frustration. Johnny thought that Ichiro took an odd battle stance, but Ichiro was no man to doubt. Ichiro came at him. Vertical slashes, horizontal swipes, and diagonal cuts that could have sliced right through concrete.

Johnny swiftly dodged every devastating blow. Each one of the attacks would have killed Johnny instantly. Johnny could feel the blood running down his left arm and dripping off his fingertips. He began to lose the feeling in his hand. Johnny clenched his left fist as hard as he could to force the feeling back into them but wasn't able to do so.

Again Ichiro attacked. First a sword strike from the left, then a stab followed by an upward swing. Johnny jumped back to avoid the strike for the left, stepped to the right of the stab and as Ichiro brought the sword upward Johnny leaned out of the way, but not quite enough. The tip of the blade caught his chin causing a small cut. Ichiro stepped back noticing the wound.

"It is only a matter of time. Give up and die with honor or you may end up in pieces," Ichiro said coldly flicking the blood from his blade. Johnny touched his chin and wiped the blood away.

"I've gotten worse cuts from a razor," Johnny replied in jest as he recalled Dash always razzing him for not being able to use a straight edge without nicking himself. Ichiro came at him again stabbing straight at his chest. Johnny avoided the sword and batted the flat part of the blade away with the back of his hand, than stepped into Ichiro. Johnny slammed his right foot down of Ichiro's left foot. Johnny used his left elbow to strike Ichiro in the face. The blow was meaningless. Johnny had barely enough movement in the arm to lift it. Let alone do any damage, but the strike was a distraction.

Johnny slammed his pistol grip down on Ichiro's forearms then crashed the butt of the pistol in to the hilt of the sword jarring it loose from his grip. The sword skittered away from them along the lobby floor and came to rest a few feet away. Ichiro shoved Johnny away and regained his composure. Johnny smiled back at him; it was a small victory, but a victory none the less.

"You think this will change the outcome? You are a good fighter Mr. Morals, but soon your body will give out and your life will be over." Ichiro balled up his fists.

"Will you just shut up and fight. I swear none of you fuckers get it. I don't need a fucking speech from a man that is tryin' to kill me!" Johnny confessed his distaste for all of Ichiro's babble. He could feel the numbness wear off in his left arm, but it was still pretty useless.

"Very well," Ichiro said and came at Johnny. Johnny moved out of the way his first punch, but shouldn't have. The blow was a feint, just a decoy to get Johnny where Ichiro wanted him to be.

Ichiro rocked Johnny's world with a right handed upper cut. The blow knocked Johnny back and nearly unconscious. The cut on Johnny's chin opened to a gash and bled down the front of his shirt. Ichiro stood there while Johnny recovered and wiped the blood from his fist.

Johnny shook his head as the daze wore off. That was no ordinary punch. There was something more behind it. Johnny wasn't one hundred percent sure but he knew how to find out. He prepared himself for another attack. Ichiro threw a left handed jab. Johnny slipped out of the way and grabbed Ichiro's fist. He moved in and viciously bit Ichiro's fist ripping the flesh from his hand as Ichiro punched Johnny with his right. The blow landed in his gut knocking the wind out of him and sending him to the ground.

Johnny spit out the chuck of flesh and gasped for air. Johnny looked at the damage he had caused. The metallic bone structure of Ichiro's hand showed through his skin. Ichiro shook his hand in pain. Johnny could tell that he must of have bone replacement, but that didn't remove the nerves.

"Cybernetics!" Johnny stated in between gasps. Ichiro moved over to him at picked him up by the collar and lifted him up.

"Yes. Cybernetics. Man cannot rival machine. Alphas or Betas," Ichiro said and punched Johnny in the stomach again with his free hand. "Gammas and now Deltas!" Ichiro grabbed Johnny's face and squeezed it. The pressure to Johnny's skull was intense. Johnny screamed in pain. Ichiro looked at him with disgust and threw him to the ground.

Johnny began to get up but was struggling. His leg, arm and face were in extreme pain, but something kept him going. Something kept allowing him to rise again. Johnny couldn't feel it, but the Beta virus was fighting just as hard to stay live as he was, eerily perhaps even more.

"My family was trying to replace what I have become," Ichiro said almost as if he was confessing. Johnny was struggling, but managed to get to his knees. "Yet out of all there test subjects. I will be the only one left alive today. My mother will finally see that there is no replacing cybernetic." Ichiro began to crack a small smile as he monologued.

"So this would be a bad time to tell you that your mother is dead," Johnny said as he wobbled up to his feet, swaying back and forth a little. A look of shock came over Ichiro's face. The look of shock slowly became cold and emotionless and grew into anger. Johnny could easily see that he had got under Ichiro's skin.

"I will tear you apart," Ichiro shouted. Johnny wasn't able to finish telling him that Dr. Maki didn't want to make any of the viruses in the first place. Maybe stop this fight so he could walk away, but Ichiro rushed at Johnny hands at the ready.

Ichiro was off balance now. His emotions were out of control. This gave Johnny a fighting chance. Ichiro came in with a left handed jab that Johnny avoided. He followed up with a right hook which Johnny ducked. Johnny they dropped to one knee and punched Ichiro square in the nuts. Ichiro howled in pain. Johnny followed up with a rising upper cut the chin. The punch knocked Ichiro to the ground.

Johnny unfortunately received the worst of it. The punch fractured Johnny's hand. Johnny grunted in pain from the snapping of the bones in his hand. He was out of time and out of options. He decided that he had to try to make a run for it. Johnny hobbled towards the exit as fast as he could, but he was no match for Ichiro. Before he could take ten steps Ichiro was on him. Ichiro grabbed him from behind and threw him against the closest cement pillar, formed in the shape of a dragon.

"Oh fuck that one really hurt." Johnny coughed and gasped for air lying face down on the tile. Johnny was now bleeding from his forehead and spit out some blood while he lay there. "Okay okay... tell you what. I'll let you walk away and you don't have to die today," Johnny joked but had figured out how to defeat Ichiro. Ichiro walked over to him and rolled him over with his foot. Ichiro grabbed him by the collar and lift him to his feet.

"I'm sorry Mr. Morals, play time is over." Ichiro sneered, preparing to kill Johnny.

"I got one last thing to say," Johnny said in a worn down voice.

"Last words... make them good ones," Ichiro said as he paused. Johnny whispered, but Ichiro couldn't hear. "What was that?" He asked. Johnny mumbled again hanging there limp. Ichiro brought Johnny closer so he could hear.

"Frankie. Repair mode," Johnny whispered. Frankie unwound from Johnny's leg, slithered up his back and over his shoulder before flowing onto Ichiro's open bite wound on his hand. He dropped Johnny to the ground and began to shake like he was having a seizure. Ichiro could feel the functioning of his hand deteriorating. The metal crawled inside his hand Ichiro began to claw at his skin tearing chunks out of his arm.

Panic began to set in his eyes as he screamed. He reached for his shoulder and yanked. Sparks, blood and lubricating fluids shot from his shoulder, but it didn't come off clean. So he yanked again tearing the arm from his body. Ichiro howled in terror as Frankie moved from his arm to his chest, the core of his cybernetics.

"Frankie cease repair mode," Johnny said. Frankie poured from Ichiro's arm socket. Changed back into a ball and rolled over to Johnny. Johnny picked Frankie up and then slowly, very slowly, stood up. Ichiro continued to scream. Johnny stepped over to him and nudged him with his good leg. Ichiro looked Johnny in the eye. The devil himself would have pissed his pants after receiving Johnny's terrifying gaze.

"I will let you live which is more than you have done for any of your victims. Remember, I let you live but Frankie can end you at any time. No more lookin' for us, no more huntin' down our friends, we're going to be left alone or I'll let Frankie finish what she started," Johnny said with a cold death stare.

Ichiro nodded in pain.

"Cause if I ever so much as think you're followin' us, I'll roll my little friend over to your door step and watch while she eats you like popcorn," Johnny said as he shook Frankie at Ichiro.

Johnny then turned around and began to walk away. He paused for a moment as he approached Ichiro's sword. The feeling began to return to his left hand. As he clenched his fist he squatted down and picked up the sword. Johnny held it up and looked at it. The blade was a piece of art and Johnny admired that.

"And I'm keeping this," Johnny said and continued to hobble away.

Luck must have been on his side Johnny thought as he walked out the door. Johnny spotted the van as it rolled up to the entrance.

"Jack. I thought we were meeting at the docks," Johnny said through the headlink.

"I told him we should wait, but he never listens," Jack replied as he waved from the driver seat. The side door of the van slide open and Dash was sitting there with a bandage wrapped around his head.

"Fucking bombs." Dash chuckled. "Some debris came raining down on me and knocked me out cold -- though it sure helped ease my fear of heights gliding down 150 floors to the ground. You're lucky I didn't fall into any power lines. Dick." Dash grinned.

"It's an improvement on your looks." Johnny laughed as he hobbled into the front passenger seat and handed Frankie over to Jack. Jack was almost in tears when he saw Frankie again. Jack set Frankie on the dashboard and the metal ball melted into the vehicle.

"Home-sweet-home, Frankie," Jack said grinning ear to ear while rubbing his hand on the dash board like he was touching a woman. "Is my baby ok?" Johnny and Dash looked at each other and shook their heads with a laugh.

"You look like shit. That's what you get for throwing me off a building," Dash said as Johnny pulled a pack a cigarette out of the glove box. He began to pat his pockets looking for a light. It was still very difficult for him to move but it was getting easier as time passed. Dash reached into his pocket and pulled out a lighter, then lit Johnny's cigarette.

"Thanks for comin' back," Johnny said through his cigarette.

" Seriously dude, we need to get you to a hospital."

"No you don't. I think that whatever this Beta thing is, it's takin' care of me." Johnny began to remove his vest and then his shirt. There was the proof. The bullet wound in his shoulder had stopped bleeding and scabbed over.

"You've got to be shitting me," Dash said as he looked at the wound. "When did that happen?"

"A few minutes ago," Johnny replied.

"No shit. Next time we get shot at I'm using you as a shield," Dash said as he looked out the back window back at Takahara Tower as they drove away. The top of the tower was still ablaze. "This is over right?"

"It's over," Johnny replied.

"Where to guys?" Jack asked as he finished caressing his van.

"The girls," They said simultaneously in a worn out tone. Jack put the van in drive and sped away from the tower, out to where Shamus was keeping them safe. They were still hold up in a large vacant apartment they had commandeered until the job was over. Johnny was so beat up he passed out on the drive there. Even with his fast recovery his body had been devastated by the assault on Takahara Tower. The Beta virus did heal him, but it still took time and the wounds were still overwhelmingly painful. It was easier for him to sleep then to try to keep his eyes open with the pain that he was in.

It was only about forty-five minutes to get there, but it was the best nap Johnny had ever had. When they arrived, Jack ran into a neighboring department store and bought Johnny and Dash some new clothes. The ones they were wearing were covered blood and grime. They then headed up the stairs to tell everyone it was all over that they could go back to their lives. They knocked on the door.

"Who is it?" Kate said with a slight tremble in her voice.

"The boys are back," Dash said excitedly. Kate sheepishly opened the door. Dash burst in followed by Johnny and Jack. "Where's Fern and Scarlet? It's all over with!" The girls were happy to see their men. Hugs and kisses were passed around for the next few moments. Shamus shared in the rejoicing and brought in a few bottles of the good stuff.

"Perhaps you boys better clean up; you still stink despite your new clothes. And where did you get those, a secondhand store?" Jack looked slightly embarrassed by the comment. "Dash, use the shower in the master bedroom. Johnny, use the one in off the hall," Fern said, pointing the way. Kate picked up Scarlet and moved toward the kitchen sink to wash off a small amount of grime that had transferred to her.

"Sorry, I'm just a happy," Dash said grinning as he looked at the mess he caused.

"I don't care about the mess. You're alive that's all that matters," Fern replied as she kissed him on the cheek and sent him off to the shower with a pat on the ass.

"Kate I'm gonna need some help... would you mind?" Johnny asked quietly. Kate smiled and followed him to the other shower. Johnny's wounds may have been healing, but he was still battered and bruised all over. It was no picnic trying to get undressed. Kate helped as best she could but Johnny was in a lot of pain. He was still having trouble lifting his left arm.

Once Johnny was undressed and in the shower she began to undress. There was so much blood on her from helping him it was the easy way to get cleaned off. Her slender body shook slightly as she was unused to the sight of so much blood. Thoughts of her friends crept into her mind. Kate needed to get the blood off so she moved Johnny out of the way and let the water wash away the blood and the gruesome memories. Johnny watched her shake as she stood in the water. Johnny did the only thing he could do and pulled her close and held her tight.

"Babe it's ok. We're safe now," Johnny told her, calming her. Johnny knew she was scared, maybe too scared to stick around after this was over. Johnny kissed the back of her neck and held her tight as the water poured over them. Her skin felt like heaven against his broken body.

"Johnny I..." She started.

"I know. You're scared, but I don't know what to tell you," Johnny replied keeping her held tightly.

"There was so much blood. I thought you were going to die too," She responded looking pained. Physically she was there, being held by Johnny, but mentally she was gone.

"But I didn't die. I'm here now. I can take you out on that date I promised you," He quickly said to try to keeper her from doing what she was going to do.

"I'm just so scared. What happens if they come back?" She asked with a whimper.

"They won't. I made a deal that will keep us safe for as long as we live," Johnny replied with confidence.

"I don't know..." She said. It was hard to see in the water but she was crying. Johnny knew it was over, even though he didn't want it to be.

"Turn around I'll wash your back," Johnny said, changing the subject. Kate nodded and let him. He finished and she got out of the shower, taking one more loving glance at Johnny. She wrapped herself in a towel and left the room.

Johnny stayed in the shower cleaning his wounds. He looked over his body and shook his head, amazed at what was happening inside of him. He also felt lucky just to be alive and have friends like Dash and now Jack. Johnny finished washing and stepped out of the shower. He dried his body off and in the process ruined his towel. As he finished he heard the water for the other shower turn off. Johnny put on a fresh pair of clothes and headed out into the living room. He could see Dash heading down the other hall naked as a jaybird. Johnny gave him a strange look.

"Forgot my clothes." Dash laughed from across the hall. Johnny laughed at the sight of his friend running buck ass through the apartment. It was good to feel at home again.

Time passed very slowly over the next few days as their lives began to return to normal. Dash and Johnny took a few odd jobs to help pay for repairs to the El Diablo Tavern and Fern needed new digs as hers was obliterated by Takahara's hit squads.

Jack was able to get the bomb in the warehouse disarmed and kept it for later use. He also swept the place for bugs and started to develop a new security system from the ground up. He began spending so much time there that he opted to make the place his new home as long as someone renovated an area for a living space.

One of the city's smaller security companies took over the city contract for police enforcement and finally stopped by Uncle Dylan's place. His death was never investigated, but his last will and testament left everything to Johnny. The money helped finish up the repairs and pay for rent. Johnny and Dash began to wonder why the attack was never investigated. They came to the conclusion that Takahara Corp. wouldn't have survived if the news had gotten out that two men were able to cause so much damage. It was announced in the News that Ichiro Takahara and had taken over as proxy head of the Neo-Japan Branch - Takahara Corp. Akiyo Takahara was given a full state funeral in the Northside of Neo-Hiroshima. The media reported his demise as, death by stroke and contributing complications from cardiac arrest. Takahara Corp covered up the destruction of the upper floors of Takahara Tower, attributing it to a freak, gas main accident.

Fern had convinced Dash that his running days were over. He managed to work a compromise with her and started his own business, using his contacts to find jobs and match them up with the right personal. The money was better and, most importantly, it allowed him to spend time with his family. He earned a reputation for landing lucrative deals for top dollar. Johnny, of course, was kept on speed dial and had first billing rights to any job. It didn't take long before Dash had become one of the best handlers in the business. His contacts began to rival Fat Montey after only a year.

Every once and awhile Johnny convinced Dash to join him on the easy jobs for old-time sake. Dash had to convince Fern to let him out on these little adventures, usually by saying that it was good exercise and he was getting a little thick around the middle. To which she usually just rolled her eyes and relented. They continued to keep an eye out for Takahara Corp., but weeks turned into months and nothing appeared on their radar.

Kate didn't stick around for long. Johnny helped her out and gave her some money so that she could get back on her feet. Shamus offered her a job once the bar was up and running again, but she declined. She left them behind and moved on -- Johnny wasn't ready to let her go. He loved her and it crushed him to let her leave.

Johnny tried to keep tabs on her so that maybe one day he could somehow make it up to her, but never quite knew how to replace what she lost. Johnny stayed in the shadows and waited for the right moment, hoping that it would come soon.

About a month after the events at Takahara tower thoughts returned back to the case that started this entire mess.

"So what are we going to do about the package?" Dash asked,

more to himself than anyone in the room.

"Let's pop it open. We're not *exactly* sure what's in it. It could be gold... or new high-tech computer bits... or," Jack began to ramble.

"No. I'm fairly certain that what's in there we really don't want to be part of," Johnny said, sliding his hand across the surface of the case. "But I'd really hate *not* to see what's in there. Jack, can you bypass these locks?"

Jack pulled out an assortment of probes and got to work. Moments later a series of clicks let them all know of Jacks success. Jack's hands hovered over the lid, anticipating what might be inside.

Dash brushed his hands aside. "I'll do the honors." Dash lifted the lid, a short whoosh of air escaped as the seal was broken. The lid was shifted aside and curls of steam formed as the cold air inside the case met the warmer air of the room. A collection of four vials sat abreast of each other, embedded in antistatic foam. The blue, grainy liquid reflected the light, giving it an almost ethereal appearance. Dash used his thumb to brush the frost off of the brass identity tag – Delta Drug: Series 4. Batch #22.

"Let's cover that back up, shall we," Johnny whispered. Who with the help of Dash set the lid back in place. "Jack, get this locked back up. And get a monitor set on the merchandise so that we can make sure the temperature remains stable inside the case."

"I'm not sure we can let Fat Montey get a hold of something this dangerous. I don't trust him," Dash said. "The question is, what do we do with it then? Destroy it? Turn it in? Sell it?"

Jack shrugged intent on rigging up a series of sensors, and attaching them to the case.

"I did find out from Dr. Maki before her death that there is no way to control the drug. It is highly unstable still and dangerous to its user after prolonged exposure," Johnny said. "We should lock this away until we know more about it. Unfortunately Dr. Maki is dead."

"And I'm fairly certain we won't be getting any more help from Takahara Corp," Jack said, miming an explosion with his hands, and making the appropriate noise.

"I'd rather this entire package wasn't' sitting around our warehouse though. Maybe we could get a lease on a smaller warehouse. Hire some cheap security to watch over the place, and with Jack installing some of his own homegrown surveillance, we shouldn't have anything to worry about," Johnny said. "I think with a little more thought this could work."

The three sat there, well into the night, discussing their options and sipping some beers.

"Has it been perfected?" Juni asked. She was now a fully grown woman at the age of nineteen. Juni sat cross-legged atop her dead uncle's desk dressed in red combat spandex, covered by a black jean jacket and was surrounded by the cloying scent of lilacs.

"Yes Ms. Takahara," the man in a lab coat replied, bowing low to the ground.

"Has this information been released to anyone but your team? Does anyone know that there is a cure?" She asked as she held up a yellow vile and stared into it. Her eyes lit up like a starry night sky.

"No Ms. Takahara," the man said. He looked nervous as sweat dripped from his forehead. Juni stood up and poked the man in the lab coat in the chest.

"Make sure to keep it that way or you'll find yourself exiting the building like my deceased uncle," she threatened. "Keep providing your usefulness and you'll keep your life, *and* that healthy paycheck."

"Yes Ma'am," he replied.

Juni performed a back summersault off of the desk and sat down in the chair from which her uncle used to manage his empire. "It is time to find the men who murdered my family and put an end to them," Juni said and waived her hand to excuse the man in the lab coat.

The man quickly began to speed walk to the door and ran into Ichiro as he limped into the room. The man cowered in fear but was hastily waved away by Juni's brother. "What have I told you about sitting in my chair?" He smirked.

"I couldn't resist." Juni stood up and did a one handed handstand on the desk.

"Juni. Stop it. Your cybernetics aren't toys," Ichiro said, rubbing his newly attached fully robotic arm. Ichiro was feeling the post-traumatic effects of having his steel bone structure torn from his body.

Juni propelled herself in the air flipping once and landing on her feet gracefully. "You're just jealous...." Juni replied and her eyes flashed darkly. "I'm sorry... I didn't mean that," she apologized not knowing what had come over her.

"It's fine. It was my own fault. I was not strong enough," he said, sighing and hanging his head. Ichiro began to say something more but kept his mouth shut. He looked down at his one good hand, flipping it palm to back before clenching it in a fist.

"We will have our revenge." Juni reassured her brother patting him on his robotic arm.

"I have a meeting," said Ichiro, as he shied away from her comfort.

"And I have a call to make," she replied. Ichiro motioned that it was ok for her to stay as he left the room. Juni dimmed the lights to the office.

Juni walked to the window and stared out over the city that would soon be her playground. She smiled to herself as she placed a phone call with her headlink.

"Who is this?" A voice growled. "How did you get this number?"

"This..." Juni began. "Is a client. I have need of some specialty personnel. If you don't think that you can handle it I can go elsewhere." Juni said, then decided to sweeten her tone. "But I heard that the Fat Man could handle *anything*." Juni sneered, listening to the heavy breathing coming from the other end of the line. She grew weary of placating disgusting fools like this, but he was a means to an end.

"Of course, of *courrrrse*!" Fat Montey guffawed. "Fat Montey can do *anythinnng*... for a price."

"Then I need someone that can handle a bit of burglary for me – cleanly, and without leaving a trail." Juni said.

Fat Montey thought for a bit, tapping his chin. "I have just the team.... A Mr. Devin O'Conner, ex sniper and one of the quietest men in the business. He's paired up with a bit of dumb muscle that trails him around like a puppy dog... Guk, or Glump, or whatever his name is... But they're reliable."

"Sounds fine. One stipulation though, I need to meet them in person, prior to the job. On my terms."

"Highly unusual but, if you have the money, I'll see that it happens."

"See that it does." Juni hung up, not waiting for a response. She looked out over the city, pressing her face against the glass window. She stood there for many moments before tears began to fall from her eyes, mirroring the rain outside. "I will avenge you mother" she whispered.

The End

© Black Rose Writing

CPSIA information can be obtained at www.ICGtesting.com
Printed in the USA
LVOW122146291211

261685LV00002B/132/P